continued . . .

"Owen and Hercules are a delight."
—Kings River Life Magazine

"The author is brilliant in not only writing character portrayals but in creating a mystery complete with twists and turns that will keep the reader trying to figure it all out. . . . I absolutely could not put it down."
—Socrates' Book Reviews

Cat Trick

"Match two magical kitties with an extremely inquisitive librarian and a murder or two, and you have all the makings of an extraordinary mystery series . . . a captivating cozy!"
—Escape with Dollycas into a Good Book

"The characters are likable and the cats are darling."
—Socrates' Book Reviews

"Small-town charm and a charming cat duo make this every cat fancier's dream."
—The Mystery Reader

Copycat Killing

"I've been a huge fan of this series from the very start, and I am delighted that this new book meets my expectations and then some. . . . Cats with magic powers, a library, good friends who look out for each other, and small-town coziness come together in perfect unison. If you are a fan of Miranda James's Cat in the Stacks Mysteries, you will want to read [this series]."
—MyShelf.com

"This is a really fun series, and I've read them all. Each book improves on the last one. Being a cat lover myself, I'm looking at my cat in a whole new light."
—Once Upon a Romance

"A fun whodunit. . . . Fans will appreciate this entertaining amateur sleuth."   —Genre Go Round Reviews

"This charming series continues on a steady course as the intrepid Kathleen has two mysteries to snoop into. . . . Readers who are fans of cats and cozies will want to add this series to their must-read lists."

—*Romantic Times*

Sleight of Paw

"This series is a winner."   —Gumshoe

"If you are a fan of mysteries and cats, you need to be reading this series now!"   —Cozy Mystery Book Reviews

"Kelly's appealing cozy features likable, relatable characters set in an amiable location. The author continues to build on the promise of her debut novel, carefully developing her characters and their relationships."

—*Romantic Times*

Curiosity Thrilled the Cat

"A great cozy that will quickly have you anxiously waiting for the next release so you can spend more time with the people of Mayville Heights."

—Mysteries and My Musings

"If you love mystery and magic, this is the book for you!"
—Debbie's Book Bag

"This start of a new series offers an engaging cast of human characters and two appealing, magically inclined felines. Kathleen is a likable, believable heroine, and the magical cats are amusing."   —*Romantic Times*

Also by Sofie Ryan

The Whole Cat and Caboodle

BUY A wHiskeR

A SECOND CHANCE CAT MYSTERY

Sofie Ryan

AN OBSIDIAN MYSTERY

OBSIDIAN
Published by the Penguin Group
Penguin Group (USA) LLC, 375 Hudson Street,
New York, New York 10014

USA | Canada | UK | Ireland | Australia | New Zealand | India | South Africa | China
penguin.com
A Penguin Random House Company

First published by Obsidian, an imprint of New American Library,
a division of Penguin Group (USA) LLC

First Printing, April 2015

ISBN 978-0-451-41995-8

Printed in the United States of America

For the gang at Starbucks

Acknowledgments

As always, I owe a debt of gratitude to my agent, Kim Lionetti, and my editor, Jessica Wade, for helping make this book the best it could be. Thanks also to Isabel for managing dozens of big and small details throughout the process. Thanks go to fellow writer Laurie Cass, who can always find something good to say about even my weirdest ideas. Thank you to all the readers who have embraced this new series. And thank you to Patrick and Lauren for their unwavering love and support.

Chapter 1

Elvis had left the building. I watched him make his way across the snow-packed front walk to my SUV, parked in the driveway. I opened the passenger door, and he dipped his dark head in acknowledgment before he disappeared inside. The cat—not the swivel-hipped singer—had been named after the King of Rock and Roll, and he'd pretty much trained everyone around him to cater to him like he was royalty, musical or otherwise.

Elvis settled himself on the passenger seat and turned to look over his shoulder as I backed onto the street, the way he always did. It was icy-cold, and my breath hung in the morning air. It was also very early. One of the best things about sharing the drive to work with the cat was the fact that he wouldn't try to engage me in conversation before I'd had at least one cup of coffee.

Lily's Bakery was the only place to get a decent cup of coffee before seven a.m. in North Harbor, Maine. We had no fast-food outlets, no drive-throughs. The slower pace of life was what attracted so many tourists, that and the gorgeous scenery along the Maine coast.

As usual, Lily was behind the counter when I tapped on the door. She kept the shop locked until seven thirty but let in regulars like me who stopped for coffee and a muffin to start the day. She smiled and came to open the door, and the warmth of the small space with its delicious aroma of fresh bread and cinnamon wrapped around me.

Lily ran Lily's Bakery with some help from her mother and another baker. She'd been selling her baking since she was twelve. The small building on the waterfront that housed the bakery had been left to Lily by her grandfather. She'd opened the business when she was twenty and had been running it, successfully as far as I knew, ever since.

"Hi, Sarah," she said. She was wearing skinny jeans and a pink thermal shirt with her long, dark hair up in its usual high ponytail. When she was in the kitchen, she kept her hair under a Patriots ball cap.

"Good morning," I said, trying not to yawn.

I could smell the rich, dark-roast coffee. I stopped by the bakery a couple times a week, and it was always made by six thirty. Lily had her morning routines, and she kept them like clockwork. She'd told me once that she got everything ready for the morning before she left the night before so she didn't have to waste time going down to the basement, where she kept a lot of her supplies.

Lily reached for the pot, and I handed her my stainless-steel mug. I looked in the glass-front display case as she poured, wondering if a chocolate éclair could be classed as breakfast food.

"You really need to have some protein at breakfast," she said.

I looked over at her. "I need some breakfast at breakfast."

She smiled, which I thought she didn't do enough of. "What's in your refrigerator, Sarah? You don't have to stick to traditional breakfast food in the morning, you know."

I took the mug she was holding out and recited the contents of my fridge. "Three eggs, two tomatoes that taste like the carton the eggs are in, and a spinach quiche that fell."

Lily looked confused. "Quiche doesn't fall."

I moved to the end of the counter for the insulated carafe that held cream and the glass-and-stainless-steel sugar-cube dispenser that looked like a futuristic spaceship.

"It does if your hands are wet when you pick up the dish," I said, adding cream and two sugar lumps to my mug. "Half the egg-and-cheese stuff went on the floor, and the spinach all slid to one end." I stirred my coffee and screwed the lid on. "And then I kind of forgot to set the timer when I put it in the oven, so the spinach turned out extra crispy." I walked back over to her. "Let's just say I don't think even the raccoons would eat it if I dumped it in the backyard."

I could see Lily was trying not to laugh. "Hang on a minute, Sarah," she said. She went back to the kitchen and returned after a minute with something wrapped in waxed paper. "Here. An apple-raisin roll with some Swiss cheese, on the house."

"Thank you," I said, taking it from her.

Lily walked me to the door. I glanced at the inky sky through the big front window. There was something smeared on the glass, I realized.

I took a step closer to the window. "Lily, were you egged?" I asked.

She nodded, folding her arms defensively over her chest. "This is the second time."

"Because of the development?"

"Yes."

About two and a half months ago, a developer from Massachusetts had proposed a mixed-use project—housing and business—for part of the harbor front, unique to the area and environmentally responsible. It had the potential to increase tourist traffic, and since all the businesses along the harbor front depended on visitors for a big part of their income, everyone had gotten behind the idea. Everyone except Lily.

"Did you call the police?" I asked. It looked like the culprit had used an entire carton of eggs on the window.

"I did," she said with a shrug. "But it happened in the middle of the night. There isn't much the police can do. No one was around, and I don't have a security camera."

She eyed the smeared glass for a moment; then she looked at me again. "It's been more than just eggs."

"What do you mean?" I asked.

"Someone switched a canister of sugar for salt in the kitchen, they canceled a delivery of cardboard cake boxes and waxed paper, and I'm pretty sure someone let a mouse loose in the store." She pulled a hand over her neck. "I can't prove any of it has anything to do with the harbor-front proposal, but realistically, what else could it be?"

"I'm sorry," I said. "Egging the windows and switching sugar for salt is childish. You don't deserve this kind of thing just because you don't want to sell the bakery."

Lily exhaled slowly. "Some people don't see it that way." Then she shook her head. "Luckily, the egg will come right off with the ice scraper I use on my windshield." She pasted on a smile that told me the conversation was over. "Anyway, I need to get back to the kitchen. Have a good day, Sarah."

"You too," I said. "Thanks for breakfast."

Elvis's whiskers twitched as I climbed back into the SUV. He eyed the wax-paper-wrapped sandwich and then looked expectantly at me.

"You can have a tiny bite of cheese when we get to the shop," I said, pulling my keys out of my jacket pocket. He immediately settled himself on the seat, looking straight ahead through the windshield, his not-so-subtle way of saying, "Let's get going."

My store, Second Chance, was a cross between a

secondhand store and an antiques shop. We'd been open for less than a year. We sold everything from furniture to housewares to musical instruments—mostly from the fifties through the seventies. Some of our stock had been repurposed from its original use, like the tub chair under the front window that in its previous life had actually been a bathtub, or the quilts my friend Jess made from recycled fabric. I often went in to the shop early if I had a project on the go. At the moment I was working on removing five coats of paint from an old wooden dresser that dated to the early 1900s.

I'd worked in radio after college until I'd been replaced on the air by a syndicated music feed and a tanned nineteen-year-old who read the weather twice an hour. As a kid I'd spent my summers in North Harbor with my grandmother. It was where my father had grown up. I'd even bought a house that I'd renovated and rented. When my job disappeared, I'd come to Gram's, at the urging of my mom, to sulk for a while and ended up staying and opening Second Chance. The store was in a redbrick house, built in late 1800s, in downtown North Harbor, Maine, just where Mill Street began to climb uphill. We were about a fifteen- to twenty-minute walk from the harbor front and close to the off-ramp from the highway, which meant we were easy for tourists to find and get to.

I parked the SUV at the far end of the parking lot. Elvis already had a paw in the top of my canvas tote, his way of letting me know he had no intention of walking across the lot to the back door. I scooped him inside the bag and grabbed my breakfast.

The first thing I did when I got inside was nudge the heat up a few degrees, grateful that my brother, Liam, had checked the old house from top to bottom before I'd bought it. He'd discovered that the old furnace was on its last legs, and I'd managed to get the seller to knock several thousand dollars off the purchase price.

Elvis and I had breakfast in my second-floor office while the workroom warmed up, and he managed to mooch two bites of Swiss cheese. After I ate, I grabbed my dust mask and left him there washing his face.

It was a busy morning, and I didn't go back to my office until it was time to leave to meet my friend Jess for lunch. Wrapped in my heavy parka, I cut across the parking lot and stepped inside the old garage we used for storage, tugging on the soft gray hat that my grandmother's friend Rose had knitted for me. I pulled my gloves out of the pocket of my jacket.

"I'm leaving," I called to Mac. "Can I bring you anything back?"

Mac was in the far corner of the building, gloves and jacket off, working on the knot that kept a pair of old brown blankets wrapped securely around two ladder-back chairs.

Mac was the proverbial jack-of-all-trades. There wasn't anything he couldn't fix as far as I'd seen. Second Chance may have been my store, but Mac was more partner than employee.

"Yeah," he said. "Maybe a turkey sandwich and some soup." He looked in my direction then and held up one hand, feeling for his wallet with the other.

I shook my head. "That's okay," I said. "I'll get it when I get back."

He smiled. "Thanks."

Mac was tall and strong with close-cropped black hair and light brown skin. He'd been a financial planner, but he'd walked away from his high-powered job to come to Maine and sail. It was his passion. All summer in his free time he had crewed for pretty much anyone who asked. There were eight windjammer schooners that tied up at the North Harbor dock, along with dozens of other boats. Eventually Mac wanted to build his own boat. He worked for me because he said he liked doing something where he could see some progress at the end of the day. He was an intensely private man, so I didn't know much more about him now than I had when I'd hired him a bit more than six months ago, but I'd always been able to count on him and I trusted him completely.

He rubbed his hands together and blew on them. "Tell Jess I should have a couple of boxes for her at the end of the week."

I nodded. "I will. I should be back in about an hour."

I walked across the parking lot, happy to see several cars parked there. January was a slow month for pretty much every business in North Harbor, but it hadn't been as quiet as I had expected. Maybe that was because we were a resale shop. Our prices weren't cheap, but they were reasonable and on most things I was willing to dicker.

I'd backed my SUV into the last space at the end of the small parking lot—which was even smaller at the moment, thanks to the mountains of snow that flanked it on two sides—so only a little snow had drifted onto the front window. As soon as the engine was running, I turned on the heater and got back out to brush the snow off my windshield. When I'd bought the used SUV in the fall, Liam had tried to convince me to choose a vehicle with seat warmers. I was starting to think I should have listened to him.

I had no trouble finding a place to park when I got downtown. North Harbor sits on the midcoast of Maine. "Where the hills touch the sea" was the way it'd been described for the past two-hundred-plus years. The town stretched from the Swift Hills in the north to the Atlantic Ocean in the south. It was set-tled in the late 1760s by Alexander Swift, and it was full of beautiful, historic buildings and quirky little businesses. Not to mention some award-winning restaurants. The town's year-round population was about thirteen thousand people, but that number more than tripled in the summer with summer residents and tourists.

North Harbor was very different in the middle of winter than it was in the summer and fall. I wouldn't have been able to park just a couple of doors down from McNamara's in August, and there would have been more than three tables occupied inside the small sandwich shop. Jess was at a table to the left of the main counter. Her hands were wrapped around a heavy mug of what I guessed was hot chocolate, and she was deep in conversation with Glenn Mc-Namara.

Jess had grown up in North Harbor, but we really hadn't been friends as kids, probably because I was a summer kid and she was a townie. We'd gotten close in college, when I'd put an ad on the music-department bulletin board at the University of Maine, looking for a roommate. Jess had been the only person to call because, it turned out, she'd taken the ad down about five minutes after I'd put it up.

Jess had been studying art history and I'd been doing a business degree and taking every music course I could manage to fit into my schedule, but we'd become fast friends. It was impossible not to like her. She had an offbeat sense of humor and a quirky sense of style.

Glenn caught sight of me first. "Hey, Sarah," he said. "Has it gotten any warmer?" He was tall with broad shoulders and still wore his blond hair in the brush cut he'd had as a college football player.

I shook my head as I pulled off my gloves and hat. "No," I said. "According to Rose, it's cold enough to freeze the brass off a bald monkey."

Glenn laughed.

Rose Jackson wasn't just one of my grandmother's closest friends, she also worked part-time for me at the shop, along with another of Gram's friends, Charlotte Elliot. Rose had been a teacher and Charlotte a school principal. I'd known them my whole life, so working with them meant I got mothered and gently—or sometimes not so gently—instructed on what I should do a lot of the time.

I loved them and I knew they loved me and only wanted me to be happy. We just didn't always agree on what that was.

I pulled my hands through my dark hair. I kept it in long layers to my shoulders. Without the layers it would have stood up all over my head in the dry air when I pulled off my hat.

"At least we dodged that storm that came down from the Great Lakes," Glenn said with a shrug of his shoulders.

Jess and I nodded in agreement. My grandmother, who had grown up in North Harbor, said that there were only three topics of conversation in town during the winter: the blizzard that had missed us, the blizzard that was headed our way, and the blizzard that we were standing in the middle of. She was more or less right.

"What can I get you?" Glenn asked as I took off my jacket and hung it on the back of my chair. The little shop smelled like fresh bread and cinnamon.

I glanced at Jess.

"I already ordered," she said.

"I'll have a bowl of whatever the soup of the day is and a cheese roll, please," I said.

He nodded. "Coffee, tea or hot chocolate?"

Out of the corner of my eye I saw Jess swipe a dab of whipped cream from the edge of her dark blue mug and lick it off her finger.

"Hot chocolate, please," I said. "But no whipped cream."

"I'll take hers," Jess immediately said, holding up her mug.

Glenn smiled. "It'll be just a couple of minutes."

I sat down opposite Jess, loosening the scarf at my neck. "So how was your morning?" I asked.

She took a long drink from her hot chocolate before she answered. She was wearing a deep-blue V-neck sweater over a lighter blue T-shirt, and her long brown hair was pulled back in a low ponytail. She was my height—about five six—and her eyes were blue where mine were brown. Jess had the kind of figure that people described as curvy, where I was usually described as looking athletic.

"Busy," she said. "I have twenty-five choir robes to alter, plus three bridesmaids' dresses and a cape to finish before Valentine's Day." She held up a hand. "And I'm not complaining. I'm not usually this busy this time of year."

Jess was a seamstress. She could and did do everything from hemming a pair of jeans to designing and sewing some spectacular gowns. What she enjoyed most was reworking vintage clothing from the fifties through the seventies. She had a funky, off-beat style and was a whiz with a sewing machine and a pair of scissors. Just about everything she restyled ended up in a little used- and vintage-clothing shop down on the waterfront that she shared space in with a couple of other women. And she made one-of-a-kind quilts from recycled fabric that we sold for her on consignment in the store. The three-quarter-length cocoa-brown hooded coat tossed over the empty chair to her left had originally been a full-length wrap coat with shoulder pads so wide it could have been worn by a linebacker for the Patriots. Jess had reworked it into something that would have been at home on the pages of a fashion magazine.

"That reminds me," I said, turning in my chair to stuff my gloves into my jacket pocket. "Mac asked me to tell you he should have a couple of boxes for you by the end of the week."

Mac and I were always looking for new items to sell in the shop. Families overwhelmed by clearing out their parents' homes had led to some great finds for us, including the claw-foot bathtub that Mac and I had made over into a chair that I hadn't been able to bring myself to sell when it was done. Occasionally we took on clearing out an entire house—something we'd just finished doing for the five children of Janet Bennett.

Since we didn't sell clothing at Second Chance, Jess often bought items she felt she could rework or turn into quilts. She'd been making her own clothes since she was teenager. She liked to say that she'd been an environmentalist before it was cool. Mac pretty much knew her likes and dislikes. Families and seniors themselves tended to just throw up their hands over closets stuffed full of old clothing, and

"Just make it go away" was something we'd heard more than once.

"That'll work," Jess said. "Thanks. Do you know what he has?"

"I think there are a couple of fake-fur vests, and I know I saw some jeans."

Her eyes lit up, and I knew she was already dreaming up ideas for everything.

Glenn came back with our lunch then: chili and a couple of sesame breadsticks for Jess, vegetable noodle soup and a roll crusted with golden cheddar for me.

"Thanks," I said as he set a tall, steaming mug of cocoa in front of me. A small bowl of whipped cream and a spoon were still on the tray he was holding. He put a dollop in Jess's cup, said, "Enjoy," and left.

"Why don't you just order a cup of whipped cream next time?" I said.

"Do you think I could do that?" Jess asked as she pulled apart one of the breadsticks. "Maybe with lots of chocolate shavings and just a couple of inches of hot chocolate in the bottom."

I made a face and shook my head at her.

She grinned back at me across the table. "So how was *your* morning?" She pointed at me with half a breadstick before taking a big bite off the end of it.

"Good," I said. "I sanded a dresser and then I worked on the website." We were running a small online store through the Second Chance website. I was constantly surprised by the things collectors were willing to buy and pay the shipping for.

I remembered something I'd wanted to ask Jess.

"Did those two vanloads of skiers stop in at the store yesterday afternoon?" I asked. "Avery gave them directions."

Avery was the granddaughter of Liz French, another of my grandmother's closest cohorts. She was living with Liz after some problems at home and going to a progressive high school that only had morning classes, so she worked most afternoons for me. Avery had an eclectic sense of style and a smart mouth, and being around her grandmother Liz and Liz's friends seemed to be good for her. It had always been good for me.

Jess nodded and wiped a bit of chili from her chin with her napkin. "They did. I sold three sweaters and two pairs of jeans." She smiled. "I love Canadians."

This winter, due to some weird configuration of the jet stream, Maine had a lot more snow than the Canadian Maritime provinces. We'd had a steady stream of skiers since the first week of December. They were responsible for more than half of my business in the last two months, and I was hoping the weather would work in our favor through February.

"Did you go running last night?" Jess asked, a contrived look of innocent inquiry on her face.

I reached for my cheese roll. "Yes, I did," I said. "Would you like to hear how many laps I did around the track, or would you rather just ask me what you really want to know, which is did I see Nick Elliot?"

She shrugged. "Okay. Did you?"

Like Jess, Nick Elliot had grown up in North Harbor. Charlotte was his mother. They were a lot alike—sensible, reliable, practical. Unlike Jess, Nick and I had been friends as kids. I'd had a massive crush on him at one time. He'd worked as a paramedic for years, but now he was an investigator for the state medical examiner's office. He was still built like a big teddy bear—assuming teddy bears were tall, with broad shoulders. He had sandy hair, warm brown eyes and a ready smile. He wasn't quite the shaggy-haired wannabe musician he'd been when we were teenagers, but as Gram would say, he cleaned up well.

I dunked a hunk of bread in my soup and ate it before I answered. "No, I didn't. Nick feels pretty much the same about running as you do."

She smirked at me across the table. "You mean he only runs if someone is giving away free cookies? Go Nick." She did a fist pump in the air.

"If you think Nick is such a catch, why don't you go out with him?" I asked.

She wrinkled her nose at me. "Not my type. Anyway, whenever you're around, he doesn't notice any other women. We could be at the pub and I could get up and dance on one of the tables in a thong while Sam and the guys did "Satisfaction," and Nick still wouldn't notice me. I think you should at least have a little fling with him."

"Well, I don't," I said dryly, "and thank you for putting that picture of you dancing at the pub in my head for the rest of the day."

"You're welcome," she said, wiggling her eyebrows at me before she bent her head over her chili again.

Jess kept insisting that Nick had had a thing for me since we were teenagers, and certainly Charlotte and some of Gram's other friends hadn't been subtle in their matchmaking efforts, but Nick hadn't made a move, which I couldn't fault him for because neither had I.

"Nick and I are just friends," I said for what felt like the twentieth time. "Between the shop and working on the last apartment at the house, I don't have time to have a relationship or a fling or anything with Nick—or anyone else."

Jess grunted around a mouthful of beans and tomato sauce. She swallowed and gestured at me with her spoon. "You make time to eat. You make time to run, for heaven's sake. You can make time for a little tongue wrestling with Nick."

"That's disgusting," I said. "I'm changing the subject. No more talking about Nick Elliot's tongue." I could see Jess was about to say something. I shot her a stern look. "Or any other part of him," I warned. "Tell me about the meeting yesterday with the North Landing people."

Her expression turned serious. "Lily still won't even talk about selling the bakery, and there doesn't seem to be any legal way the town council can expropriate the land. And there doesn't seem to be any way to rework the plan around her either."

"Was she even at the meeting?" I asked.

Jess shook her head. "No, and it's a good thing she wasn't. Time is getting short and people's tempers are even shorter." She played absently with the end of a breadstick. "You know how tense things have been around town for the last couple of weeks. It was even worse last night. Jon West isn't going to wait much longer. If he can't build here, he's going to take the project somewhere else. He wants North Landing to be his showpiece, a way to entice other towns and cities to build similar projects, but he isn't going to wait forever. Some people are pushing for the council to go to court and find a way to force Lily to sell under eminent domain."

Jon West owned North by West, the development company floating the harbor-front project. I had a vintage light fixture at the shop that he'd expressed an interest in having us refurbish for the hotel that was planned as part of the development.

"I don't see how that would work," I said, tucking a loose strand of hair behind my ear.

"Me neither," Jess said. "And even if it did. It would be so ugly." She dipped the end of her breadstick in her soup and took a bite. "The weird thing is there was a proposal for the waterfront almost five years ago, right after Lily opened, and she didn't have a problem with that."

"People change," I said. "She's being hassled at the bakery, you know."

"How do you know?" Jess asked.

"I stopped for coffee this morning. Someone had egged the big front window."

Jess just shook her head.

"I wish there were some way to change Lily's mind." I pushed my empty bowl away. I couldn't read the expression in Jess's eyes—frustration, maybe, mixed with a little sadness.

"It's not going to happen," she said flatly. "As far as Lily is concerned, the development will destroy the charm of the waterfront. I think she's wrong, but . . ." She shrugged. "On the one hand, I kind of admire her for sticking to her principles. On the other hand, I think the development would be good for business, and it's not like I have a money tree in my backyard."

I reached for my cup. "Vince said pretty much the same thing to me yesterday." Vince Kennedy played in The Hairy Bananas with Sam Newman, who owned The Black Bear pub and who had been a second father to me since my own dad died when I was five.

Jess ate the last spoonful of her chili and nodded. "Lily holding out is a lot worse for him. He'd be able to unload that old building his father still owns. He'd be free of the taxes, and I'm guessing with his father in that nursing home, they could use the money."

"Yeah," I said. "I think the development offer on that old warehouse is pretty much the only offer Vince has had in the last four years."

"I have a feeling this is just going to get uglier than it already is," Jess said. "I wish Lily could see what holding out is doing to the town. People are desperate to make North Landing happen." Her mouth twisted to one side. "And when people get desperate, they do stupid things."

Chapter 2

I checked my watch. I needed to get back to the shop. I got Mac's soup and sandwich, plus a cinnamon-cranberry muffin for myself. Jess wrapped herself in her chocolate truffle coat and wrapped me in a hug.

"We're still on for Thursday-night jam?" she asked.

"Absolutely," I said.

"If you get a better offer and you need to bow out, that's okay," she said as she pulled out of the hug, a smile twitching at the corners of her mouth.

I put a hand on one hip and gave her a wide-eyed look of mock surprise. "What could be better than spending the evening with you?"

She laughed and shook her head. "You're such a suck-up," she said. "I'll see you Thursday night."

Thursday-night jam was a musical jam session Sam hosted every Thursday night in the off-season at The Black Bear. You could count on Sam and the guys from The Hairy Bananas being there, and from time to time other people would show up with a guitar or bass and sit in for a few songs.

Mac was in the main workroom/storage area when I got back to Second Chance.

"You'll probably need to warm up that soup in the microwave," I said, handing him the brown paper takeout bag.

"I'm sure it's fine," he said, setting down the screwdriver he'd been holding.

I could hear voices, agitated voices, coming from the store.

"Do I want to know what's going on in there?"

"I've been asking myself that same question," Mac said with a smile. "So far the answer is no." He hooked a nearby wooden stool that I'd just primed the day before and sat down, lifting the container of soup from the bag and pulling off the lid.

I leaned against the dresser he'd been working on. "You don't have a spoon," I pointed out.

"Not a problem." He lifted the waxed cardboard cup to his lips as though it were a cup of coffee.

I glanced over toward the door that led to the main part of the building. I could still hear the voices. I couldn't really make out more than a few odd words, but I recognized Rose's voice along with Avery's and Liz's.

Rose was a tiny white-haired dynamo, barely five feet tall in her sensible shoes. She—along with Charlotte—worked part-time for me, mainly because they were both reliable and hardworking, and I wasn't good at saying no to Gram.

Mac leaned over and set his soup down on the floor. "I'll go see what's going on, Sarah," he said.

I put out a hand to stop him. "It's okay," I said. "I'll go."

He raised an eyebrow. "You sure?"

"This is not my first rodeo," I said, straightening up and pushing back the sleeves of my sweater.

"Okay. Yell if you need backup."

There were no customers in the store. Charlotte was behind the cash desk with a cloth in her hand and a set of sherry glasses on the counter in front of her. She still had the bearing and eagle-eyed gaze of the high school principal she'd been. Even in flats she was taller than I was. She had soft white hair and warm brown eyes behind her glasses. Right now those dark eyes looked troubled.

When I'd left for lunch, Charlotte had told me that she was going to dust and polish all the glassware in the store. Now she was frowning and her glasses had slid halfway down her nose. Rose had her apron in one hand. The other hand was on her hip, and she was looking up at Liz, who had several inches on petite Rose.

I knew by her stance and the way her chin was jutting out that Rose was arguing about something with Liz. Liz was standing in the middle of the room. She was wearing a vivid cardinal-red coat and a soft, butter-colored hat. As always, she looked polished and elegant. Her nails were manicured and her blond hair curled around her face. Unlike Rose and Charlotte, Liz refused to let her hair go gray.

"If the Good Lord hadn't intended me to be blond, he wouldn't have created Light Golden Blonde, number thirty-eight," she'd said emphatically to Rose when the latter had suggested Liz let her hair "go natural."

Beside Liz, Avery was engulfed in an oversize black parka I knew she'd bought for eight dollars at Goodwill.

"Oh, for heaven's sake," Liz said, waving one hand as though she were shooing away a bug. "Just call him."

"No," Rose said. I knew that tone and that body language. Liz should have as well. The two of them had been friends for most of their lives even though they were very different. Rose dressed for comfort; Liz was all about style. Rose favored sensible shoes, and Liz had never met a pair of heels she didn't like.

"Call who?" I asked.

Rose turned to look at me over her shoulder. "No one," she said.

"Josh Evans," Liz countered.

I looked at Rose. "Why do you need a lawyer?"

When Arthur Fenety had been murdered back in the fall and their friend Maddie Hamilton was arrested for the crime, Rose, Liz and Charlotte—unhappy with the way the police were handling the case—had investigated, with some help from Alfred Peterson, who had to be the world's oldest computer hacker, and, well, me. Nick had argued vehemently with his mother about it. I'd tried my best to rein them in, but somehow I'd gotten pulled into the investigation myself. Josh had taken on Maddie's case when I'd asked, and Liz had quietly covered the bill.

"I don't need a lawyer, dear," Rose said. "As usual, Liz is overreacting."

"What would be the harm in at least talking to him?" Charlotte asked. As a former school principal, she was often the voice of reason.

Rose pointed a finger from Liz to Charlotte. "Both of you need to have your hearing checked because I've told you twice now. Josh is a very nice young man, but I don't need a lawyer."

Liz made an exasperated snort and shook her head.

I turned to Avery. "What's going on?"

She shrugged. "Rose got kicked out of her apartment. Nonna and Charlotte want her to make a stink about it."

I turned back to look at Rose again. "You were evicted?" I said.

Silently, she pulled an envelope out of her pocket and held it out to me.

I took out the single sheet of paper inside. It was an eviction notice. Rose had until the middle of February to vacate her apartment at Legacy Place. There was no reason given.

Legacy Place was the former Gardner Chocolate factory—"A little bite of bliss in a little gold box." In the early nineties the company had built a new manufacturing facility just on the outskirts of North Harbor. The old factory had had a number of lives in the next twenty years, and then about three years ago the Gardner family had renovated the building into a much-needed apartment complex for seniors. Rose derisively called the place "Shady Pines."

"Rose, they have to at least tell you why they've asked you to leave," I said, gesturing with the envelope. "Maybe it's not a bad idea to call Josh."

Josh Evans had grown up in North Harbor. Not only had he been Maddie Hamilton's lawyer when she was accused of Arthur Fenety's murder, but he'd known Rose—and Liz and Charlotte and my grandmother—since he was a kid. I knew he'd be willing to help.

Rose laid a hand on my arm. "I don't want to fight this," she said. "I don't want to make a big fuss."

I knew she'd only originally agreed to the move to the seniors' apartment complex to put her daughter's mind at rest. Getting evicted was the perfect out for her. I looked at her without saying anything. Her cheeks grew pink and her gaze slipped away from mine. I was right.

I looked at the letter again. It was dated the second week of January—two weeks earlier. "How long have you known about this?"

"A while," she hedged.

"Why didn't you say something?"

"She's stubborn," Liz said, a frown forming between her perfectly groomed eyebrows.

I turned my head to look at her. "Pots and kettles, Liz," I said, raising one eyebrow.

Her mouth moved, but she didn't say anything else.

"I wanted to get my ducks in a row before I told you all," Rose said, looking around at all of us. She sounded a little less defiant and a little more embarrassed than before.

"And did you?" I asked gently.

She sighed. "Not exactly."

"Rose, do you have somewhere else to live?" Liz asked.

"Not yet." Her chin came up. "I'm still weighing my options."

"Well, while you're weighing them, you can move in with Avery and me," Liz said, nodding her head as though everything were settled, which I knew it wasn't.

"Say yes," Avery immediately said, a huge smile stretching across her face. "Please. Right now I'm the only one who cooks. If Nonna made a cake, even a dog wouldn't eat it."

Liz shot her a look. She could actually cook. She just didn't see why she should.

"Sorry, Nonna, but that's true," Avery said with an offhand shrug.

"Thank you both, but no," Rose said firmly. She looked directly at Liz. "How long have we been friends?"

"Not as long as it feels, sometimes," Liz retorted.

"If we lived together, I'm sure I'd try to smother you in your sleep by the end of the second week," Rose said, her expression completely serious.

Liz narrowed her blue eyes. "Are you implying I'd be difficult to live with?"

"I'm not implying it," Rose retorted. "I'm coming right out and saying it. You would be difficult to live with. I don't want to ruin our friendship, and I don't want to go to prison because I put a pillow over your face." She leaned toward me. "Although I could probably get off for justifiable homicide."

"I heard that," Liz said. "And I am not difficult to live with."

Beside her, Avery gave a loud snort.

Liz fixed her gaze on her granddaughter and held up two perfectly manicured fingers. "Two words. Boarding school."

I knew she wasn't serious. So did Avery.

Avery held up her hand, the fingers spread wide apart. "Five words, Nonna," she countered. "You can't program the DVR."

"Rose, would you live with me?" Charlotte asked.

Rose half turned to smile at her friend. "Thank you," she said, "but you don't have anywhere to put me, and I'm not putting you out of your room."

An ice dam on the roof of Charlotte's house just after New Year's had caused a leak in her spare room. The roof had been patched and Nick had pulled up the soggy carpet, but the ceiling and one wall still needed to be repaired, and given Nick's schedule, who knew when that would be.

Rose held up a hand. "And before anyone gets any ideas, I'm not living in sin with Alfred. He already offered."

Avery opened her mouth to say something, but Rose cut her off.

"And we're not getting married, either, in case anyone has any ideas." She leaned toward me again. "Remind me that I need to get some Bengay. I think Alfred pulled something getting up off his knees."

I couldn't help smiling at the thought of stoop-shouldered, bald-headed Alfred Peterson, whose pants were generally up around his armpits, getting down on one knee to propose to Rose.

"Everyone, please, there's no need to overreact," Rose said in a louder voice. She gestured toward a notepad sitting on the counter by the sherry glasses Charlotte had been dusting. "I went online and made a list of apartments for rent. I'm sure I'll find something."

"You wouldn't have to find something if you'd stop being so pigheaded and move in with me," Liz retorted.

Charlotte had been studying Rose's list. She looked up, caught my eye and gave her head a slight shake.

Charlotte knew North Harbor better than I did. If she didn't think any of the places on that list were acceptable, that was good enough for me.

I rolled my neck from one side to the other. My shoulders were tying themselves in knots. "We'll find something for you somewhere," I said to Rose. Maybe Jess would know of a place, I thought. Or Sam.

"Why can't Rose just take that extra apartment you have?" Avery said.

Elvis had wandered in from somewhere, and he

loudly seconded her suggestion as she bent down and picked him up.

"Oh, I can't do that," Rose said. "And Sarah's not finished renovating that apartment anyway."

My house, an 1860s two-story Victorian, was divided into three apartments. I lived in one. My grandmother lived in the other when she wasn't traveling with her new husband, John. The third apartment was where my family—my brother, Liam, my mom and my stepfather—stayed when they came to visit. I hadn't finished the renovations in that space, but I wasn't that far from being done, either.

Liz walked over to the cash desk and picked up the pad with Rose's list. She scanned the page.

"You can't live in any of these places," she said. "Two of them are too far from downtown, and another is so—" She made a face. "Well, let's just say even the cockroaches won't live there."

"We don't have cockroaches here. It's too cold," Rose said matter-of-factly, shaking out her apron.

I sighed softly. Rose was family. They were all family—Rose, Charlotte, Liz and Avery. A family that was more like the Addams Family than the Waltons sometimes, but family nonetheless. I loved them all.

I turned to look over my shoulder at the door to the workroom. Somehow I'd known Mac was there, leaning against the doorframe, arms folded over his chest. A look passed between us.

Sometimes it felt as though Mac could read my mind. This was one of those times. I dipped my head ever so slightly in Rose's direction. Mac gave me an almost imperceptible nod in answer to my unspoken question.

Rose and Liz were still arguing. I came up behind them and wrapped my arms around Rose's shoulders. "Come live with me," I said. "Mac will get the apartment ready, and since we won't be living in the same space, you won't have to put a pillow over my face in the middle of the night."

"I can't," she said. "You're young. I'll cramp your style."

I laughed until I realized she was serious. Then I gave her a hug. "Rose, I don't have a style. I work. I run. I go home. Say yes. Please. It'll get Liz off your case, and it will put my mind at ease."

She hesitated. "All right. Yes."

Charlotte and Liz beamed. Avery cheered. Even Elvis gave an enthusiastic meow.

I glanced back at Mac, who smiled at me as well.

It really was the best solution. And really, what could go wrong?

You'd think I'd know better than to ask that question.

Chapter 3

Liz came back just before five to pick up Avery. It had turned out to be a busy afternoon, not Canadian skiers this time, though. We'd had a busload of Japanese tourists on a snow tour through New England. They'd taken great delight in posing for pictures next to the snowbanks in the parking lot, and they'd bought every refurbished quilt and vintage table-cloth in the shop.

Avery was vacuuming and Rose was out back with Mac. I walked over to Liz, put both hands on her shoulders and rested my chin on them. She smelled like lavender talc.

"Are you sure you want to do this?" she asked.

I knew she meant letting Rose have the apartment.

"I'm sure," I said.

"I'll pay for whatever you need to get the place ready."

"No, you won't," I said. "I already have every-thing. Liam got me a great set of kitchen cabinets for a song from a rehab he did. They were only a year old and they're just like new. Mac's going to do the work, and we'll work out some kind of compensation."

My brother, Liam—who, strictly speaking, was my stepbrother; our parents had married when we were little—was a building contractor. He was very involved in the small-house movement.

"I think you're going to have to be creative about that," Liz said.

I nodded, making my chin bounce against my interlaced fingers. "I know. So thank you for the offer, but I have it all covered."

"You're a stubborn child," Liz said. She turned her head and narrowed her eyes at me, but I could hear the affection in her voice.

I stretched forward and kissed her cheek before I dropped my hands and straightened up. "That's because I spent my formative years with all of you."

"Well, at least let me take you out to Sam's for supper," Liz said. "Avery is going over to Rose's to bake." Unlike Liz, Rose loved to cook. Not only was she teaching Avery to bake, but she was trying to teach me some basic cooking skills. So far Avery was the better student.

Supper with Liz or my specialty, a scrambled-egg sandwich with the two cardboard tomatoes from my fridge. It was an easy choice.

"Okay," I said.

We agreed on a time, and I went to cash out.

Liz left with Rose and Avery.

"Would you like a ride?" I asked Mac.

"I'm good," he said, pulling up the hood of his parka. He gestured at the large chandelier that was sitting on a tarp in front of a section of shelving. "What do you think? It's pretty much cleaned up."

The chandelier was cast bronze, an Art Deco–style from the 1920s, according to my research. The circular body of the light was about two feet across, with a cutwork design of four phoenixes rising from the ashes. Behind the cutwork was a red glass shade. We'd bought it from a department store in Portland that was closing. And Jon West had expressed interest in buying it. If the harbor-front project went ahead, the beautiful old light could end up in the lobby of the proposed hotel.

I walked over for a closer look. "Oh, Mac, it looks good," I said. What I'd been afraid was patina caused by aging had turned out to be just dust and grime. Now that both the metal and the glass were clean, the beauty of the light was even more apparent.

"Glad you like it," he said. "We should be able to turn a decent profit. And you might want to thank Avery. She spent a lot of time working on that glass shade with a toothbrush."

"I will," I said.

I locked up my office, and when I came back downstairs, I found Elvis was sitting by the back door, waiting for me.

"Looks like it's just you and me," I said. I opened the door, and he stuck his furry black nose outside and promptly sat down.

"Let's go," I urged.

He looked up at me and meowed.

I knew what he wanted. "You can walk," I said.

He craned his neck around the door for another look at the parking lot. Then he looked at me again, tipping his head to one side so I couldn't miss the ropy diagonal scar that cut across his nose.

"Just because you have that battle scar doesn't mean I should carry you," I said.

The vet had no idea how Elvis had gotten his war wound. "I'll bet you the other guy looked worse, though," he'd said.

Elvis was still watching me. He didn't even twitch a whisker.

I pulled on my gloves. "Anyway, I can't carry you. I already have a load." In addition to my purse, I had a large tote bag full of table runners that I was hoping my homemade stain fighter would work on.

Elvis got up, walked over to the canvas carryall and put a paw on top.

"No. You can't ride in there. I don't want cat hair all over those runners."

He dipped his head, licked his chest several times and then shot me an expectant look.

I blew out an exasperated breath. I was arguing with a cat. A cat! And who was I kidding? He was winning.

I'd had Elvis for the past seven months. He'd just appeared one day, down along the harbor, mooching from several different businesses, including The Black Bear. He had shown up at the pub about every third day for a couple of weeks. No one seemed to know who owned the cat. That scar on his nose wasn't new; neither were a couple of others on his back, hidden by his fur. Sam had managed to con me into taking the cat. I was pretty sure Elvis had been in on the scam, too.

He was very social, I'd discovered. He'd quickly made himself at home in the shop, charming customers who could easily get distracted by his war wounds and end up spending more than they'd intended. I'd quickly realized that Elvis's skill at sales wasn't his only ability. Strange as it sounds, he had an uncanny knack for figuring out when someone was lying. When someone was stroking his fur, if they were not being completely honest about whatever they happened to be talking about, he somehow knew, the knowledge evident in the disdainful expression on his furry face.

Mac had pointed out that researchers had discovered dogs had a part of their brains devoted to decoding emotions in people's voices, so why couldn't Elvis decode lies from the truth? Jess's theory was that Elvis was the feline version of a polygraph. Somehow he was responding to changes in a person's heartbeat, breathing and skin. It was as good an explanation as any. The problem was the kitty lie detector acted as one only when it suited him.

I slid the strap of my purse over one shoulder, put the tote bag over the other and bent down to pick him up. "This doesn't mean you've won," I said. "It just means I don't want to stand here all night."

"Murr," he said. He looked up at me, a guileless look in his green eyes. We both knew who had won.

"Why do I even have these . . . discussions with you?" I said to him. He regarded me thoughtfully, as though he couldn't figure it out, either.

Juggling purse, bag and cat, I managed to get the door locked and hurried across the lot to the SUV. I put everything, including Elvis, on the passenger side. The cat shook himself and then got settled on the seat. As I pulled out of the lot, he looked both ways. Whoever Elvis had belonged to before me had clearly driven around with him a lot. He'd look both ways at an intersection or a stop sign, and he'd even turn to check over his shoulder when I backed up. Once he'd meowed loudly at me when I'd run a yellow light. It was like having a little furry backseat driver.

Once we were home, I got Elvis some fresh water and a little something to eat. Then I went into the bedroom to change. It was cold, but I wanted to walk downtown to meet Liz instead of taking the SUV, so I put on leggings under my jeans, along with a lavender turtleneck and a heavy cable-knit sweater over that. I stuck my feet into my favorite fleece-lined booties and went out to the kitchen.

"Want to go take a look at the apartment?" I said to Elvis. He was washing his face, but he took a couple more swipes behind his ear and came over to me.

"Merow!" he said with enthusiasm.

I'd ended up with my house after a series of trades that had started when I'd cleaned out an old barn and the owner had told me I could have the rusting Volkswagen Beetle I'd discovered inside just for getting it off the property. Eventually I'd ended up with the chance to buy the old Victorian plus a pretty decent down payment for it. My apartment was on the main floor at the front. Gram had the second-floor unit. I wasn't sure if she and her new husband, John, would keep it, or if they'd eventually want something bigger. At the moment they were in New Orleans for the winter, building houses for the charity Home for Good. I missed Gram, but I hadn't seen her so happy in a long time.

The apartment Rose would be taking overlooked the backyard. Like Gram's place, it had a covered verandah. I let myself into the unit and stood in the kitchen, looking around at all there still was to do. It was the room that needed the most work. The bottom cupboards were in place and so was the countertop, but the doors hadn't been hung, and there was no sink or taps and no upper cabinets at all.

The walls were going to need to be touched up as well. Elvis was nosing around in the living room where the cabinet uppers were stacked on a tarp. The walls and the ceiling in there needed a couple coats of paint.

"Did I undersell how much there still is to do?" I asked the cat.

He looked around the room and made a sound halfway between a burp and a snort. I bent over and scooped him up. "Thank you for that vote of confidence," I said.

He leaned over and licked my ear.

Elvis was contentedly ensconced in front of *Jeopardy!* when I headed out, the TV set on a timer to shut off when the game show was over. He watched the show faithfully, Monday through Friday. I had no idea why he liked it so much. Maybe it was the theme music, maybe it was host, Alex Trebek, or for all I knew, maybe Elvis was playing along at home.

I got to The Black Bear about five minutes before Liz. The place was only about a third full, typical for a Tuesday in January, I knew. Sam gave me a hug and showed me to a booth along the back wall. He was tall and lean. His shaggy hair was a mix of blond and white, and he was usually wearing a pair of dollar-store reading glasses.

"Is Jess meeting you?" he asked.

I shook my head. "No. Liz."

"What can I get you while you wait?"

"I'm not driving," I said. "So maybe a glass of wine."

"I have this new hot-toddy recipe," Sam said, running his fingers over his beard. "Want to try it?"

I eyed him suspiciously. Sam's drink concoctions had a tendency to lead to a person waking up wearing a sombrero, with their cheek drool-stuck to the table and no memory of the previous twelve hours.

"What's in it?" I said.

"Cranberry juice, apple cider, Patrón, Drambuie and some fresh lime," he said, ticking off each ingredient on his fingers.

"Tequila and apple cider?" I shook my head. "I think I'll just stick with a glass of white wine."

Sam leaned over to plant a kiss on the top of my head. "Good choice," he said. "I'll send someone right over with it."

Liz arrived just as my glass of wine did. "I'll have a cup of coffee, please," she said to our waiter. "And it's one check. Mine."

He nodded. "I'll be right back."

Liz tossed her coat onto the seat of the booth and slid in next to it.

"What are Avery and Rose making?" I asked.

"Some kind of five-layer lemon cake with the raspberry preserves Rose put up last fall. Avery picked all the berries for her."

"It sounds good," I said, rubbing my hands, which were still cold, together. Maybe I should have ordered the hot toddy after all, I thought.

"It probably will be," Liz said as the waiter came back with her steaming mug of coffee. "I don't have the patience to teach Avery how to bake. Not that I bake anyway."

We both ordered the hot turkey sandwich. I knew the turkey would have been roasted earlier in the day, the gravy hadn't come out of a can and the thick slices of multigrain bread had come from Lily's in the morning order.

Liz looked around. "It's quiet," she said. "I was hoping we'd have a few more buses of tourists from that snow tour."

"I talked to the bus driver from today's group," I said. "There should be a couple more buses through on the weekend."

"And if we get a little more snow, we should see more skiers," Liz said, reaching for the tiny pitcher of cream the waiter had brought when he'd brought her coffee.

"Were you at the meeting about North Landing last night?" I asked.

"Oh yes." She tapped one peach-hued nail on the table. "You know, even with the Japanese tourists and the Canadian skiers, off-season revenue for most of the businesses in town is down close to ten percent."

I wasn't surprised. Although I hadn't been in business last winter, my profits were off about eight percent from my estimates. Luckily, the online store was making up the difference.

I traced the rim of my wineglass with a finger. "Do you think there's any way the town can force Lily to sell the bakery?" I asked.

"No," Liz said with a shake of her head. "I don't see how they can make eminent domain—or anything else for that matter—work. A good lawyer could argue against the public-use clause."

I exhaled loudly. "Is there a chance that Lily can be persuaded to change her mind?"

Liz laughed, but there wasn't any real humor in the sound. "Name someone who hasn't tried. A couple of people spoke to Caroline, for all the good it did—which was none."

Caroline was Lily's mother. I sometimes saw her running at the track when I was there. I had no idea how she felt about the development project. I did know that Caroline was the kind of person who'd support her daughter no matter what her own opinion was. My own mother was the same way.

The waiter arrived then with our sandwiches. They came with a side of cranberry chutney and another of apple carrot salad.

Liz picked up her knife and fork, cut a bite of her sandwich and ate it. "Oh, that's good," she said. She set down her fork and reached for her coffee. "You know, if the development were to go ahead, I could live in one of the new apartments, eat here whenever I felt like it and never have to lay eyes on one of Avery's kale frittatas again."

"Kale is good for you," I said, putting a forkful of cranberry chutney on top of my sandwich.

"Yes, I'm sure you eat it all the time," Liz said, raising her eyebrows over the top of her glasses.

"Avery is good for you, too," I said.

"Point to you," she said with a smile.

"Would you really sell your house and move into an apartment?" I asked.

"Maybe." She shrugged. "Avery won't be with me forever, and if you tell Rose this, I'll smack you with my purse, but I don't think I'd like Legacy Place any more than she has."

I made an *X* on my chest. "Your secret is safe with me."

We ate without talking for a couple of minutes. Then I thought of something I'd meant to ask Jess. "Liz, isn't there some way the development could just be built around Lily's Bakery?"

Liz put down her fork and knife, looked around for our waiter and, when she caught his eye, pointed to her empty coffee cup. "You're not the first person to think of that, and no, it can't. You see, the basements of the buildings on either side are connected to the basement of the bakery. At least they were when the buildings on that whole end of the street were constructed. There are fire doors between each one, but they're connected."

I frowned at her. "Connected? How?"

"From the bakery and the bookstore right on down to that old building that belongs to Eamon Kennedy, at one time the basement was all just a big common dirt cellar for storage. Rumor has it that space was part of the underground railway at one point."

"I had no idea," I said.

Liz shrugged. "Most people don't, but my first husband was a bit of a history buff. I've crawled around just about every old building in town. Frankly, I think it's a part of North Harbor history we should talk more about."

I tried to imagine Liz in her high heels and perfect manicure crawling around the dirt-floor basement of some old building. The mental image made me smile, and I bent my head over my plate.

"Never mind grinning, missy," Liz said tartly as though she'd just read my mind. "Just because I clean up well doesn't mean I can't get down and dirty."

I lifted my head and smiled at her. "I'll remember

that," I said. I took another sip of my wine. "If the basements are all closed off now, why couldn't the developer just tear down the other buildings and leave the bakery?"

The waiter came with more coffee. Liz added cream to hers and stirred before she answered. "I'm no structural engineer, but as I understand it, it has to do with the integrity of the common outside stone walls. Basically, if the other basement walls are taken down, Lily's will collapse as well, like a row of dominoes. Without her property, Jon West can't get a building permit to tear down the buildings around the bakery."

She picked up her cup. "There was some talk about just working around the bakery anyway, but since the engineer's report details the possible damage to the building if they go ahead, Lily would be able to sue, well, practically everyone if her basement collapsed. She could keep the whole project tied up in court for years."

"No wonder there's so much animosity toward her," I said, skewering a chunk of turkey and swirling it through a puddle of gravy on my plate.

"You heard about the—I don't know whether to call them 'pranks' or 'vandalism,'" Liz said.

I nodded. "I didn't just hear. I saw."

Liz frowned at me. "What do you mean 'saw'?"

"I stopped in for coffee. It looked as though someone had hurled about a dozen eggs at the front window."

"What's the world coming to?" Liz asked, shaking her head. She tried the apple carrot salad and gave a murmur of approval. "That kind of childish behavior isn't going to fix anything."

I couldn't help playing devil's advocate. "I know," I said, nodding my agreement, "but when some people get frustrated, they also get stupid."

"Stupid is as stupid does," Liz retorted, pushing up her glasses with one finger. "I'm frustrated with the whole situation, but you don't see me sneaking around in the middle of the night toilet papering the bakery."

"Someone toilet papered the bakery?" I said, my fork paused in midair.

Liz made a dismissive gesture with one hand. "No, no, no. I was just trying to make a point about how ill-advised some people's behavior can be. The Emmerson Foundation holds the mortgages on two of the buildings that would be coming down for the development. Both of them are in default, and I don't see the owners coming up with the money anytime soon. If the North Landing project falls through, the foundation will be out more than a million dollars. That's money that was earmarked for upgrades to the Sunshine Camp."

I leaned against the back of the booth. "Oh, Liz, I had no idea that much money was involved."

"Well, it isn't exactly something I've been trumpeting all over town." She twisted her gold wristwatch around her arm. "I did do something that in retrospect was ill-advised, though."

"What was it?" I asked, crossing my fingers figuratively if not literally that I wasn't going to have to call on Josh Evans's legal skills once I heard her confession.

Liz sighed. "When I said a couple of people talked to Caroline, well, I was one of them."

"Oh, Liz," I said softly.

She waved a hand at me. "I know. It was a stupid idea, trying to get to Lily through her mother. Caroline was nice about it, nicer than I probably would have been in the same position."

I pulled my hands through my hair, gathered it all at the nape of my neck and let it fall on my shoulders again. It had been a long day and I was getting tired.

"What time were you at the store this morning?" Liz asked, clearly trying to change the subject away from Lily and the waterfront development.

"Oh-dark-thirty," I said.

One well-groomed eyebrow went up, but Liz didn't say anything.

"I'm still sanding paint off that old dresser, and I wanted to put the last coat of clear wax on the chair I've been working on so Mac can take it down to Jess. She's going to reupholster it for me."

"And did you?"

I nodded, reaching for my wineglass.

"Good," Liz said. "Then there's no reason to get up with the chickens tomorrow morning."

"Except I have to pick up five dozen rolls for the hot-lunch program at the school first thing in the morning." I held up a finger. "Remind Avery that I'm picking her up early, too. She's going to help at the school, since she doesn't have any classes herself tomorrow."

"I'll remind her," Liz said. "When you consider what tuition costs at that private school of hers, you'd think they'd be in classes a little more often."

I didn't say anything. I just looked at her across the table.

She set her cup down. "Don't worry. I'm not going to make a speech about how in my day I walked four miles to school barefoot through six feet of snow, uphill both ways."

"I thought it was five miles," I said, raising an eyebrow at her.

Liz grinned. "Maybe if I'm lucky Avery won't have time to make me one of those hideous green-juice concoctions for my breakfast." Her blue eyes narrowed, she tipped her head to one side and looked thoughtfully at me.

I shook my head. "Don't even think about sending that child out to my car with some kind of organic kale smoothie," I warned, "or Rose won't be the only one you'll have to watch around your pillows!"

Liz laughed. She had a great laugh, smoky and husky, and it made me glad all over again that I'd decided to come back to North Harbor after my radio career had gotten derailed.

We finished the meal talking about my grandmother and John and the house-building project they were working on in New Orleans. We both passed on dessert.

"Where are you parked?" I asked when we stepped out on to the sidewalk in front of The Black Bear.

Liz pointed down the street.

"I'll walk you down," I said, hooking my arm through hers.

She stuck out her foot in a black leather ankle boot with a two-inch spike heel. "Are you suggesting I can't walk in these? Or are you afraid I'm too decrepit to make it on my own?" she teased.

"Maybe I'm afraid I'm too decrepit to make it to the corner," I countered.

As we came level with Lily's Bakery, I caught sight of Lily inside, wiping down the top of a small round table by the front window. And she caught sight of us. *Don't come out,* I thought. But she dropped the cloth on the table and headed for the front door. I let out a breath, and Liz patted my arm with a gloved hand.

"It's all right, Sarah," she said softly.

Lily stepped in front of us on the sidewalk, blocking our way. Her dark-brown eyes flashed with anger, and the color was high in her cheeks.

"You had no right to try to do an end run around me by going to my mother," she said to Liz, her normally soft voice laced with anger. Her long brown hair was pulled up in a high ponytail. She didn't have a jacket on, only a white-and-blue-plaid shirt over a thermal tee and jeans, but she didn't seem to notice the cold.

"You're right," Liz said in a calm, steady voice. "And I'm sorry."

"That doesn't change anything," Lily said. Her hands were clenched into fists at her sides. "I'm not selling. Stop pressuring me. Stop hassling me. And stay the hell out of my business!" She turned and disappeared back into the bakery.

I felt a tremor go through Liz's arm and I didn't think it was due to the cold.

"I've never seen Lily that angry," I said.

Liz swallowed and looked back over her shoulder at the little shop as we started walking toward the car again. "Neither have I," she said. "I should have known Caroline would tell her."

"That was very nice, apologizing to her like that."

"I shouldn't have gone to her mother," Liz said, giving me a sideways look. "I don't know why I thought it would make a difference. Lily's her baby. Of course she's going to stand by her."

"It'll work out," I said as we came level with Liz's car. "If this project doesn't work out, maybe some other developer will be interested. Maybe someone will come up with a smaller project, a different one."

Liz smiled at me. "Sometimes you're so like your grandmother," she said. She let go of my arm and touched my cheek for a moment before pulling out her car keys. "Can I drive you home?" she offered.

I shook my head. "Thanks, but it's not windy and my coat is warm. I think I'll walk. But thank you for dinner."

"You're welcome, my dear," she said. "I'll make sure Avery is ready in the morning. Have a good night."

I waited until Liz pulled away from the curb. She looked in her rearview mirror and waved at me. I waved back; then I stepped to the curb and looked both ways, planning to jaywalk instead of going back to the corner to cross.

"You're not planning on trying to cross the street, are you?" a voice said behind me. "Because that would be against the law, and I'd be forced to make a citizen's arrest."

I turned to see Nick Elliot standing behind me. He was wearing a black quilted jacket, a black-and-red knitted cap over his sandy hair and a big smile.

I folded my arms over my chest. "Let's just say, hypothetically of course, that I was thinking about crossing here instead of at the corner: How would you be planning on apprehending me? I'm pretty fast."

He frowned in mock seriousness. "Trying to avoid capture would be a waste of time. I know where you live." He paused. "And I'd tell my mother on you."

I held up a hand. "Okay. You win. I'll walk to the corner. I don't want any trouble with Charlotte Elliot."

Nick laughed, his chocolate-brown eyes gleaming. I started across the sidewalk toward him and stepped on a small patch of ice. My foot skidded out from under me, and I pitched forward, right into Nick's arms.

"I've got you," he said, holding me tightly.

My hands had landed on his chest. I caught the scent of his Hugo aftershave, the same one he used to wear when we were teenagers. Jess swore the reason he still wore it was because he was still hung up on me. I thought habit was the more likely reason. That and I'd noticed Charlotte had bought it for him at Christmas.

"You all right?" Nick asked.

I was suddenly aware that his arms were still around me. And it was wonderfully warm, pressed up against his broad chest.

"I'm okay," I said, taking a small step back out of his embrace.

Nick kept one hand on my arm. "Be careful. That's not the first patch of ice I've seen tonight."

I smiled up at him. "See? If I'd crossed the street, I'd be fine."

He grinned. "No one ever said staying on the straight and narrow was easy."

My mouth moved, but I didn't say anything for a moment. Then I shook my head. "Nope," I said. "I was trying to work in 'heading down a slippery slope into a life of crime,' but I can't do it."

Nick laughed. "What are you doing down here anyway?"

"I had supper with Liz at The Black Bear. I was just on my way home. What about you?"

He gestured over his shoulder. "I was at the bookstore." He raised an eyebrow. "Are you parked close by, or did you walk?"

"I walked," I said.

"So did I." He smiled. "Can I walk you home?"

"I don't know," I said, working to keep a straight face. "Can you?"

Nick laughed and shook his head. "You spend too much time with my mother." He raised an eyebrow. "Seriously. I'll walk you."

"You don't have to do that," I said. "I promise not to break any laws on the way there."

He smiled at me. "Do you remember what I told you the last time I walked you home?"

That had been more than three months ago. But I remembered. "You said, 'I am my mother's son.'"

"Uh-huh," he said, turning up the collar of his jacket, "and you said that we both get that same look when we've got our minds set on something."

"In other words, don't argue."

He nodded. "Yes."

I pulled up the zipper of my coat, pulled the sleeves down, and tied my scarf a bit tighter at my throat.

With a hand still on my arm, Nick moved me to his left side and tucked my hand in the crook of his elbow. "Just so you don't get any ideas about breaking the law when we have to cross the street." The smile went all the way up to his dark eyes.

We walked back to the corner, crossed over and headed down the street in the direction of my house. I was acutely aware of the warmth of Nick's body beside me, and it seemed I could still smell his aftershave. My heart seemed to be beating a lot faster than made sense.

This was stupid, I told myself. This was Nick I was walking arm in arm with, not some romance-novel cover boy. Nick, whom I'd known since I was a kid. Nick, who once wiped his nose on my *Mighty Morphin Power Rangers* T-shirt.

I realized he'd just said something to me and I'd missed it. "I'm sorry. What did you say?" I asked.

"I just asked if you and Jess were going to be at the pub Thursday night. Where were you?"

"I was just thinking that you still owe me a T-shirt. A *Mighty Morphin Power Rangers* T-shirt, size medium."

"I don't think so," he said.

I leaned sideways and looked up at him. "Excuse me. I beg to differ. You wiped your nose on mine. You got boy cooties—and worse—all over it."

He stopped walking. "First of all," he said, holding up one gloved finger, "my mother washed that T-shirt. It was fine. Second of all, I was making social commentary when I wiped my nose on your shirt."

"Social commentary?" I said, struggling not to laugh.

Nick pulled himself up to his full six-foot-plus height. "Yes. Social commentary. Maybe you don't remember, but you tried to say that those Mighty Morph-whatever Power People could take on the Justice League. Wiping my nose on that shirt was my way of showing my disdain for your opinion."

"Mighty Morphin Power *Rangers*," I said, putting the emphasis on the last word. "Not Power People. And for your information, the Rangers could have wiped the floor with the Justice League."

Nick gave a snort of laughter. "Not likely."

"I have one word for you," I said. "Megazord."

Then I pressed my free arm diagonally across my chest.

"What? Are you about to swear some kind of oath? The code of terrible teenybopper kids' shows?"

"The *Mighty Morphin Power Rangers* is classic TV," I said. I tapped my jacket with one finger. "I have a T-shirt on under this, and I'm protecting it from you."

Nick started to laugh, and he pulled me back against his side. "I missed this, you know," he said as we started walking again.

"Being reminded about your dubious taste in superheroes?" I teased.

He scrunched up his nose at me. "No. I mean being with someone who knows me so well. It's nice."

I nodded. "Yeah, it is."

He reached over and gave my hand a squeeze.

"And, yes, Jess and I are planning on Thursday-night jam. You want us to save you a seat?"

"Please," he said. "I'm not on call."

I bumped him with my shoulder. "Are you bringing your guitar?"

"Are you?" he countered.

"Point taken," I said.

"We should get together and play sometime," Nick said. "My mother thinks you spend too much time working."

I laughed. "She says the same thing about you."

"That's because she wants grandchildren." He steered me around a slippery patch on the sidewalk.

"She told you that?" I asked.

"Not directly. She just points out every baby she sees when we're out anywhere."

I bumped his hip with mine. "Oh, you poor thing," I said with mock concern.

"I'm not going to get any sympathy from you, am I?" he said.

I shook my head. "Nope. I work with your mother and Rose, and Liz is in the store all the time. They're always trying to stage-manage my life." I smiled up at him. "Suck it up, big guy."

He laughed and pulled his hat down over his forehead a bit more with his free hand. "So what's new with you?"

"Not much," I said. "The store's been a little quiet, but we're getting more traffic on the website."

"Do I dare ask what's happening with Charlotte's Angels?" he said. "If I ask Mom, she changes the subject."

After they'd "solved" Arthur Fenety's murder last spring, Rose, Liz and Charlotte had decided to open their own detective agency, Charlotte's Angels, Discreet Investigations, the Angels for short. They'd set up their office in the sunporch at the store. Winter had moved them inside to the far end of the back room.

"They haven't had any big cases," I said. "I think they found someone's missing teeth."

Nick sighed. "Tell me you're kidding."

"I wish I were," I said.

We turned a corner. "I thought they'd give up this whole private detective business."

I shook my head. "Liz, Rose and your mother. You really thought they'd just 'give up'? Did you grow up somewhere else?"

He made a face. "I know. Wishful thinking on my part. Tell me how the work is going in the old garage. When I talked to Liam, he said he got you some shelving for storage." Nick and my brother were good friends.

"He did," I said. "Four big wall units. They're in great shape and the price was terrific. All I need now is for him or Dad to come for the weekend and help me get them up. It's more than Mac and I can do alone."

"Let me know if I can help," he said.

"I will. Maybe I can lure him to town with the chance of hanging out doing gross boy stuff with you."

Nick nodded. "Now that I think about it, it's been way too long since Liam and I have spent the evening down at Sam's. I'm a pretty good wingman, if I say so myself." He raised an eyebrow and gave me a sly smile when he said "wingman."

"I don't want to talk about Liam's love life," I said, shaking my head. "I don't want to think about it. As Avery would say: Ewww!"

We walked in comfortable silence for a moment.

"Did you miss it when you were gone?" I asked. "North Harbor. Everyone."

"You know, at the time, I would have said I didn't." He looked down at me. His mouth moved as though he were trying out the feel of what he wanted to say before he said it. "Now I realize I did," he said. "More than I knew."

We talked about the changes in North Harbor in the years we'd both been away, and suddenly I realized we were in front of my house.

I let go of Nick's arm. "Thank you for the walk home." I yawned, tried to stifle it and failed. "I'm sorry," I said. "It's not the company. It's just been a long day."

He smiled. "You're welcome. And thank you for *your* company." He looked up for a moment at the blue-black night sky shot with stars. "It's good to be home," he said when his eyes finally met mine again.

We looked at each other, the moment stretching out between us. Then Nick cleared his throat and glanced over at the house. I'd left the outside light on. "You'd better get in. It's cold out here." He leaned forward and kissed my forehead, just below my hat.

I headed for the steps, fighting the urge to touch the spot with my fingers. I turned at the door and raised one hand in good night. Nick did the same and then turned and headed down the sidewalk.

I gave in and put my fingers to my forehead. Was it just my imagination that I seemed to still be able to feel the warmth of his lips?

Avery was waiting by the side door of Liz's house in the morning, standing under the outside light, huddled into her giant parka and big polar fleece mittens, hugging a square tin covered with pink peonies to her chest.

"It's so freakin' cold," she said as she climbed into the passenger side of the SUV. "Can I have hot chocolate? Please, please, please?"

"Yes," I said. "If Lily doesn't have any made, we'll stop somewhere and get you some. How did the cake turn out?"

She threw back her hood and smiled. "So excellent." She set the rectangular tin on the seat between us. "This is for coffee-break time this morning," she said. "There's enough for everybody."

I smiled at her. "Thank you, Avery. You didn't have to do that."

"Yes, I did," she said, fastening her seat belt. "Rose gave me that look. You know the one I mean, where she wants you to do something nice, but she doesn't say it because she wants you to do it without being told."

I did.

Avery flipped through the radio stations as we drove down to the bakery. I parked directly in front of the shop and we got out. I peered through the front window, but there was no sign of Lily at the counter getting ready for her day.

"That's odd," I said.

Avery shrugged. "Maybe she forgot we were coming."

"Maybe," I agreed, although that wasn't like Lily at all. Then again, neither was last night's outburst.

Avery tried the door. "Hey, Sarah, this is open," she said.

That was wrong as well. I felt a prickle of apprehension. "Go wait in the car," I said, stepping past her.

She gave me her "stupid adult" look. "Uh, not likely," she said, following me inside.

I called out Lily's name a couple of times, but there was no answer.

"Maybe she's in the kitchen and has her iPod on or something," Avery offered.

It was possible, although I'd never seen Lily with an iPod.

I pushed open the swinging door to the kitchen. The lights were on, but there was no sign of Lily anywhere. And there were no loaves of bread cooling on racks. No cinnamon rolls waiting to go in the oven. Something was wrong. Very, very wrong. Then I saw the door down to the basement was open.

I turned to look at Avery. "Just stay right here," I said. "Without giving me a hard time for once. Please." Something in my voice or my face must have told her not to argue this time.

I walked over to the open basement door, my heart pounding loudly in my ears. Lily was at the bottom of the basement stairs. There was blood on two of the steps. I didn't go down to check on her. I could tell from the angle of her neck that she was dead.

Chapter 4

I turned around and hustled Avery back out to the SUV.

"What's wrong?" she asked.

"Just go," I said, putting one hand in the middle of her back and pushing her ahead of me while I fished my cell phone out of my pocket with the other.

We got as far as the sidewalk before Avery braced her feet. She swung around to face me and crossed her arms over her chest. "I'm not going anywhere until you tell me what's going on," she said. She had the same stubborn look I'd seen many times over the years in her grandmother's eyes.

"There was . . . an accident," I said, choosing my words carefully.

"You mean Lily's dead," she said flatly, "because if she were just hurt, you'd be in there helping her."

I took a deep breath and exhaled slowly. "Yes," I said. "Lily's dead. Please go sit in the car while I call 911."

Avery looked over at the bakery. "All right," she said after a moment. She started for the SUV.

"Avery," I called after her.

She stopped and looked back over her shoulder at me. "Keep your phone in your pocket for now, please." I didn't want her to text her friends with the news before the police had a chance to contact Caroline.

After a moment's hesitation she nodded. "All right."

I turned my back to the SUV, swallowed against the sudden sting of tears and called 911.

The first patrol car arrived in minutes. I explained about finding Lily's body. The officer asked me to stay outside and went in to have a look for himself. After that things got very busy, very quickly. Avery and I waited in the SUV and watched the action swirl around us. When I saw Michelle's car pull in at the curb ahead of us, I nudged Avery.

"I'm going to talk to Detective Andrews for a minute," I said.

Detective Michelle Andrews and I had been best friends growing up, at least for two months of the year. We were both summer kids in North Harbor, and each year we'd just pick up the friendship where we'd left off the previous summer. Then at fifteen Michelle had suddenly stopped talking to me. It wasn't until last winter that I'd found out why. Now we were slowly rebuilding our relationship.

"So stay here," Avery finished. "Yeah, I know."

Michelle smiled when she caught sight of me.

"Hey, Sarah. What's going on?" she asked. She was wearing a dark navy parka and heavy-soled boots. A cardinal-red hat was the only spot of color I could see on her. Michelle was tall and lean with red hair and green eyes. Everything looked good on her.

"I came to pick up five dozen rolls for the hot-lunch program at the elementary school." I stopped for a moment, seeing Lily's body at the bottom of the basement steps in my mind. "Lily . . . Uh, there was no sign of Lily anywhere. I found her at the bottom of the basement steps. She's dead."

Michelle's eyes shifted to the bakery for a moment and then came back to me. "Did you touch the body?"

Lily had already gone from being a person to a body. I reminded myself that Michelle was just doing her job. "No," I said.

She frowned. "How did you know she was dead, then?"

This time I was the one who looked away for a moment. "I don't think anyone's neck could be at that angle and still be alive," I said quietly.

"I'm sorry, Sarah," she said, laying her hand on my shoulder for a moment.

I brushed a strand of hair back off my face and took a deep breath, trying to hold back the tears that were threatening again. "It's all right. Better it was me that found her and not her mother."

Michelle nodded. "Okay, tell me what happened, from the beginning."

There really wasn't that much to tell, but I went over everything that had happened from the time I'd picked up Avery until the patrol car arrived. As I finished, Nick Elliot's black SUV angled in at the curb in front of Michelle's car. He got out, grabbed his gear from the backseat and walked over to us.

"Hey, what's going on?" he asked.

"It's Lily Carter," Michelle said.

He swore, almost under his breath. Then he looked at me. "Sarah, what are you doing here?"

"I was picking up rolls for the hot lunch at the school," I said, rubbing my gloved hands together. "I, uh, found her."

"Hey, I'm sorry." His free hand moved as though he was going to touch my arm, and then he stuffed it in his jacket pocket like he'd suddenly thought better of it.

"Sarah, where's Avery?" Michelle asked, looking around.

I pointed toward the SUV. "She didn't see anything," I said. "We both came back outside as soon as I realized Lily was dead."

"I'm just going to talk to her for a second," she said.

I realized she probably wanted Avery to corroborate my story. Friends or not, she had to do her job.

She looked at Nick. "I'll see you inside."

He nodded.

I watched Michelle walk down the sidewalk to my car. Avery was already getting out. I turned back to Nick.

"What happened?" he said, shifting his weight from one foot to the other.

I pulled my scarf a little tighter around my neck. It was so cold our breath hung in the early-morning air like little smoke signals. "I don't know. When we got here, there was no sign of Lily. The door was unlocked—which was wrong. Lily never unlocks that door before seven thirty. We went in and . . . she was at the bottom of the basement stairs."

Nick swiped a hand over his chin. "If they're like the stairs going down to most of the basements along here, they're an accident waiting to happen— skinny steps, high risers. I don't know why we haven't had more accidents like this."

I looked down at the sidewalk and scraped at a chunk of ice with the toe of my boot.

"What is it?" he asked.

I looked up at him. His head was tipped to one side, and there was concern in his brown eyes.

"Nick, maybe this sounds crazy, but I know Lily's morning routine. I'm in here early at least a couple times a week, getting rolls for the school or coffee and a muffin for myself. She wouldn't have left that front door unlocked, and she wouldn't have been on those stairs, not in the morning. She always got everything ready for the next day before she left at night."

Nick shifted the silver case he was carrying from one hand to the other. "She could have forgotten about the door, and people don't always stick to their routines."

I shook my head. "You didn't know Lily. She did things the same way all the time. All the time. She told me once she thought maybe she was a little OCD." I stamped my feet on the brick sidewalk. The cold was beginning to seep through my heavy boots. "If it were anyone else, I'd agree with you, but not Lily. And you have to have heard how much upset there's been over her refusing to sell for the North Landing project."

"Wait a minute. You think someone killed Lily?" he said, a frown forming between his eyebrows.

I remembered what Jess had said about desperate people doing stupid things. Killing Lily went way beyond stupid. "I don't know," I said finally. "I just can't shake the feeling that there's something off about this."

Nick did put a hand on my arm then. "Sarah, I promise, if there's anything even a little suspicious about Lily's death, we'll look in to it."

"Thank you," I said. I glanced over my shoulder. "I should check with Michelle and see if Avery and I can go."

"I'll call you later," he said. "I might have some questions."

"I'll be at the shop all day," I said, managing a small smile.

We walked back to Michelle and Avery.

"You two can go," Michelle said to me as we came level with the SUV, "but I'll need to talk to you later."

I nodded. "You know where to find me."

Michelle and Nick headed for the front door of the bakery. I walked around the SUV to get in the driver's side and couldn't help looking back at the building. Nick was just going in the door. He turned and looked back at me, raising a hand when he caught sight of me. I lifted my own hand in return.

Avery had already fastened her seat belt. Now she shifted in her seat. "What did the detective ask you?" she said.

"She just wanted to know what happened."

"Yeah, that's what she asked me, too," she said. She slumped back against the seat as I pulled out of the parking spot, navigating carefully around the glut of police and other investigative vehicles.

"So do you think that developer guy killed her?" Avery asked.

I almost drove though the stop sign at the corner.

"Nobody said Lily was killed," I said firmly. Even as the words came out, I was aware that, technically, I'd said it to Nick.

"Oh, c'mon, Sarah," she said, sliding down so she was sitting on her tailbone with her knees pressed up against the dashboard. "I know what's going on around town, and I know Lily was the only person keeping that development thing from happening. And now, big surprise, she's dead. What are the odds of that happening?"

I reached over and flicked her knee with my thumb and index finger. "Sit up," I ordered. "If I have to stop fast, you'll find out what the odds are of you choking on your shoulder belt."

She made a face, but she straightened up.

There were no cars behind us, so I turned to look at her before I crossed the intersection. "I don't know what happened to Lily. Neither do you. Let the police do their job. It doesn't do anyone any good to speculate."

"Okay," she said cheerfully. "But I'm right. I told you there was something creepy about that old guy last fall and then he ended up dead."

The "old guy" Avery was referring to was Arthur Fenety. He'd come into Second Chance a few days before his death. Avery had pronounced him "skeevy" at the time, and in truth I'd agreed with her, although I hadn't said so.

I was uncomfortably reminded that his death was the reason Rose and Alfred Peterson, along with Charlotte and Liz, had gone into business as Charlotte's Angels. They'd had only two cases since Fenety's murder: the missing set of false teeth I'd told Nick about and a would-be suitor who wasn't the woman she'd pretended to be—or, it turned out— even a woman at all. I knew Rose was going to be all over Lily's death if she thought there was anything suspicious about it. I also knew there was no point in telling Avery to keep her suspicions to herself. Like most teenagers, she had the ability to suddenly lose her hearing with respect to certain subjects.

We drove over to McNamara's. I parked in front and turned to Avery.

"I know. Keep a cork in it." She must have seen the surprise on my face. "That's what Nonna would say," she said. "And I will. Lily's mom and her friends shouldn't find out about what happened to her from someone telling someone telling someone else."

"Thank you," I said. Sometimes Avery could be surprisingly thoughtful.

I bought her a hot chocolate and a scrambled-egg-and-ham sandwich from Glenn McNamara. Then I asked him if he had enough rolls in his freezer to sell me five dozen, explaining only that there had been a problem at Lily's without saying why. When he found out they were for the hot-lunch program, he wouldn't take my money.

"A few rolls aren't going to break me, Sarah," he said with a smile.

"I owe you," I said, smiling back at him.

The smile got bigger, and he raised his eyebrows at me. "Someday, and that day may never come, I will call upon you to do a service for me," he said in a pretty good Marlon Brando impersonation.

I laughed. "Anytime, Glenn, as long as it doesn't involve doing anything with a horse's head."

It was almost time to open the store. I decided to detour there first and then take Avery and the bags of frozen rolls to the school after that. I'd already called to let the vice principal know that we were running a bit late, again without saying why.

"As soon as Mac gets here, I'll run you over to the school," I said to Avery as we pulled into the lot at the shop. "You can call me when you're done."

"Okay," she said cheerfully. She'd finished the sandwich in about four bites, but she was still nursing the giant hot chocolate.

Mac and Rose came in together about ten to nine.

"Avery, dear, what are you doing here?" Rose

asked when she caught sight of the teenager. "Aren't you supposed to be at the elementary school?"

"Yeah, we got held up," Avery said.

"What happened?" Rose asked as she took off her coat.

I shot Avery a warning look, which she either didn't catch or—more likely—decided to ignore. "Well . . ." She let out a breath. "Lily's kind of dead."

"Dead?" Rose repeated, her eyes widening.

Mac caught my eye, and I gave a slight nod.

Rose put a hand to her chest. "Oh, my word," she said. Then she looked at me. "What happened to her?"

"I don't know," I said. "Michelle and Nick are there."

"But Lily's so young."

I could see the thoughts turning in her head, or as Jess had once described it, the hamsters running on their wheels.

I walked over to Rose and took her coat from her, laying it across the counter by the cash register. "This is not a case, Rose," I warned. "This is a job for the police."

She nodded at once. "Oh, of course, dear," she said.

I didn't believe her for a moment.

Chapter 5

We heard very little about the investigation into Lily's death for the rest of the week. Both Michelle and Nick came by separately to ask Avery and me a few more questions, but they were both tight-lipped about what they'd discovered so far. It was Nick's job, as an investigator for the medical examiner's office, to figure out how and why Lily had died, and Michelle's to investigate if it turned out a crime had been committed. The fact that no one had said immediately that her death was an accident made me wonder if my suspicions were right.

Rose *seemed* to be staying out of things. She didn't try to wheedle information out of me with cookies and hot chocolate. She didn't try to eavesdrop when Michelle came by with her follow-up questions. She seemed to be doing exactly what I'd asked her to do. Which told me she was up to something.

Cleveland, one of the trash pickers I regularly bought from, came by on Friday with a battered old dining room hutch in the back of his truck. Most of the faux walnut finish was worn off. There were watermarks on the exposed wood and more than a few scrapes and gouges.

Mac stood in the parking lot while I climbed in the back of the half-ton and took a closer look at the piece of furniture. "Tell me you're not going to buy that," he said.

"It's solid wood," I said.

"Good," he countered. "We can burn it for heat if it gets any colder."

I made a face at him.

He just shook his head. "You're on your own with this one, Sarah," he said, heading back to the shop.

"Fine with me," I called after him. I was feeling restless. It had been a while since I'd had a big project to work on. And maybe it would take my mind off what had happened to Lily.

Cleveland and his cousin carried the hutch into the work area, and I paid him twenty dollars for it.

"Did you see the look on his face?" Mac asked after the two men had left. "He thinks he put one over on you."

"Oh, ye of little faith," I said, circling the big piece of furniture. It had three shelves, scrollwork at the top and two louvered doors on the bottom. It stood about five and a half feet high. I was already thinking about possible ways to refinish it.

Mac held up both hands. "I'm not going to say another word."

"You can tell me what a genius I am when this is done," I said.

I took some photos of the hutch so I could study them over the weekend and decide what exactly I wanted to do.

I ended up spending most of the weekend working on the apartment kitchen with Mac. We got the upper cupboard boxes hung and all the doors attached on Saturday. Then, while Mac installed the sink, I painted the living room ceiling. By late Sunday afternoon I was wiping out the insides of the cupboards while Mac screwed on the hardware.

"I never would have gotten so much done without you," I said to him. He was kneeling on the floor, using the cordless drill, and I was halfway up the small stepladder. We both had dust on our jeans and bits of sawdust in our hair—me more so than Mac since he kept his dark hair cropped close to his head.

"I don't mind," he said. "I didn't like the idea of Rose living somewhere she might not be safe." He grinned. "Or if she moved in with Liz, where Liz might not be safe." He fastened the last doorknob and stood up, stretching one arm up over his head and then the other. "Can I help you?" he asked.

I shook my head. For a moment I'd gotten sidetracked watching his muscles move under his black T-shirt. "Thanks, but this is the last one." I wiped the bottom cupboard shelf and dropped my cloth back into the bucket. Then I climbed down, wiping my damp hands on my jeans.

"It looks like a kitchen now," I said with satisfaction, turning slowly to take in the whole space.

"That it does," he agreed.

"Am I crazy, Mac?" I asked, reaching for the bucket that had been balanced on the ladder's paint shelf.

"Are you talking in a general, existential sense, or do you have something specific in mind?" he said, a teasing edge to his voice.

"Both." I set the bucket on the floor and leaned against the counter. "What if Rose drives me crazy? What if I drive her crazy?"

He picked up the drill and began to unscrew the bit. "You'll work it out. You can talk to Rose. She's reasonable."

I shot him a look.

"Most of the time," he amended. He put the bit back in a small plastic case and set the drill itself in the bottom of his toolbox. "Have you always been close the way you all are?" he asked. "If that's not too personal a question."

"It's not," I said. "And yes, we pretty much have. When my father died, Rose, Liz and Charlotte kept my mom and Gram and me going. They didn't just wrap their arms around us. They wrapped their lives around us. They'd always been part of my life, but they became family. Then, when Mom met Peter, my stepfather, they made him and Liam family as well. Do you remember the fairy godmother in Cinderella?"

He nodded.

"That's what they've always been like, more opinionated and no magical powers, but otherwise that's pretty much it."

"It sounds nice," he said, setting the toolbox over by the door.

I shrugged. "It was, although I didn't always think so when I was a teenager." I started to laugh.

Mac narrowed his eyes. "What?" he asked.

"When we were thirteen, Michelle and I wanted to go see Aerosmith in concert down in Portland."

"Michelle. You mean the detective."

I nodded. I couldn't stop laughing. "They took us. Gram, Liz, Rose and Charlotte. All four of them, plus Michelle and me in Liz's big ol' Lincoln Continental. They all had Aerosmith T-shirts and jeans. They had every single CD, which they played all the way there and all the way back, and they sang along with every song. Loudly."

"Liz in an Aerosmith T-shirt?" Mac asked. "No. You're kidding me, right?"

I shook my head, but I couldn't stop grinning at the memory. "Oh, it gets better. We had great seats— some contact Liz had through the foundation. During 'Walk This Way,' Steven Tyler came down off the stage. He was maybe four feet away from us. Remember, Michelle and I were thirteen." I laid a hand on my chest. "We could barely breathe, we were so excited."

"I sense there's more," Mac said, the hint of a smile pulling at his mouth.

"He started dancing with Rose."

"Rose?" His eyes darted from one side to the other.

"Uh-huh. With a whole lot of hip action."

Mac started to laugh as he stretched an arm up

over his head. "You're telling me that Rose Jackson was dirty dancing with Steven Tyler at an Aerosmith concert?"

"There are photos," I said. "And the band was filming the concert for some reason, so somewhere there's video of Rose, as she put it, 'getting down with Steven Tyler.'"

Mac was shaking with laughter now, one arm wrapped across his chest.

I held up a hand. "There's more. You've seen that purple scarf she wears sometimes, with the silver Aztec design?"

He nodded.

"Tyler gave it to her. He slid it off his own neck and wrapped it—there's no other word to use— seductively around her neck."

Mac grinned at me. "Let me guess. You were scarred for life."

I wrinkled my nose at him. "No. That happened when he kissed her. And I don't mean a peck on the cheek."

Mac pulled a hand over his neck. "Don't tell me Steven Tyler slipped Rose the—"

I held up a hand and shook my head. "No, no, no!"

"Well, that's not so bad," he said with a shrug. "Tyler was probably just trying to be nice to a fan."

"Who frenched him," I said, raising an eyebrow for emphasis.

Mac's mouth opened and then closed once more without making a sound. He started laughing again.

I couldn't help laughing again myself. "I can still see Steven Tyler's expression," I said.

"Hey, for all you know, maybe he liked it," Mac said, his dark eyes gleaming with humor.

"Yeah, that's the thing," I said, making a face. "I'm pretty sure he did."

"Oh, now I'm never going to listen to 'Walk This Way' quite the same way ever again." He pushed away from the counter and straightened up.

"Do you have any grandparents-slash-crazy-senior-citizens in your family?" I asked, bending down for the bucket.

"I think Rose and Liz and Charlotte—and your grandmother—are pretty much one of a kind," Mac said. The broom was leaning in the corner by the door to the hall, and he reached for it.

"I can do that," I said.

"So can I," he said.

I took the bucket of dirty water into the bathroom to dump it, realizing that he hadn't actually answered my question. I wasn't surprised. Mac was a master at deflecting personal questions, and I'd never pushed it.

My cell phone rang as I stepped back into the kitchen. It was Jess.

"Are you still working in the apartment?" she asked.

"We're just about done," I said, pulling my hair free from its ponytail.

"I have a shower curtain and a window curtain for the bathroom and a roman shade for the kitchen."

"Aw, Jess, you're an angel," I said. "Thanks."

"Hey, no problem." I pictured her in her sewing room, her feet probably propped up on the table. "Have you eaten yet?"

"No," I said. My stomach chose that moment to growl, reminding me that all I'd had was a banana for lunch.

"Mac still there?"

"Yes."

"Okay. You guys stay where you are. I made pork and cabbage. I'll bring some over, along with the curtains. I really wanna see how the place looks."

A bowl of Jess's pork and cabbage sounded a lot better than anything I would have come up with for supper.

"We'll be here," I said.

"See you in ten," she said, ending the call.

I turned to Mac. "Jess is bringing supper. And unlike me, she can cook. Can you stay?"

He hesitated for a moment and then nodded. "Thanks. I'd like that."

There was a round wooden pedestal table in the living room that we'd moved out of the kitchen. Mac and I each grabbed an end and we set it back in the corner.

"What are you going to do with this when Rose moves in?" Mac asked. He tipped his head to one side and studied the table. At the moment it was painted a muddy shade of brown.

"Take it back to the shop and strip it," I said over my shoulder as I headed back into the living room for the folding chairs that had been doubling as kitchen chairs.

"What are you thinking about for a finish?" he asked, coming to the doorway to take two of the chairs from me.

"I'm thinking a whitewash if the wood is in decent condition."

He nodded slowly.

"Remember those white chairs we got at that yard sale in the fall? The ones with the cat-scratched fabric seats?"

"They smelled like cigarette smoke."

I nodded. "I'm thinking of painting them lavender and getting Jess to make me new seats in some darker purple fabric."

"That could work."

I rinsed my cloth in the sink and wiped a fine layer of dust off the top of the table.

"I was holding on to this for Jess," I said. "She wanted it for the new shop, but now that North Landing is pretty much dead, there won't be a new shop."

"You really think the development isn't going to happen?" Mac asked. He moved around the kitchen, picking up small bits of wood we'd discarded as shims when we were installing the cupboards.

"It'll be months before Lily's estate is settled."

"True, but everything probably goes to her mother. She could sign an agreement to sell to the developer when the property is finally hers."

"She could," I said, taking the cloth back to the sink to shake it out.

"But you don't think she will."

I looked at him over my shoulder. "Lily was so against selling. I don't think Caroline will do it. They are . . . were very close." I hung the wet cloth over the tap and turned, leaning against the counter. "What do you think about the whole proposal? Do you think it's a good idea? Is it sound financially?"

It occurred to me that I could have—maybe should have—asked Mac for his thoughts sooner. He had been a financial adviser for many years before he'd decided he'd rather sail and make things with his hands.

"I just saw a preliminary prospectus," he said, bending down to pick up two thin shims that had somehow slid into the living room. "But what I saw looks good." He straightened up.

"But?" I said.

He exhaled quietly and turned the two scraps of wood over in his hands. "The research seems to be solid. There's definitely an interest in development on the scale West is proposing. His financing is solid."

I sensed a little hesitation. "But?"

"West's carrying a lot of debt for a small company. If this deal falls through, it could break him." Mac shrugged. "Those are just my thoughts based on a quick read-through of the simplified prospectus. I could be wrong."

But he probably wasn't. When Mac gave his opinion, it was after he'd taken the time to think things through.

Jess tapped on the door then so I didn't have a

chance to say anything. She had a gray garment bag in one hand and a red insulated cooler in the other. Mac took the cooler and I grabbed the garment bag, taking it into the bathroom and hanging it over the shower rod because there really wasn't anywhere else to put it.

"The blind is out in my car." Jess gestured at the red bag. "The food and everything you need is inside," she said. She waved her hand in the direction of the hall. "I'll just go get the blind and we can eat."

Right on cue my stomach growled.

Jess laughed. "I'll hurry."

I unzipped the top of the insulated cooler. She'd brought everything—bowls and forks, three small wineglasses and a huge stoneware crock of her pork and cabbage. Tucked in the outside pocket of the bag was a small bottle of apple cider.

Mac opened the cider and poured a glass for each of us while I dished out the pork and cabbage. It was still hot.

"It smells good," Mac said as he moved behind me with the glasses.

"Thank you," Jess said from the doorway. She set the blind on the counter and kicked off her boots. "Oh, this looks nice," she said approvingly, looking around the room.

"Thanks," I said.

She leaned around the living room doorway. "Umm, I like that color on the walls."

The living room, bathroom and bedroom were a creamy, buttery shade that warmed the small rooms.

"That's because you picked it out," I teased.

"And I do have good taste," she retorted.

She shook off her coat and hung it over the back of the chair. "Let's eat," she said.

The meat and sweet cabbage in a spicy sauce was as delicious as I'd promised Mac it would be. About halfway through the meal, Jess ran her hand over the tabletop.

"I hate it, but you might as well sell this table," she said with a sigh. "There's no way North Landing is going to happen now."

I turned to her, my spoon halfway between the bowl and my mouth. "What do you mean by 'now'? Has something happened?"

She looked from Mac to me. "Right. You've been working here all day, so you haven't heard."

"Heard what?" I asked. I felt the bottom fall out of my stomach, as though I'd just rolled over the top of a roller coaster. I knew what she was going to say before she spoke.

"Lily's death has officially been called a homicide."

I rubbed the space between my eyes with two fingers. "You know what this means, don't you?" I said.

Jess looked confused. "No," she said.

Mac gave me a sympathetic smile. "It means the Angels are going to be spreading their wings."

Chapter 6

I was lying on the couch with Elvis sprawled across my chest, trying to read—and failing because someone's big, furry head kept getting in the way—when my cell phone rang later that evening. I put the book on the floor and reached for the phone while Elvis raised his head and glared at me.

"You could always go lie somewhere else," I said.

He narrowed his green eyes at me and flopped back down again.

It was Nick on the phone. "Hi," he said. "Am I taking you away from anything important?"

I folded one arm behind my head. "No. I'm just basically being a lounge chair for a cat. What's up?"

I heard him exhale slowly and pictured him swiping a hand over his chin. "I didn't know if you'd heard: Lily's death has been ruled a homicide."

"I know," I said. "Jess told me." I'd been trying not to think about what she'd said, but I hadn't really succeeded. "Do you think it could have anything to do with the development proposal?"

"That's not really my job," he said. "That's Michelle's department."

Elvis yawned and rolled partway onto his side.

"I know," I said. "But you have to have an opinion. C'mon, Nick. I'm not going to tell anybody."

He sighed. "At this point I don't know."

Neither one of us said anything for a moment. "Someone pushed her down those stairs," I said after a moment of silence.

"You know I can't tell you that," Nick said.

"I didn't ask you anything," I said, sliding up into a halfway-sitting position. That was too much moving around for Elvis. He jumped down to the floor and stalked away, flicking his tail at me because he didn't have fingers. "And I'm not going to repeat any conversation we have. I'm just saying, *hypothetically*"— I put extra emphasis on the last word—"someone must have pushed her."

"Hypothetically, yes," Nick said dryly.

I stretched out one leg and then the other. "But whoever it was didn't just come up behind her and give her a shove. *Hypothetically*."

"Why do you say that?" he asked, and I could hear a note of caution in his voice.

"She was lying on her left side. If she'd been starting down the steps and someone had given her a push, she most likely would have landed on her right side."

For a moment he didn't say anything. When he did finally speak, it was just one word. "Because?"

I grabbed a pillow and stuffed it behind my back.

"Lily went up and down those steps a dozen times a day. So she probably didn't use the railing. I go up and down the stairs at the shop easily that many times in a day, and I know I don't."

"Okay," he said.

"If someone had pushed Lily, her instinct would be to grab for the railing. It's on the left side. If she couldn't get her balance, she'd be leading with her right side as she fell and she'd land on that side. Which she didn't."

"No, she didn't."

"Someone hit her," I said slowly, the idea just occurring to me, making my heart sink. "She was at the top of the stairs. She was turning, and whoever killed her hit her on the back of the head. The momentum and the fact that she wasn't turned completely around means that she would most likely have ended up landing on her left side."

I waited for Nick to say no, to tell me I was wrong.

He didn't.

"But how do you know she didn't just hit her head on one of the steps?" I asked. I knew Nick was very good at his job, and if he said Lily's death was murder, then it was. I just didn't want it to be. I hated to think that the last moments of her life were filled with fear.

Nick let out another breath. Was he stretching his arms up over his head? I wondered. "Okay," he said. "Let's say someone did hit Lily over the head—and I'm not saying that's what happened, just to be clear."

"I know," I said, nodding even though he couldn't see me.

"The injury wouldn't be up in the same place as it would be if she'd fallen, and it wouldn't look the same."

"What do you mean it wouldn't be in the same place?" I asked.

"Did you take any anatomy classes?" Nick asked.

"In high school."

"So you don't know any of the bones in the skull."

"Yes, I do," I said a little indignantly.

My high school biology teacher had had a full-size skeleton in the lab that he'd named Clyde, which we'd all thought was made of some incredibly realistic plastic or resin. There was a bit of an uproar my senior year when it came out that Clyde had been a real person and an alumnus of the school—and really had been named Clyde.

I'd always liked Clyde. Once I'd even done the Macarena with him when the teacher was out of the room.

I pictured the skeleton's bony head now. "The bone in the front where the forehead is, that's the frontal bone," I said. "The bottom part of the jaw is the mandible. The top of the head and the upper part of the back of the head are all parietal bone. And below that is the occipital bone."

"Very good," he said.

I couldn't help smiling as though I'd just gotten a gold star from the teacher. "Thank you."

"If Lily had slipped and hit her head, we'd expect

to see an injury where the occipital bone and temporal bone meet or a bit above that, but not a lot above that area." He didn't even bother to say "hypothetically."

"So if the injury was higher than that, it suggests someone hit her," I said.

"Exactly."

"Okay, but you said the injury wouldn't look the same," I said. "What do you mean?"

"Did you ever hit a piñata with a baseball bat?"

"Liam's tenth birthday party. *Samurai Pizza Cats.*"

I heard something fall in the bedroom. I was guessing that Elvis had jumped up onto the small table I kept beside the bed and had nosed one of my books onto the floor. He'd done that before when he felt my attention was focused somewhere other than on him.

"Pizza what?" Nick asked.

"*Samurai Pizza Cats.* They were three cyborg cats—"

"Let me guess," he interjected. "And they liked pizza."

"Close," I said. "They worked in a pizzeria."

"Of course. How could I have missed that?" Nick laughed then. "I can't wait until the next time I see Liam." He cleared his throat. "When you swing, the end of the bat is moving faster than the part closer to your hands."

"Right." I heard what was probably another book hit the floor in the bedroom.

"So when it makes contact with the piñata, it does more damage than the shaft does farther down the length of the bat."

"Because it has more momentum."

"Exactly."

I couldn't say anything for a moment as I tried not to think about the fact that we were really talking about Lily and not a papier-mâché container shaped like a cat.

"You okay?" Nick asked.

"Uh-huh." I swallowed down the lump that had suddenly tightened in my throat. "Help Michelle catch whoever did this, please?" I whispered.

"I will," he promised.

I cleared my throat. "Nick, you know that Rose and your mother and—"

"I know." I could hear a combination of frustration and resignation in his voice. "I'm beating my head against the wall, thinking I can find a way to convince them to stay out of this—aren't I?"

"Yes."

He laughed. "You couldn't hedge even a little bit? Throw me a bone?"

"Your mother, Rose, Liz—they're all stubborn women. You know that. Put the three of them together and they become an immovable object." I pulled my legs up and wrapped one arm around my knees. "You saw what happened when Arthur Fenety died and Maddie was a suspect. Nothing you or I said made any difference."

I imagined him grimacing and raking a hand through his hair. "And after that little experience, you know what I found?" he asked.

"No," I said.

"Gray hair. A little clump of gray hair, right in the front. You can't see it, but it's there. My mother is giving me gray hair."

I smiled. "She says the same thing about you."

He laughed.

"I'll keep an eye on them," I said. "I promise."

We said good night and I ended the call. I got up and went into the bedroom to check on Elvis. He was curled up on the lounge chair, head on his paws. Two paperbacks had mysteriously fallen onto the floor.

"I know you're awake," I said quietly. One ear twitched, and then he opened one eye, looked at me for a moment and closed it again. I bent down and picked up the books. One of them was a small cookbook Rose had given me full of simple recipes.

"They just use basic ingredients," she'd said. "The kind of things you already have in your kitchen." After she'd looked around my cupboards and refrigerator, she'd amended that to "things most people already have in their kitchens."

I was certain Rose wasn't thinking about cooking right now. She was probably sitting with a cup of tea and Alfred Peterson, figuring out how the Angels were going to investigate Lily's death. I'd told Nick I'd keep an eye on them. I just wasn't sure how I was going to do that and not get sucked into their investigation, because I definitely wasn't getting involved in a murder investigation again.

Famous last words.

*   *   *

When I got to the shop in the morning, Rose and Alfred Peterson were waiting for me. Mr. P.'s pants were tucked into pile-lined lace-up boots. He was wearing a faux-fur trimmed hat with earflaps, a heavy gray wool overcoat with a green-and-blue fringed scarf I knew Rose had knitted for him wound around his neck and at least two pair of mittens, as far as I could tell. He looked like the Pillsbury Doughboy on his first time out in the snow.

"Hey, Mr. P.," I said. "What are you doing here?" It wasn't like I didn't know the answer to my question.

"Rose and I are going to start working on the case," he said.

I pulled the key out of the lock and looked at Rose. "You have a case?"

She squared her shoulders. "I know you have to have heard that Lily's death wasn't an accident."

"I have," I agreed, kicking snow off my boots before I stepped inside and turned on the lights.

"We're going to investigate," she said.

"Do you have a client?"

I saw a look pass between Rose and Mr. P. She wiped her feet on the mat before looking at me again. "Not yet."

"Rose, the police are going to be investigating, along with the medical examiner's office. Both Michelle and Nick are very good at what they do."

It was the wrong thing to say, which I realized as soon as the words were out.

"And we aren't?" Rose said. She held her head high, chin stuck out a little.

"I didn't say that," I said, trying to keep the frustration I was already feeling out of my voice.

"But you were thinking it," she countered.

"Rosie, I don't think Sarah meant any harm," Mr. P. said gently.

"You don't think we can figure out who killed Lily," Rose said, her tone more than a little indignant. She looked so tiny in her blue coat with the collar turned up and her blue-and-red cloche pulled down over her forehead to her eyebrows, but I knew she could do just about anything when she set her mind to it.

"Nice try," I said, "but you're not going to guilt me into saying I think what you're doing is a good idea." Elvis squirmed in my arms, and I set him on the floor. He headed for the doors into the store.

"I wasn't trying to guilt you, dear," Rose said. She gave me her innocent, cookie-baking grandma look.

"Good to know," I said mildly.

Elvis was standing not very patiently in front of the double doors, and I knew that if I didn't start the morning routine soon, he'd start protesting more aggressively. And loudly.

"I have a list of parcels that need to be packed," I said to Rose. "Would you start on that, please?" I glanced at Alfred. "Mr. P., would it be too much trouble for you to go up to the staff room and put the kettle on?"

"I'd be happy to, my dear," he replied. He sat down on the old church bench Mac had put by the back door and started taking off his boots.

I headed for the store. After a moment Rose followed me. She touched my arm as I flipped on the lights.

"I see what you're doing," she said.

"What I'm doing is turning on the lights."

She made a face at me. She looked like a little gray-haired elf with her cheeks rosy from the cold. "You think I'll give up if you don't argue with me. Very sneaky." She was trying to look angry but couldn't manage it.

"I learned at the feet of the masters," I said. I leaned over and kissed the top of her head and then headed for the stairs trailed by my furry sidekick.

Elvis climbed up on the credenza I used for storage in my tiny office and watched me while I took off my outside things and put on my shoes. I kept a bag of cat kibble in my desk. I fished out a couple of pieces and gave them to him, leaning against the long, low piece of furniture while he ate and then gave his face and paws a quick cleaning. Once he was finished, he rested his head against my arm and looked up at me with his green eyes. I reached over to rub the side of his face.

"I didn't win that one, did I?" I said.

He made a soft *murp* that either meant "No, you didn't," or "Don't stop what you're doing."

After a minute I picked the cat up again and set him on the floor. "Time to earn your keep," I told him.

He headed for the main floor like a cat with a purpose, stopping only to pull the door open a little wider with one paw.

Downstairs I gave Rose the list of items that needed to be packed, and she headed out to the storage room to get started. "Mac's out back," she said. "He says he may have a customer for those hammered-tin ceiling panels you two salvaged from Tucker's farm."

The tin panels she was talking about had come from the kitchen ceiling of an old farmhouse that was about to be torn down. The owner had told us we could have whatever we could carry out of the house for free. Mac had immediately zeroed in on the kitchen ceiling. He'd carefully pried down all the three-foot-by-three-foot squares, insisting that they hadn't been painted but were just covered in a layer of dust, grease and grime, baked into place by the heat of the old kitchen woodstove. If he had a possible sale for them, we'd soon be finding out if his guess was right.

Mr. P. touched my arm as I stood there deep in thought. I turned and he held out a blue mug decorated with a grinning Cheshire Cat. "I thought you might like something a little stronger than tea," he said with a smile. He had another mug in his other hand. I was guessing that one was for Mac.

"Thank you," I said, taking the cup from him.

I took a sip. The coffee was strong and hot, just the way I liked it. "You make a good cup of coffee," I said.

"I'm good at all sorts of things," he said. Then he winked at me and headed for the back room.

I watched him go, trying to decide whether he'd just flirted with me or if it was just my imagination.

I managed to spend the next forty-five minutes working on my trash-picked hutch. Mac was right that the piece was in horrible shape, but I still felt confident that with work—and a lot of sandpaper—I could turn it into something that would catch a customer's eye.

Nick showed up about ten thirty. I was hanging a banjo up on the wall with the other instruments.

"Nice," he said, leaning over my shoulder for a closer look. "Where did you get it?"

"Would you believe it was trash-picked?"

He frowned. "Seriously?"

I nodded, turning the banjo a little to the left so it was hanging straight. "I have a couple of Dumpster divers who come in pretty regularly—trustworthy guys, at least so far. One of them brought this in just before Christmas. I had to have it restrung, but otherwise it was in good shape." I smiled at him. "You didn't come here looking for a banjo, did you?"

He brushed a few flakes of snow from his hair. "I was hoping I could talk to you. It's about Lily. There are a couple of questions that have come up . . ." He let the end of the sentence trail off.

"Sure," I said. "Hang on. I'll get Mac to watch things here and we can talk in my office."

"Thanks," he said.

Mac was spreading the hammered-tin panels on a tarp on the floor. Mr. P. was down by the far wall, doing something on his computer that I fervently hoped was legal. Rose was stuffing shredded paper curls into a small box at the workbench.

"Good morning," Mac said when he caught sight of me. "I'm just about set to try your magic degreaser potion on these."

I took a couple of steps closer to him. "Could you watch things out front for me?" I asked, keeping my voice low. "Nick's here. He has more questions about Lily."

"No problem," Mac said, brushing off his hands. He followed me back into the store.

Nick was studying our collection of Valentine's Day cards from the fifties and sixties. Avery had arranged them between two thin sheets of plexiglass that Mac had mounted on the wall with mirror clips.

"Do you remember when we were in school we used to give little cards like these to each other?" Nick asked. "And those little heart-shaped candies with sayings in the middle."

"I remember those," Mac said with a smile. "Never give one that says 'Be Mine' to three different girls." He shook his head.

Nick nodded in sympathy. "Yeah, it's pretty much the same deal with cards that say 'My Sweetness.'"

I crossed my arms over my chest. "See? That's why little girls grow up to be big girls who stay home on Valentine's Day with a chocolate cheesecake and a Ryan Gosling movie marathon."

Nick put a hand to his chest in mock woundedness. "It's not our fault. We were wild stallions. We couldn't be tamed with just one saddle."

"Absolutely," Mac agreed.

I rolled my eyes at the two of them. "We'll be up in my office," I said.

Mac nodded. "Take your time. Good to see you," he said to Nick.

Nick smiled. "You too."

With Nick in my office, the space seemed even smaller. I gestured at the love seat. I'd finally surrendered my red womb chair to the store, where it had sold in two days, replacing it with an armless chair I'd reupholstered in a vivid green-and-black-geometric print. I pulled it closer and sat down. Nick took off his wool topcoat, tossed it over the arm of the love seat and sat down as well.

He was wearing a charcoal suit with a crisp white shirt and a red tie. Avery would have said he looked so fine. She would have been right. He was a very handsome man, but he still had a bit of the small-town-boy quality.

"I'm just trying to clear up a few loose ends," he said. He pulled a notepad and a pen out of the pocket of his coat. "You said that Lily had a routine she followed in the morning."

I nodded. "She did. I think she had routines for everything. She told me once that she got everything ready the night before so she could start baking as soon as she got in the next morning. I think that was one of the reasons she hired Erin Lansing as an assistant baker. They worked the same way."

Nick wrote something on the notepad and looked up at me again. "Tell me about the argument Lily had with Liz the night before she died."

I should have guessed someone would have told the police about that. "Isn't it your job to figure out how Lily died and Michelle's to catch the bad guy—if there is one?" I asked.

"It is," he said, "but there is some overlap in what we do. Tell me about the argument, Sarah."

"It wasn't really an argument."

"So what was it?"

Before I could answer, there was a tap on my door and Rose bustled in carrying a cup of tea in one hand. One thin, star-shaped ginger cookie was tucked onto the saucer.

"Hello, Nicolas," she said. "It's awfully cold outside. I thought you might like a nice, warm cup of tea."

He smiled and took the cup from her. "Are you sure this isn't a bribe so you can pump me for information?" he asked.

"If I were trying to bribe you, I would have brought more than one cookie," she said, smiling sweetly at him.

"How did you know Nick was here, and why didn't you bring me a cookie?" I said.

She reached into the pocket of her apron, pulled out something wrapped in a red-and-white-polka-dot napkin and handed it to me. I could see the curved edge of a round cookie peeking out the top.

"I knew Nick was here because I heard you tell Mac when you asked him to watch the front of the store." One eyebrow went up. "People underestimate me because I'm old." She smiled sweetly at me and left.

"How could she have heard me tell Mac you were here?" I said to Nick.

He'd broken his cookie in half and was about to dunk it in his tea. "I don't know," he said.

"I have ears like a wolf," Rose called from the hall.

Nick laughed and put the entire piece of cookie in his mouth. I shook my head in defeat, leaned against the back of my chair, broke off a bit of my own cookie and ate it.

"Lily and Liz, that Tuesday night," Nick prompted.

"Right," I said. "I was walking Liz to her car. We'd had supper together at Sam's. When we came level with the bakery, Lily saw us through the front window and came out." I stopped and exhaled slowly. "She was very angry."

"About?"

"Liz had gone to her mother to see if Caroline would agree to talk to Lily about selling the bakery for the development."

"What happened when Lily confronted Liz?" Nick asked, taking a drink of the tea. The cup look very small in his large hands.

"Nothing really," I said. "Liz apologized. Lily had her say and went back inside. The whole thing was over in less than a minute." I broke another piece off my cookie and ate it. Then I leaned sideways to peek out my office door and make sure Rose wasn't still lurking in the hallway. There was no sign of her.

I straightened up. "Seriously, Nick. Liz isn't really a suspect, is she?"

He finished writing in his notebook, closed it and

put it and the pen back in his coat pocket. "I can't tell you that," he said, softening his words with a smile.

"How about blink once for yes and twice for no?"

"How about I need to get back to the office?"

He stood up and so did I.

I saw his gaze flick to the door. "She's not there," I said. I reached over and closed the door. "Better?"

He nodded and reached for his coat. "Sarah, I know you said that it's pretty much impossible to keep Rose and my mother and the rest of them out of this case, but it would be a really bad idea for them to get involved. There's a lot of emotion tied up in this whole development proposal. Things could get ugly."

"Hang on. You think Lily's death is tied to the development?"

His mouth moved. For a moment I thought he wasn't going to answer me. Then he sighed and said, "I didn't say it had anything to do with the North Landing proposal."

"All right," I said.

It didn't seem like a good time to point out that he hadn't said it didn't, either.

"This is something 'the Angels' should keep their wings out of," Nick said as he wound his scarf around his neck.

I rolled my eyes at him. "And you and I have had so much success convincing them to stay out of things in the past."

The collar of his coat was folded under on one side. I reached over and fixed it, smoothing it flat with my hand. He smelled wonderful. Hugo after-shave, of course, and something else. Oranges?

Nick smiled down at me. "Thanks," he said. "I never quite mastered getting all dressed up."

"I think you mastered it just fine," I said.

Suddenly the room seemed too warm, and I took a step back from him. I still had half a cookie in my hand, and it seemed like a good time to finish it.

He smiled. "When you talk to Jess, tell her the nachos are on me this week."

I laughed. "I think you're going to regret that offer."

There were no customers in the store, but Liz and Charlotte were downstairs, both wearing their coats, standing by the big front window and talking to Rose. The three of them turned to look at us.

"Hi, Mom," Nick said, smiling at Charlotte. "I didn't know you'd be here." He started toward her. She met him halfway, reaching out to put a hand on his arm.

I joined them. I could see by her stance and the expression on her face that Rose, to use an expression of my grandmother's, was loaded for bear. Her eyes were fixed on Nick.

"What's going on?" I asked.

Charlotte glanced back at her friends.

Rose pulled her gaze away from Nick to me. "The police have a suspect, and we have a *client*." She put a little extra emphasis on the word "client."

"Who?" I asked.

Liz turned to face us. "Me."

Chapter 7

"What?" Nick looked as surprised as I felt. I felt certain he hadn't known.

"Nick has to leave," I said. "I'm just going to walk him out." I waved my finger in the general direction of all of them. "We'll talk about this when I come back in. Don't go anywhere. Please."

"I'll talk to you later," Charlotte said to Nick, giving his arm a squeeze. She looked at me, and then her gaze slid to the front door, her way of asking me, without saying anything, to get Nick out.

I all but pushed Nick to the front door.

"Sarah, I had no idea," he said. He glanced back over his shoulder at his mother, Rose and Liz.

"I believe you," I said, "and so will they when they've had time to calm down, but for right now . . . just go. Please?"

He pulled his gloves out of his pocket. "Okay," he said. "But call me if . . . if they decide to do something stupid, or . . ." He shrugged. "Just call me later, okay?"

"I will," I said. Out of the corner of my eye, I saw Rose looking in our direction. If Nick didn't move soon, I was afraid there was going to be a confrontation I'd just as soon avoid.

I put my hand on his chest and gave him a little push. It was that or hip check him through the heavy wooden door with its leaded glass window, and that seemed like a bit too radical. Rose was coming toward us. "Go," I urged.

He went.

I made a beeline for Rose, draped my arm around her shoulders and turned her back around.

She tried to shake me off, but I'd been expecting that.

"Sarah, I wanted to have a word with Nicolas," she said, clearly annoyed at me.

"I can see that," I said. "I'm trying to stop you."

"I can see *that*," she retorted.

However, I was bigger than she was, so I frog-marched her across the room, reaching out to catch Liz's hand with my free hand. "Are you all right?" I asked.

"Of course I am," she said.

"Want to tell me what's going on over a cup of tea?" I'd learned a long time ago that the three of them didn't do anything without a cup of tea.

Charlotte passed behind me. "The kettle's on," she said, resting her hand on my shoulder for a moment. "I'll go make a pot."

I half turned. "Thank you," I said. I turned back to Rose. "I'm guessing Mr. P. is going to join us?"

"Alfred is part of the team," she said, a bit of a huffy edge in her voice.

"Go get him, then," I said. Monday mornings this time of year were pretty quiet, so we might as well have our tea in the shop. I decided I could keep an eye out the front window for customers.

I turned to Liz. "Are you really okay?" I said.

"No," she said. "I'm damned angry." She narrowed her eyes at me. "Are you going to try to stop us from looking into Lily's death?"

I shook my head. "Nope. I know a waste of time when I see it."

That made her laugh. "You are a very smart girl."

Charlotte came down with the tea just as Rose returned with Mr. P., who was carrying a couple of folding chairs. Once everyone had somewhere to sit and a cup of tea, I turned to Liz. Elvis had wandered in from somewhere and was settled on her lap. "Okay. What happened?" I asked.

"Right after Avery left for school this morning, Michelle Andrews showed up at my door with another police officer," Liz said. "She wanted to talk about what happened last Tuesday night, when you and I were walking to the car and Lily came out of the bakery." She made a sweeping gesture with one hand. "They already know."

"So you told Michelle what happened?"

"Yes," Liz said. She was stroking Elvis's fur, and he looked like he was following her every word, head tipped to one side. And for all I knew, maybe he was.

"Then what?" I prompted.

"Then she asked me about the conversation I had with Caroline."

"Wait a minute. You went to Caroline?" Charlotte said, smoothing her apron over her lap. "I thought your disagreement with Lily was about the development."

Liz looked at her and then reached for her tea and looked away. She was a little pale under her expertly applied makeup. "It was," she said. "I just left out the part about talking to Caroline because you told me it was a bad idea."

"I'm not saying I told you so," Charlotte said gently.

Liz looked at me. "I explained to Detective Andrews that all I did was remind Caroline how important the harbor-front development could be for the town. I didn't ask her to pressure Lily, and she didn't really say anything to me, either way."

"You said you're a suspect," Charlotte said. "What else happened?"

Liz took a sip of her tea and set it down before answering. "She asked me what I did after I left Sarah."

"You went home," I said. "Didn't you?"

Liz nodded. "I did." She was scratching the side of Elvis's chin and he was leaning into her hand, blissed-out.

"So did you tell Michelle that?" I asked, tracing the inside of the curved handle on my cup with one finger.

"No," Liz said. "I told her that if she had any more questions, she should contact my lawyer."

"Why?" Charlotte asked.

Liz turned in her direction. "Because she was wasting time asking me questions that I'd already answered. Twice. She should be trying to figure out who really did kill Lily. She thinks I pushed that child down the bakery stairs over money?" She gave her head a shake. "That's ridiculous!"

"So call your lawyer," I said. "I'm guessing in this case that would be Josh Evans."

Liz nodded.

"So call him," I said, dipping my head in the direction of the phone, which was sitting on the counter next to the cash register. "Avery can corroborate that you were home and Michelle can move on."

"Avery wasn't home," Liz said, bending her head over her cup again.

"Where was she?" Charlotte asked, leaning forward in her chair. Rose was studying her friend, a small frown adding lines to her face.

"She spent the night with Elspeth." Elspeth was Liz's niece, which made her Avery's first cousin once removed or second cousin or something. She was also one of Avery's mom's closest friends.

"Liz, did you stay home all night?" Rose asked.

We all looked at her, but Rose kept her gaze on Liz.

"What kind of a question is that?" Liz grumbled.

"A question that deserves an answer, just like the ones Sarah's been asking you."

It hit me then that Liz had said that she had gone home, but she hadn't said she'd stayed home.

"Did you stay home?" I said.

"No," she finally mumbled.

Rose and Mr. P. exchanged a look.

"Where did you go?"

Elvis was leaning against Liz and she was still stroking his fur.

"Nowhere really," she said. "The house was so quiet without Avery and it wasn't that cold, so I went for a walk." She looked out the window for a moment. "I know it looks bad, but I didn't do anything to Lily. I swear."

I looked at Elvis, still contentedly sitting on Liz's lap. Nothing in his demeanor said he thought that she wasn't telling the truth—that was assuming his lying radar was working. Not that I needed anyone—human or feline—to tell me that Liz was telling the truth. I leaned over and put my hand over hers. "I know that," I said.

"We all know that," Rose echoed.

But how exactly was I going to convince the police?

"The first thing we need to do is come up with some legitimate suspects," Rose said. "I think we need to know a little more about Lily. Did she have any enemies? We know a lot of people were angry because she wouldn't sell the bakery. Have you all forgotten that?"

Liz made a dismissive gesture with her perfectly manicured left hand. "You really think someone here in town killed her over that?"

Rose's gray eyes flashed with intensity. "You

think that couldn't happen? People have been killed over cheese, for heaven's sake."

"Cheese?" Liz repeated, the skepticism clear in her voice. Elvis's ears twitched and he looked around. He liked cheese.

"Yes, cheese," Rose said indignantly, color rising in her cheeks. "I read it online. It was somewhere in France. A man stabbed his next-door neighbor and buried the body in his basement. It was over some rare type of sheep's milk cheese."

"You think Lily stabbed somebody and buried the body in her basement and that was why she didn't want to sell the bakery?" Liz asked. As if he could see where this was going, Elvis jumped down from Liz's lap and came over to me, sitting down by my feet where he was out of the crossfire, and washing his face.

Rose made a face and set her cup down again. "Now you're just being foolish," she said. "The basement at the bakery is finished, all concrete and stone. Lily couldn't have buried anyone down there. And where on earth would she find a curd knife in North Harbor?"

Charlotte looked over at me, a smile pulling at her lips. Rose and Liz were away, and if one of us didn't stop the conversation dead, they could keep going for at least a half hour. I gave a slight shrug. I didn't have anything.

"You know, the development isn't the first time Lily has been at the center of a controversy," Charlotte said slowly.

I looked at her again. "Excuse me?"

Liz was nodding. She tapped her cup with one pale turquoise nail. "That's right. I'd forgotten about the business with young Caleb."

"You weren't here then," Charlotte said to me. "It was, let me see, must be four years ago now. Lily's ex-boyfriend, Caleb Swift, disappeared after taking out his sailboat, the *Swift Current*."

I frowned. "What do you mean, disappeared?"

"He sailed out of the harbor, and about eighteen hours later the boat was found adrift. There was no sign of Caleb."

I held up a hand. "Wait a minute. I remember Gram telling me something about that. There was no sign of a struggle on the boat, no blood, nothing out of place."

"He was just gone," Charlotte said.

"Caleb was a descendant of Alexander Swift," Liz continued, "and his grandfather Daniel's only heir. He was the golden boy of that family—smart, handsome, athletic, and he'd been sailing since he was six."

Rose drank the last of her tea and set her cup down, her "discussion" with Liz forgotten. "Daniel Swift always believed that Lily knew more than she was admitting about why Caleb took his boat out the night he disappeared."

"I don't understand," I said, leaning over to pick up Elvis. He settled himself on my lap and looked from me to Charlotte as though he were interested in our conversation. Maybe he was, for all I knew. "What does—did—Lily have to do with the disappearance of her former boyfriend?"

"He went to see her the night he vanished," Charlotte said, setting her tea down on the small table between us. "There's some security footage of him leaving the bakery, headed in the direction of the waterfront. It's not very good quality. The Levengers had an old camera set up." The Levenger family owned the Owl & the Pussycat bookstore next to Lily's Bakery.

"A couple of Caleb's friends seemed to think he was a bit obsessed with getting Lily back," Liz added.

Elvis looked at me. I reached over to give him a scratch behind his left ear, and he started to purr.

"What did Lily say?" I asked.

"She said that Caleb had just dropped by to pick up some things of his she still had—a sweatshirt, a camera." Charlotte shrugged.

"Caroline confirmed her story. She got to the bakery a few minutes after Caleb did." Liz brushed a few cookie crumbs off her sleeve.

"She's Lily's mother," Rose said, getting up and bustling around collecting the cups. "What else is she going to say?"

"You think that both of them were hiding something?" I asked.

Charlotte shook her head. "I don't know."

Liz handed Rose her cup and got to her feet. "What really matters is that Daniel Swift thought they were."

Chapter 8

Rose and Mr. P. headed to the back room to start looking for more details about Caleb Swift's disappearance. Liz pulled out her phone, I assumed to call Josh Evans's office. Charlotte came over to me and put her arm around my shoulders. "I'm sorry you're stuck in the middle, but we have to do this. Liz needs our help."

One of the things I'd always loved about Charlotte and Rose and Liz was their sense of family. They knew it was more than blood or a piece of paper like a marriage license. They knew that family came from the heart. So what right did I have to tell them not to help Liz? And it wasn't like I could stop them anyway.

I looked at Charlotte. "I'm not in the middle. I'm one hundred percent on your side."

Her eyes narrowed. "Are you sure?"

I smiled. "Absolutely. And I'm just going to say one thing about Nick. For all he huffs and puffs and roars, he's on your side, too."

Charlotte gave my shoulders a squeeze. "He's still going to have a cow," she said.

I grinned at one of Avery's expressions coming out of Charlotte's mouth. "It won't kill him," I said.

Mac poked his head in then from the back room. "There are two buses pulling into the parking lot."

"Canadians," Charlotte said with a gleam in her eyes.

"Thanks," I said to Mac. "Would you tell Rose I need all hands on deck? The case is going to have to wait for a while."

He nodded. "Sure."

Charlotte was right. The two busloads of people were Canadians, on their way back from catching a couple of Bruins games in Boston.

I'd already decided that the stereotype about Canadians being exceptionally polite was true, and this group was no exception.

"If it's not too much trouble, could I try that guitar?" a man in his mid-forties asked me, pointing to a black Epiphone Limited Edition Special-I electric guitar that we'd had in the shop for only about a week. I'd found it, minus both E strings, at an estate sale. Now that it was cleaned up, with a new set of strings, I knew it would be a good instrument for a beginner.

"Do you play?" I asked the man as I lifted down the guitar. He was wearing a black knit Bruins beanie with a gold pompom and the team logo on the front.

He shook his head. "I don't, but my grandson started lessons a couple months ago. I think he has some talent." He smiled. "I may be a little biased."

I smiled back at him. "The tone isn't as good as a more expensive instrument," I said, running one hand over the smooth, dark finish. "But that's something a beginner probably isn't going to notice. The action is good, and it's fun to play."

"So you play," he said.

I nodded. "I do, but I'm pretty rusty."

He smiled. "Would you play something, please? Just so I can hear what it sounds like?"

I was rusty, although my fingers weren't quite as out of practice as I'd been letting on to Sam and Nick. I'd gotten my guitar out several times in the last couple of months and sat on the bed, playing around with it while Elvis listened and seemed—at least some of the time—to bob his head along to the music.

Elvis had gotten his name, via Sam, because the latter claimed the cat had once sat just inside the door of The Black Bear while Sam and the guys did a set of the King's music, leaving only when they segued into their Rolling Stones set. The next morning he was back in the narrow alley beside the shop, watching Sam as he took a pile of cardboard boxes to the recycling bin. "Hey, Elvis. Want some breakfast?" Sam had asked after tossing the last box in the bin. The cat had walked up to him and meowed a loud yes. I was a little skeptical about the story, but Elvis the cat clearly had an affection for the other Elvis's music.

"Okay," I said with a smile. "Just don't judge the guitar by the guitar player."

I did a quick check on the strings to make sure they were in tune. Then I exhaled slowly and played the first few notes of Boston's "Amanda." I sang along softly, more out of habit. When I got to the end, the customer applauded—and so did the rest of the shop. I had no idea anyone else was listening. I felt my face getting warm.

Mac caught my eye from behind the cash register. "Nice," he mouthed.

I raised a hand in acknowledgment of the applause. "Thank you," I said. I turned back to my customer.

"I'll take it," he said. "And if that's rusty, you must be *wow* when you're practiced."

In the end we sold three guitars, all the quilts we had—both the antique ones and the ones Jess had made from recycled fabric—about half of our vintage postcards and most of Avery's new collection of candles—tea lights made from miniature silver trophies she'd found at the curb on garbage day, to which she'd added beeswax votives.

Mac helped me restock and reorganize at the end of the day. The tour director had told him a bus of skiers would be coming through tomorrow, and she'd suggest to their tour leader that they stop at Second Chance.

"We should put a *We Heart Canadians* sign on the door," Rose said, brushing lint off the front of her apron.

"You certainly do," I said. "I saw you flirting with that older man with the . . . interesting hair." The man in question had been wearing an ill-fitting curly hairpiece that was the color of Elvis's fur.

"I wasn't flirting," she retorted, giving me her stern teacher look. "I was being charming."

I held up a hand. "I'm sorry. I stand corrected."

"But that hair was unfortunate." She sighed and shook her head. "I did work it into the conversation that I believe hair is not necessarily a sign of virility in a man." She gave me a sly smile. "But you know what they say about men with big feet—don't you, dear?"

Behind me Mac made a strangled sound like a dead car battery failing to turn over.

"What do they say about men with big feet?" I asked, knowing I was going to regret the question.

"They wear big shoes." She laughed, then patted my arm and headed for the back room.

After work I took Elvis home and changed into my running clothes. The cat climbed up on the chair I kept for him by the window, looked outside at the wind blowing the snow around and then turned to look over his shoulder at me. It might have been my imagination, but it almost looked as though he gave a little shiver.

"I'm going to the track," I said.

He yawned.

"Why is it no one ever wants to go running with me?" I asked.

He yawned again.

My favorite shoes were at the back of the closet by the front door. The laces of the left shoe seemed to be caught up on something, and I knelt down to un-snag it.

"I could have gotten a dog, you know," I said. "Maybe a great big German shepherd. German shepherds like to run."

A furry black face seemed to materialize in front of me. Elvis stared at me unblinkingly, his way of expressing how ridiculous replacing him with a dog would be.

"Okay," I said. "So I'm not really going to replace you with a dog."

Satisfied, he turned around and headed for the bedroom.

"But I could," I called over my shoulder.

"Merow," he answered without looking back.

I ran three miles, faster than my usual pace, using my frustration to drive my legs. About two laps from finishing, I looked up to see Nick standing by the doors, holding two cardboard takeout cups. He smiled as I ran by and lifted one of the cups in a mock toast to me. I really hoped they held hot choc-olate and that one of them was for me. I held up two fingers to signify two more laps and he nodded.

I was ready to slow down. I should have slowed down, but something about Nick standing there watching made me keep up the pace until the very last step.

"I'm tired just watching you," he said, walking over to me as I stretched by the railing.

"You're welcome to join me anytime," I said, rais-ing an eyebrow in invitation. "I could train you."

"You could kill me," he said, handing me one of the takeout cups, which was hot chocolate with marshmallows half-melted on top. I wasn't crazy about whipped cream on my cocoa, but I loved marshmallows.

"Wait a minute," I said after taking a sip. "This is from McNamara's." I eyed him suspiciously. "What do you want?" Glenn used steamed milk, sugar, cocoa and melted chocolate in his hot chocolate. It tasted rich and decadent and not at all like something made with hot water and powder from a paper packet.

Nick gave me that little-boy look that he'd been using to get out of trouble since he actually was a little boy. "Hey, I just wanted to do something nice for you. You're so suspicious."

"Well, thank you," I said. I took another sip of the hot chocolate. It was good—chocolaty and not too sweet. "But you're so transparent, your head may as well be a giant round fishbowl. What's up? Spill."

"Please keep this under your hat," he said, his expression suddenly serious.

I nodded, wondering what I was swearing myself to silence over.

"Liz called the bakery the night Lily died."

"Damn!" I whispered. I turned away for a moment and then looked back at Nick. "I take it she didn't tell you or Michelle when you talked to her."

"No, she didn't," he said. "You know I don't think that Liz had anything to do with Lily's death, but . . ." He didn't finish the sentence. He didn't need to.

I shook my head and wrapped my hands around the cup to warm them. "This kind of thing makes her look bad."

Nick nodded.

"I'll talk to her," I said, although I wasn't sure how exactly I was going to urge Liz to tell the police something I wasn't even supposed to know about.

"The Angels are on the case," I said, mostly to change the subject. I watched his face over the top of my cup. "I couldn't come up with any way to dissuade them."

He gave me a wry smile. "I know. Mom called me. I know you tried." He shook his head. "She also told me that if I gave you a hard time about it, she'd use a certain photo of me in a"—he gestured with his free hand—"sort of loaded diaper as her Christmas card next year."

I crossed an arm over my midsection and tipped my head to one side to study him. "Your mother plays hardball," I said.

"Yes, she does," he said with a smile.

"So that's why you brought me this." I held up my cup and then took another sip from it. "It's a bribe."

"Guilty as charged," he said with a shrug.

I wrinkled my nose at him. "I really need to see that photo of you before I can promise anything."

"How about having supper with me instead? That would get me some more brownie points."

His cell phone buzzed then. He handed me his cup and fished in his pocket, pulling it out and studying the screen. "Hang on a second," he said, taking a few steps away from me.

I sipped my hot chocolate and waited. The call took less than a minute. Nick walked back to me, putting his cell back in his pocket. "I'm sorry," he said. "I have to go. Rain check on supper?"

"Sure," I said. I handed him his cup. "And I'll talk to Liz."

"Thanks," he said. "I'll walk you out."

I gestured at the cubbies on the end wall. "I have to get my coat and boots. You go ahead."

"Okay," he said, zipping his jacket and pulling on his gloves. "I'll see you Thursday night." He rolled his eyes. "Assuming no one dies and I don't get called in to work."

I nodded. "We'll save you a seat."

He left and I walked over to the cubbies, stopping to stretch my calves again before I switched my running shoes for boots.

I came out of the doors to the track just as Michelle got to the top of the stairs from the main level.

"Hi," I said.

She stopped on the top step. "Hi. Do you have a minute? I need to talk to you about something."

"Sure," I said. "Have you eaten yet? We could have supper if you have time."

Her expression turned cautious. "Are you cooking?" she asked as we started down.

"Would it be bad if I were?" I said, working to keep my expression serious.

Her mouth moved before she answered. "Cooking was never your strength," she finally said.

"I could be a lot better cook now than I was when we were teenagers," I said. Michelle and I had just reconnected after a very long period of estrangement. She had no way of knowing I still couldn't cook any better than I had when we were fifteen. Back then she'd helped me bury more than one of my cooking creations in my grandmother's backyard.

She narrowed her eyes at me. "Are you?" she asked. Her clear green eyes stayed locked on my face, and after a few seconds I felt a tiny twinge of sympathy for any suspect that had ever been questioned by her.

I made a face. "Rose has been trying to teach me."

"So that's no?" she said.

"That's no."

She pushed back the sleeve of her jacket and looked at the heavy gold watch she was wearing on her left arm. There was something familiar about it, but I couldn't place it. Michelle hadn't worn the watch when we were teenagers. She hadn't worn any watch at all. But it still looked familiar.

"Actually, I don't have a lot of time," she said. She gestured at the main level ice surface behind her. "Is it okay if we just go sit inside where they're practicing and talk? The heat'll be on."

The TV was on the timer so Elvis would be able to watch *Jeopardy!*. He had to be the show's most faithful viewer. I had no idea why. It was just one of his little quirks I'd discovered since he and Sam had conspired to put us together.

"Sure," I said.

Michelle and I were still building a friendship that had derailed—although I hadn't known why—when we were fifteen. It had been only last fall when I'd found out she'd heard my thoughtless comment to Nick that I'd wished her father, who had just been sentenced to jail for embezzlement, was the one who was dead, instead of my own father, who had died when I was small. She hadn't stayed around long enough to hear me take the words back less than a minute after, and when her father died two weeks later, she hadn't been able to forgive me. I was glad that we were working on a new friendship. I'd missed her. Even though Jess and I had become very close, Michelle—like Nick—was a connection to my childhood. I was very glad to have it back.

There were maybe a dozen people watching the boys' high school hockey team scrimmage. Michelle and I took seats in the top row of one of the end sections. She unzipped her jacket and stuffed her gloves in her pockets. In her cream cable-knit sweater with her hair pulled back in a high ponytail, she looked so much like the teenage girl she used to be.

"I know you've gone through it more than once," she said, "but please, tell me again about Liz and Lily in front of the bakery. Did you see anyone? Did anyone stop on the sidewalk or come out of a store?"

I told the story again, noticing that she seemed to be particularly interested in who might have seen the confrontation. Was that a good thing? Was she looking for witnesses to corroborate our story?

I shifted sideways in my seat. "Michelle, I'm not trying to tell you how to do your job, but you're looking in the wrong place if you think that Liz had anything to do with Lily's death."

"I know," she said.

Chapter 9

"You know?"

She nodded. "Yes." Her phone buzzed then. She held up a finger and retrieved the phone from her pocket. After glancing at the screen, she put it back and smiled at me. "Sorry," she said.

"How do you know?"

"Her neighbor across the street is a techie. He has a security system with cameras mounted outside his house." She held up her right thumb and finger about an inch and a half apart. "Tiny little things. They scan the yard and the street every thirty seconds. A little weird if you ask me, but perfectly legal. They caught Liz coming and going, and she wasn't gone long enough to get to the bakery and kill Lily."

I felt the last of the tension I hadn't really been able to run out drain from my body. "I'm really glad to hear that," I said. "Thanks for telling me."

Michelle smiled. "You're welcome."

I let out a sigh of relief. Liz was off the hook, and I didn't need to have that conversation about the phone call she'd made to Lily that I wasn't even sup-posed to know about.

"Sarah, you probably have more influence with Liz than pretty much anyone," Michelle said, the smile fading. "Could you remind her what a bad idea it is to keep things from the police—anytime—but especially in a case like this?"

"What do you mean?" I asked, even though I knew what she was going to say. Had Michelle somehow managed to read my mind?

"Liz made a phone call to the bakery the night Lily confronted the two of you, the night she was killed. I'm guessing it was just to apologize again, but she didn't tell us." She made a face. "Not very smart of her."

"I'll talk to her," I said, "but I'm not making any promises."

Then it struck me: If Michelle knew that Liz wasn't a suspect, then why had she wanted to hear my story about her encounter with Lily? "You think maybe the real killer was there, outside the bakery somewhere, and saw what happened?" I said.

She just looked at me with those calm green eyes. She didn't say a word.

I waited. She still didn't say anything. "Can't you at least wave your scarf at me if I'm on the right track?" I asked.

"You mean like semaphore with accessories?" she said.

I laughed, picturing her spelling out "yes" or "no" in the air with the fringed ends of her scarf.

Michelle tipped her head to one side and regarded me, a smile starting at the corners of her mouth. "I'm not Nick. Your charm doesn't work on me."

I laughed. "Trust me. It doesn't work on Nick, either."

"Are you sure?" she said. "Because I saw him on his way out of the rink tonight. When I said I was looking for you, he wanted to know why. I thought he was going to start beating on his chest with his fists."

I couldn't help laughing even harder. "I think that has more to do with the fact that Nick thinks of me as family than with my so-called charm."

Michelle rolled her eyes. "Of course."

Below us the scrimmage seemed to be over. The players were gathering at the opposite end of the rink. "So how long have you been involved with the hot-lunch program?" Michelle asked.

"I took over from Gram when she went on her honeymoon." Down on the ice the coach had the boys doing speed drills. "Sam and Lily and Glenn—plus a couple of restaurant owners—have done most of the work. Glenn bailed me out the other morning when Lily was . . ." I didn't finish the sentence. I cleared my throat. "Have you heard whether or not Caroline is going to keep the bakery?"

"You mean is she going to sell to North by West for the development?"

"Actually, I didn't, but do you think she will?"

Michelle shrugged. "I don't know."

I wondered if she thought Lily's death had anything to do with her opposition to the North Landing project. I knew there was no point in asking.

Michelle reached for her jacket and pulled it on. I zipped up mine.

"Let's get together sometime soon," I said. "Sometime when we don't have to talk about one of your cases."

"I'd like that," she said with a smile.

We hugged. It was still a little awkward, but it got less so every time I saw her.

Jeopardy! was just ending when I got home. Elvis was on his favorite chair in front of the television. I peeled off my running clothes and had a shower, letting the water work on my stiff shoulders for a moment. My brother had talked me into a low-flow showerhead that somehow used air to make the spray of water feel more intense. I had no idea how it worked. But I liked it for loosening my muscles after running.

The phone was ringing when I came out of the bathroom. I sprinted for it, doing a hurdle over Elvis, who was sprawled in the middle of the hallway.

"Don't get up," I called over my shoulder to him.

His response was to roll onto his back and paw the air like he was in some very slow-paced exercise class.

It was Sam. "Hey, kiddo," he said. "Are you going to be there for the next fifteen minutes or so?"

"I'm going to be here for the rest of the night," I said, grabbing a clean pair of socks from the bed and pulling them on my bare feet.

"Then is it okay if I stop in for a minute?"

"Sure."

"See you in a few, then."

I got dressed in leggings and a heavy sweatshirt and decided to throw a load of towels in the washer. It was closer to twenty minutes before Sam rang my bell. I opened the door to find him standing next to a tall, blanket-wrapped . . . something and Alfred Peterson.

"Hi," I said. I pointed at the bundle. It was close to five feet high, the old wool blankets lashed together with elastic bungee cords. "What is that?" Elvis was peering around my ankles.

"It's, uh . . ." Sam swiped a hand over his mouth. He was wearing a gray hand-knitted hat—probably made by Rose—and bits of his salt-and-pepper hair were poking out from underneath. He shrugged. "I don't know what it is. I just loaded it and drove it here."

Mr. P. leaned sideways and smiled at him. "Thank you, Sammy. I've got this."

Sam pointed through the open doorway. "You want this inside?"

Mr. P. hesitated. "Well, if it's not too much trouble," he said.

Sam shook his head. Then he wrapped his arms around the blanket-wrapped . . . thing and muscled it into my living room, setting it in the middle of the floor. He put an arm around my shoulders and kissed the top of my head. "Enjoy, kiddo," he said.

I closed the door behind him. "Alfred, what is

this?" I asked, gesturing at the blanket-wrapped bundle that seemed to be taking up all the extra space in my living room.

"It's a thank-you," the elderly man said.

"For what?"

"For giving Rosie the apartment. For sharing your home with her."

"You don't have to thank me for that," I said, wondering what on earth he'd done. "I love her. I don't want her living somewhere that isn't safe."

"Yes, I do," he said.

He was still bundled up in several layers against the cold. "Why don't you take your coat off and have a seat?" I said.

"Just for a minute," he said. "I'm meeting the boys for poker later."

He pulled off his navy blue cap and unwound the long scarf from around his neck. I took them and his heavy woolen overcoat. Underneath he was wearing a bulky striped sweater and another, thinner scarf. He could have led an expedition to the North Pole and not been cold.

Mr. P. took a seat on the sofa, and Elvis immediately settled at his feet. "Sarah, did you know that I was married for fifty-two years?"

I sat down in the chair opposite him. "No. I didn't," I said.

"My wife's name was Kate. She was beautiful and feisty—like Rose." He smiled. "When she died, I thought I'd never meet anyone else I could love. I didn't even want to. And then Rose came into my life."

"She's special," I said.

"Yes, she is," he agreed. "And stubborn. She didn't want any of you to know she couldn't find a place to live." He reached down and stroked Elvis's fur. "I'm very grateful for what you and Mac are doing—fixing the apartment and letting her live here." He indicated his thank-you gift in the middle of the room. "Please, accept this as my way of saying thank you."

I wasn't quite sure what to do. "What is it?" I asked.

"Merow," Elvis said.

"Elvis thinks you should see for yourself," Mr. P. said. "I agree."

"All right," I said. I got to my feet, brushed off my hands and started removing the elastic bungee cords that were holding the two wool blankets in place. They fell to the floor, and for a moment I just stood there, speechless.

It was a cat tower. And not just any cat tower. It stood about five feet high with a sleek, curved S shape. At the top was a smooth, curved platform topped with a Berber carpet square. About a foot below that was another level, and there was a third underneath that, maybe three feet off the ground. On the bottom, on one side was a hidey-hole, about two feet square with a circular opening. It too was topped with a square of carpet. On the opposite side of the S curve, a rectangle of sisal had been attached, perfect for sharpening claws. All I could think was that it looked so elegant, not a word I would have used to describe a cat tower before this.

"Oh my word," I whispered. I was speechless, something that rarely happened. I looked at Mr. P., my mouth hanging open.

"Mrrr," Elvis said. He made his way across the floor and poked his head in the hidey-hole entrance.

"No, you can't go in there," I said.

Being a cat, he immediately decided that was exactly what he wanted to do and did.

"It's okay, Sarah," Mr. P. said. "It's for Elvis."

I shook my head. "It's beautiful. It really is. But I can't keep it. It's way too expensive."

He looked genuinely puzzled. "No, it isn't. It's just a little wood and some carpet samples. I already had all the lumber, and Vince got me the carpet."

"Wait a minute," I said. "You *made* this?"

Mr. P. nodded.

I looked at the cat tower again. "But it's all . . . curvy." I gestured with both hands.

"Oh, my dear, that part was easy," he said. "All I had to do was put the wood in the steam box. We have one at the seniors' workshop." He gestured at the tower. "The finish is water-based and nontoxic, by the way."

Elvis climbed out of his new little house and jumped up on top of it. Another leap and he was on the first level above the floor. He lay down and looked around. "Mrrr," he said approvingly.

"This is beautiful," I said, still feeling a little at a loss for words. "This is art. I had no idea you could do this."

"So you like it?" he said, raising an eyebrow.

I nodded. "Yes, I do. And so does Elvis."

"You'll keep it, then?"

"I'd be honored," I said. "Thank you for the thank-you."

"You're very welcome," he said. He was already putting on his coat.

"Could I drop you at your poker game?" I asked.

He waved me away. "Thank you, but the game is at Harry's and he lives just around the corner." He pulled on his hat and wound the long scarf around his neck again.

Elvis jumped up another level and looked around rather like a monarch surveying his kingdom. "Mrrr," he said again, clearly pleased.

"You're welcome, Elvis," Mr. P. said. He patted my arm. "I'll see you tomorrow."

I showed him to the door and after he left turned back around to find Elvis at the top of the tower. "You're so spoiled," I said.

He gave me an unblinking green-eyed stare that told me he wasn't going to dignify my remark with a comment.

I reached up and lifted him down, which got me a lot of cat grumbling. "I'm just going to move it over by the window." The tower was heavy, but I managed to get it across the floor so it was just to the right of the window. I held out a hand. "Go ahead," I said to Elvis once it was in place.

He made his way up two levels and settled himself with an exhalation that sounded a lot like a sigh of contentment. I folded the two blankets, which I recognized as belonging to Sam, and put them and the bungee cords in an empty grocery bag. I hung it on the front doorknob so I wouldn't forget to return everything to him.

I remembered then that I hadn't put any towels in the bathroom. I went to the storage closet to grab some clean ones. The back wall of the closet was the only wall I'd be sharing with Rose when she moved in, and I knew that Liam and Dad had used sound-muffling drywall and insulation when it had been built, so I felt confident Rose wouldn't be able to hear me and I wouldn't be able to hear her, either.

Elvis had jumped down from his perch and followed me because he was nosy that way. He poked his head into the closet the way he usually did, so we both heard the noise at the same time. It was a scratching, scrabbling sound.

I scowled and swiveled my head to look at the cat. He eyed the wall and then looked at me.

"If that damn squirrel got back in, we will be having squirrel stew for supper tomorrow night," I said forcefully. I swear the cat made a face.

"Okay, so I don't actually know how to make squirrel stew," I hissed. "I'm trying to make a point."

The sound stopped. We waited, both of us warily watching the closet wall. Less than a minute later it started again.

Late in the fall my dad had replaced the bedroom window in the back apartment. A squirrel had jumped in through the opening. Dad had chased it all around the small bedroom, but it was Mom who had saved the day by putting a piece of bread spread with peanut butter on a chair outside the window. Once the squirrel had taken off with its treat, she'd stood guard with a leaf rake until the new window was in place.

Elvis was sniffing the closet wall. He pawed at it and looked at me. "I don't know how it got in," I said in answer to what I imagined was his unspoken question. "Maybe while Mac and I were carrying in the ladder yesterday." I turned and headed for the kitchen and my shoes, the cat on my heels. He followed me out into the entryway. There was a small pile of long boards, trim pieces we hadn't needed for the cupboards stacked in the hallway. I took a section about three feet long from the top of the stack. I didn't really want to hurt the squirrel, but when I saw it, I was going to swing that plank like I was Big Papi swinging for the Green Monster in Fenway. Elvis looked at me and licked his lips. He was in.

I unlocked the apartment door and eased it open, trying to be as quiet as I could. The sound was even louder in the apartment. It sounded like the squirrel—or whatever it was—was trying to dig its way out of the closet. I motioned to Elvis to go ahead of me, which he did, creeping across the kitchen like a furry black ninja. My plan was for Elvis to spook the squirrel into running and then I would chase it down the hall and out the front door, which I'd already opened.

The scratching sound seemed to be getting louder. It occurred to me that maybe it wasn't a squirrel back there. But as long as it wasn't a black bear, my money was still on Elvis. I eased my way over to the living room doorway and nodded at the cat. He darted around the corner to the bedroom doorway. I waited. No squirrel shot out of the bedroom with a cat in hot pursuit. The scratching sound began again. I crossed my fingers—figuratively since I was holding the length of wood with both hands—that Elvis didn't have a skunk cornered in there, and I launched myself into the bedroom swinging the board in front of me—narrowly avoiding taking off the top of Rose's head.

She turned and smiled at me. "Oh, hello dear," she said.

Chapter 10

My heart was pounding so hard it took a few seconds for me to get my breath. I'd come way too close to actually walloping Rose with my makeshift squirrel eliminator. "Rose!" I exclaimed. "You almost gave me a heart attack. What are you doing in here?"

"I'm trying to get this dang-blasted curtain rod out of the closet," she said. The rod was the long wrought-iron one that belonged over the living room window.

"Merow!" Elvis said sharply.

"I'm sorry, Elvis," Rose said, inclining her head toward him. "Excuse my language."

"Let me see," I said. I poked my head around the closet door for a closer look. Each end of the rod had a pointed finial, and one of the points was wedged in the back corner of the space.

I twisted and maneuvered and in a couple of minutes I had the curtain rod free.

"You are a darling girl and very, very smart," Rose exclaimed, clapping her hands together.

I blew my hair back off my face. "How did you get in here?" I asked. Elvis had gone into the closet, maybe to make sure for himself that there weren't any squirrels in there.

"I borrowed the extra set of keys that Isabel keeps at Charlotte's," she said.

"And does my grandmother know you borrowed the keys?"

"Well, of course not," Rose said, giving me a slightly condescending look. "She isn't even in town." She started patting her coat pockets.

"What did you lose?" I asked, brushing a dust bunny off the knee of my leggings.

"Nothing," she said. "I'm just looking for—" She found something in her left pocket. "Never mind, dear. Here it is." She pulled out a tape measure. "Hold this end for me, please."

I took the end of the metal tape, and Rose went to the other end of the curtain rod. She peered at the numbers and her lips moved, although no sound came out. Then she smiled. "That's going to work just fine," she said.

I looked blankly at her.

"I have some panels that I was hoping would work in the living room window. And they will." For the first time she noticed the board I'd been carrying. "Oh my goodness," she said, her eyes widening. "Did you think I was someone breaking in?"

I bent down to pick up the plank. "I thought you were a squirrel."

Her eyes darted around the room. "A squirrel?"

"One got in this room last fall when Dad put in the new window. I thought maybe it had gotten in again on the weekend when Mac and I were bringing in the paint and the ladder."

Rose looked at the piece of cupboard trim in my hand.

"You weren't going to hurt a little squirrel—were you, Sarah?"

The length of wood—which had seemed so small in the hallway when I was headed to confront a vicious rodent—suddenly felt like an oversized club now that I was standing here with Rose.

"I . . . I wasn't going to hurt it," I stammered. "I was only going to herd it outside again." I made the motion with the piece of wood and noticed that Elvis had already slipped out of the room.

"Well, I'm glad to hear that," she said, putting the tape measure back in her pocket. "Squirrels are environmentalists, you know."

She leaned over to pick up one end of the curtain rod.

"I, uh, didn't know that," I said, taking it from her and following her out to the living room, where Elvis was sitting under the window, not looking at all like a cat who a few minutes ago was licking his whiskers at the thought of squirrel kebobs for a little evening snack.

"Oh yes," Rose said. "Squirrels are the animal kingdom's equivalent of Johnny Appleseed." She tipped her head to one side and smiled at me, making a wide circle with one hand. "They spread seeds far and wide and help maintain genetic diversity in a lot of plant species."

I nodded silently. I had the niggling feeling that Rose was screwing with me, but nothing showed in her face.

I set the curtain rod down on the floor under the window. "Is there anything else you need to do while you're here?" I asked.

She shook her head and began to button her coat. "That's all."

I smiled. "I'll get my coat then and I'll drive you home."

She waved away the suggestion with one hand. "I walked over here. There's no reason I can't walk home."

"It's cold," I said.

"It was cold when I walked over," she replied, squaring her shoulders under her blue coat.

"Rose, am I going to have to pin you down and tie you up with that cord"—I pointed to a window blind lying on one of the folding chairs, its cord spilling onto the floor—"and wrestle you into the car? Because I could do it."

Rose reached over and patted my cheek with a gloved hand. "Fine. I'm going to let you drive me home because I don't want you to be embarrassed when a little old lady takes you down."

We started for the door. "You think you could take me down?" I said.

"Well, of course I could." She gave me a look that,

had it come from Avery, would have also come with the comment, "Well, duh."

We stepped out into the small hallway, and I locked the door.

"When you have gray hair and wrinkles people tend to underestimate you. It's one of the pluses of being old," she said, "which is good, because some of the minuses are a pain in the hind end."

"I don't underestimate you," I said, waggling my eyebrows at her. "But you may be underestimating me. I've spent most of my life around you and Gram and Charlotte and Liz." I gave her a sly smile. "I've learned a few things from all of you." I winked at her and went in to get my coat. I caught sight of the cat tower by the window. I poked my head back out in the hallway and beckoned at Rose. "I want to show you something."

"Oh, my dear, that's a lovely cat climber," she said. She looked down at Elvis. "You're a very lucky cat."

He murped agreement.

"Sarah, where did you get this?" Rose asked.

"Alfred made it for me," I said. "As a thank-you for me letting you have the apartment. You just missed him."

Her face turned an adorable shade of pink. "Oh my goodness," she said, putting a hand to her cheek.

"He's crazy about you, Rose," I said.

She smiled. "I know."

"Rose Peterson has a very nice ring to it," I teased as I got my jacket from the closet.

"Never you mind about my love life, missy," she said tartly.

I looked at her over my shoulder. "Oh, so your love life is off-limits, but it's okay for you and Liz and Charlotte to meddle in mine."

She pulled herself up to her full height of almost five feet. "Yes, it is. We're not meddling. We're just sharing the benefit of our experience with you."

I laughed and pulled on my hat. "Why do you always get the last word?" I asked.

Rose smiled. "Because I'm old and very cute." She winked at me.

I kissed the top of her head much the way Sam had done with me. "That you are," I said, grabbing my purse.

"Before I forget, I have some good news," I said as I pulled out of the driveway. "Liz isn't a suspect in Lily's death anymore."

"That's wonderful," Rose exclaimed. "How do you know?"

I told her about meeting Michelle.

"This doesn't mean we're stopping the investigation."

I was at a stop sign and there was no one behind me, so I turned to look at her. "Why is this so important to you?" I asked. "You barely knew Lily. And Liz is in the clear now."

"We can make a difference," she said. "And when you get old, you get invisible."

I shook my head. "I don't understand. You're not invisible, Rose. Not to me."

She nodded. "But you're the exception, dear. Old people make younger people nervous. They see that we're slower and more forgetful. And nothing is where it's supposed to be anymore without surgery or spandex."

She put her hands on the front of her coat and made an upward motion like she was hiking up her chest, and I had to bite my tongue so I didn't burst out laughing.

"Sarah, I know that you're the one who figured out who killed Arthur Fenety, but we all helped," she said.

She was right. They had. They'd driven me crazy in the process, but they had.

"We made a difference in the world beyond making baby quilts and selling cookies to get new playground equipment. I liked the feeling."

"Those other things matter, Rose," I said. I looked both ways and crossed the street.

"And so does this," she said.

I sighed softly. "So what's next?"

"You're really not going to try to shut us down?"

I shot her a quick glance. I could tell from the brief glimpse of her body language that I'd be wasting my time. I'd always been wasting my time trying to stop them. So was Nick.

I didn't even try to stifle a smile. "I told you I've learned a few things from all of you, and one of them is to know when I've been beaten. So no, I won't. What will you do now?"

Rose sighed softly. "It's looking more and more

like Lily's death has something to do with the harbor-front development," she said. "It certainly has brought out the worst in some people."

"Money usually does," I said. I glanced over at her again.

She nodded. "That and sex," she said.

"Right," I agreed, keeping my eyes fixed on the road through the windshield. I was *not* going to get into a discussion involving sex with Rose.

"I know this is a good thing for Liz and for Eamon Kennedy and for a lot of the businesses along the harbor front, but I wonder sometimes if this proposal is good for the town."

I did glance over quickly at her then. "It could be good for bringing in more tourists."

"I know," Rose said, folding her hands in her lap. "I meant the division it's caused in town isn't good for any of us. Whatever happens, those kind of wounds tend to linger."

We drove in silence for about a minute or so.

"Sarah, do you think that man—Jon West—could have killed Lily because she wouldn't sell the bakery to him?" she asked.

I exhaled softly. "I don't know," I admitted. "People have committed murder for a lot weaker reasons."

"Maybe what happened was an accident," she said, "and the person got scared and ran."

"Then whoever it was, they need to come forward. The longer they wait, the worse it gets."

"It's not always easy to do the right thing," Rose

said softly. "It takes you down the road less traveled, and that's a bumpy trip."

I nodded without speaking. I wasn't sure what road we were on as far as the investigation into Lily's death, but I was certain we were in for a rough ride.

Chapter 11

Tuesday passed quietly. I spent most of the morning working on the old dining room hutch.

"What do you think?" I said to Mac, pushing the dust mask I had been wearing onto the top of my head and wiping my hands on my old jeans.

He walked around the piece. "It seems sturdy enough."

"The middle shelf is cracked." I pointed to the split that ran the length of the wood. "Could you cut me a new one?"

He nodded. "Sure. Do you want me to try to match the wood?"

I shook my head. "No. That doesn't matter."

Mac grabbed a tape measure from the worktable. "So you're painting the shelves?"

"I'm painting the whole thing." I ran my hand over the side of the unit. "The wood isn't exactly pretty."

Mac looked past me toward the shelves on the back wall. "Do you remember that desk we cannibalized when we were working on the armoire?" he asked.

I squinted in the direction of the shelves. "If you're thinking about using the wood from the bottom of the leftover drawer for a shelf, I don't think it's long enough."

"No," he said. "I was thinking that maybe you could use the drawer pulls on this piece."

I pulled my dust mask off completely. "I don't remember what they look like," I said.

"They're Victorian ring pulls," he said. "Let me see if I can find them."

The chandelier Mac and Avery had been cleaning up was still on the tarp, taking up a lot of the room's space. "Are you finished working on this?" I asked.

"Almost," Mac said, looking up from a box he'd just lifted down. "I need to replace a couple of screws that were stripped when I took the glass shade out."

"I had a call from a developer in Bangor," I said. "He's renovating an old building, turning it into a restaurant. I think he'd take the chandelier if Jon West doesn't want it for his new hotel."

"Give me another day," Mac said. "Then you can call West and see what he wants to do."

"Fine with me," I said. A day wasn't going to change anything with respect to the future of the waterfront development, as far as I could see.

"Carl Levenger is coming in sometime today to get that table," Mac said, pointing at a rectangular wooden table over by the door to the shop. We'd sanded the table smooth and stained it light oak with the legs painted a medium gray color called iron ore.

Carl Levenger owned the Owl & the Pussycat bookstore. He'd bought the table for the back of the store, where his various reading groups had their meetings. Carl showed up about quarter to twelve. He walked approvingly around the table.

"I still really like it," he said. Carl was a former university professor in his late fifties who had taken early retirement a couple of years ago and come home to run the bookstore when his father died. The Owl & the Pussycat had been started by Carl's grandfather.

Mac began to wrap the top of the table in a couple of old blankets we kept for just that purpose, and Rose stepped in to help him.

Carl smoothed a hand over his bald pate. "I heard you were the one who found Lily," he said. "I'm sorry. She was good person."

I nodded. "Yes, she was."

"We'd talked about going in on a better security system." He shook his head. "I wish now we had. Maybe then the police could have caught whoever it was who was hassling her and Lily would still be alive."

Mac helped Carl load the table in the back of his van. Rose touched my arm. "It's almost lunchtime," she said. "How about a fresh pot of coffee?"

I smiled at her. "That sounds good." She started for the stairs, and I watched Carl pull out of our parking lot and start down the street. Was he right?

Was the solution to Lily's murder as simple as finding out who had been harassing her?

Jess showed up about four o'clock with new three new quilts. She poked her head around my office door. "Do you have a minute? I need your opinion on something."

"Sure," I said, coming around my desk. "What is it?"

She grinned. "I'd rather show you than tell you."

I followed her downstairs. Asia Kennedy was standing in the middle of the shop with Charlotte and Avery. Vince's daughter was wearing a sock monkey hat with a black quilted jacket, a denim skirt and a wild pair of burgundy-pink-and-orange-argyle knitted leggings.

"Hi, Asia," I said. "How's the guitar?"

I'd just sold the fifteen-year-old a used Fender acoustic with a black finish. She'd clearly inherited some of her father's musical ability.

Asia smiled shyly at me. "It's awesome," she said.

"I'm glad," I said, smiling back at her. I turned to Jess. "So what did you want me to see?"

"Me," Asia said, sticking out one leg.

"Did you make those?" I asked Jess.

She nodded. "Remember that box of sweaters you sold me?"

I leaned forward for a closer look at the diamond-pattern tights Asia was wearing. She turned her leg from one side to the other. "Those were a sweater?" I said.

"Yep," Jess said.

"I want a pair," Avery clamored. "Please, please, please."

"Which you have to pay for," Charlotte said.

"I will. I promise," Avery said, putting a hand over her heart.

Jess smiled. "Come down to the store and I'll let you look through the sweaters and pick which one you like."

Avery started jumping up and down and grinning.

Jess held up a hand. "And I'll give you the same deal I gave Asia. You can have the leggings for free as long as you wear them to school and tell everyone where they can buy a pair."

"You're kinda like a walking billboard," Asia said with a shrug.

"Deal," Avery immediately agreed.

Jess looked at me. "So will you and Mac keep an eye out for more sweaters the next time you get hired to clear out someone's house?"

"Absolutely," I said.

"You want a pair to go running in?" she asked, lowering her voice, her blue eyes gleaming.

"Absolutely not," I said.

Mac and I put a second coat of paint on the living room walls of Rose's apartment after supper. I told Mac the story of thinking I was going to do battle with a rowdy squirrel in the apartment and discovering Rose instead.

He laughed. "I have a feeling living next to Rose is going to be interesting."

I shook my paintbrush at him. "Don't use that word," I warned. "The last time you did that, I ended up with a detectives' office in my sunporch and a senior-citizen computer hacker using my Wi-Fi."

There was a teasing gleam in his dark eyes. "But think how boring life would be without them."

"You're probably right," I said, pulling my paint can a little closer. I was doing the edging and Mac the roller work.

I realized that I hadn't told Mac about the cat tower. "Hey, I didn't tell you what Mr. P. did last night."

"Do I want to know?" Mac said. One eyebrow went up and he grinned.

"You probably do," I said. "He made a cat tower for Elvis to thank me for letting Rose have this apartment. I'll show it to you when we're done. It's more like a piece of sculpture."

"I didn't know Mr. P. knew anything about woodworking," Mac said, putting his roller back in the tray for more paint.

I moved along the floor a little farther. "Maybe you should try picking his brain," I said. "He knows how to use a steam box. Didn't you say that's how you bend wood when you're making a boat?"

Mac nodded. "I will. Thanks for the suggestion." He worked his way down the wall. "He really is crazy about Rose."

"Did you know he was married? He told me he and his wife were together for fifty-two years." I used the edge of my T-shirt to wipe a dab of paint off the trim because I couldn't find the rag I'd been using.

"I knew Alfred had been married," Mac said, putting more paint on his roller, "but not for that long." He tipped his head to one side and studied the stretch of wall he'd just painted. "It's funny. When we get married, we're making a commitment that's forever. If it's a good marriage, forever isn't long enough."

"And if it's not a good marriage?"

"Then it just feels like forever."

"That sounds like experience talking," I said. I kept my eyes on the edge of the wall above the baseboard.

After a moment Mac said, "It is."

"Which kind of forever did you have?" I asked. I continued to work my way along the tape line above the trim, wondering if he'd answer the question or evade it.

"Both, I guess," Mac said after another silence. "At different times it was both."

Mac had been married. It was the first bit of personal information he'd shared in the time I'd known him. Somehow I knew not to ask anything else right now.

I did a little more work on the hutch first thing in the morning at the shop. Cleveland showed up with two boxes of trash-picked old Dick and Jane readers. Charlotte poked through both cartons and her eyes lit up. She looked up at me and nodded.

Cleveland and I dickered over price for a few

minutes. In the end he got a little more than I wanted to pay but not as much as he'd asked for. As my grandmother would have put it, we were both a little happy and both a little had.

"These are wonderful," Charlotte said. "They're in excellent shape. They didn't spend a lot of time in a classroom." She beamed at me and pushed her glasses up her nose.

"Would you go through the boxes and catalog them for me," I asked. Charlotte loved books. I knew she was the right person for the job. She'd handle the books with care and make meticulous notes on each volume.

"I'd love to," she said.

"I'll carry the boxes inside for you," Mac offered.

"Could you watch things here for about an hour?" I asked when he came back to the workroom. I'd told Michelle I'd talk to Liz, and I hadn't done that yet. I didn't want to put it off any longer.

"Sure," he said. "Charlotte and I can handle things here. Take your time."

I drove down to McNamara's and bought a couple of lemon tarts. Then I pulled out my cell phone and called Liz. "I have two of Glenn's lemon tarts," I said when she answered. "I'm willing to share if you're willing to make coffee."

"The lemon-cream-cheese filling or lemon meringue?" she immediately asked.

"Do you care?"

Her warm laugh came through the phone. "I'll go turn the coffeepot on."

Liz and I sat at the round wooden table in her huge kitchen. I could see why Avery liked to cook there. The space was a cook's dream with stainless-steel appliances and granite countertops.

"So what did you want to talk to me about?" Liz asked after she'd had a bite of her lemon tart.

"Why do you think I want to talk to you?" I said, adding cream to my coffee.

"You brought a bribe, and it's the middle of the morning." She gave me a fake smile across the table.

"All right. I did come to talk to you."

"About?"

"You called Lily the night she died, the night she confronted us on the sidewalk in front of the bakery," I said.

"What if I did?" Liz asked. She leaned back in her chair and crossed one leg over the other.

"You didn't tell the police."

She drew in a breath, held it for a moment and then let it out slowly. "I don't suppose there's any point in asking you who told you that?" she said.

I shook my head. "Nope."

"It was either Nicolas or Michelle Andrews."

"It doesn't matter who told me," I said, watching her across the polished wooden table. "What matters is that it was a dumb thing to do. You withheld information from the police, Liz."

She shrugged. "Which they could find if they did their job—which they did. No harm done."

I glared at her. "Yes harm done. It's a bad idea to

keep things from the police, especially when they're investigating a murder in which you're a suspect!"

Liz tapped a pale pink nail on the edge of her cup. "I didn't tell the police because I knew it would make them suspicious, which they were when they found out, which just proves my point." She picked up her cup and took a drink, watching me over the rim.

"How did you convince Josh it was a good idea to keep that information from the police?" I asked. I was fairly certain I knew the answer.

Liz glanced over toward the windows above the sink. She looked a little sheepish.

"Liz," I said, an edge of warning in my voice.

Her gaze came back to me. "All right. I didn't exactly tell him. I didn't want him to have to lie."

I pulled a hand back through my hair and sighed.

"Don't give me that look," she said. "I protect the people I care about. You know that, Sarah."

There was a knock on the back door then. It opened and Elspeth Emmerson, Liz's niece, stepped into the kitchen.

"Hi, Sarah," she said when she caught sight of me.

"Hi," I said.

"Am I interrupting something?"

I shook my head. The conversation with Liz was going nowhere.

"No," Liz said. "We're just having coffee. Come sit down and I'll get you a cup."

Elspeth joined us at the table. She was in her late

twenties, and she reminded me a lot of her aunt. She had the same big heart and probably didn't own a pair of sensible shoes. She was wearing skinny black pants tucked into black stiletto ankle boots, and her long blond curls fell below her shoulders.

Liz made a move to get up.

I laid a hand on her arm. "I've got it," I said.

I got a cup and saucer from the cupboard and poured Elspeth a cup of coffee.

"Thanks," she said as I set it in front of her. She set a manila envelope on the table. "Dad asked me to give these to you," she said to Liz.

Liz slid the envelope across the table, glanced at it, and left it next to her plate. "Thank you, sweetie."

"How's business?" Elspeth asked me as she added sugar to her coffee.

"Down from summer and fall," I said, "but the skiers have helped."

"Us too," she said, taking a sip from her cup. Elspeth ran a successful spa and salon, Phantasy, which drew tourists to town for the relaxation and pampering they offered. "Last week a tour guide called. There was some problem with the grooming equipment where they were skiing, so they brought twenty-four people over for spa manicures. And Glenn McNamara supplied lunch." She brushed her hair back from her face. "That was something Lily used to do for us." She stared into her cup for a moment. "Her death was a horrible thing."

"You went to school with Caleb Swift, didn't you?" I asked. "Lily went out with him for a while."

Elspeth hesitated for a moment; then she nodded. "I did."

A look passed between her and Liz.

"What's going on?" I said.

Elspeth pressed her lips together for a moment. Then she looked at me. "I knew Caleb," she said.

Liz looked concerned, but she didn't speak.

Either way it was Elspeth who shook her head. "It's not a big deal, Sarah. Caleb and I went out for a while. He was a jerk, the proverbial entitled rich kid. Which I should have seen." She rolled her eyes and gave me a self-deprecating smile. "I didn't have the best taste in men back then."

I smiled in sympathy. "I'll tell you about some of the guys I dated in college sometime."

We talked about some ideas Elspeth had for luring more tourists to town during the off-season. I finished the last of my coffee and stood up. "I'd better get back to the shop," I said. "It was good to see you, Elspeth."

She smiled. "You too."

Liz walked me to the back door. I wrapped my arms around her in a hug. "I love you," I said.

She smiled. "Everybody does."

Mr. P. showed up at Second Chance just after lunch, when Avery arrived for her shift. It turned out that the two of them had walked to the shop together.

"Am I a distrustful and suspicious person for thinking that it can't be a good thing having those two in cahoots?" I said to Mac when they came in, heads together.

"They could be working toward world peace," he said with a slight smile.

I turned and raised an eyebrow at him.

The smile got a little wider. "Or world domination," he added. He looked at his watch. "Do you have time to go over the list of things you want to put an offer in on from the Thomas estate?"

"Yes," I said. "Just give me five minutes to get Avery working on some new teacup gardens."

Charlotte was at the cash desk with a pencil and a pad of paper, working on an idea for a window display for Valentine's Day. Our window displays changed a lot, usually because Charlotte or Avery had come up with a new idea. But since their ideas seemed to bring customers into the store, I didn't mind if they changed the window every second day.

I touched Charlotte on the shoulder as I passed her. "Come up with any ideas yet?" I asked. All I could see on the paper were some scratched-up hearts and the word "love" crossed out several times.

"What exactly did you have in mind for the window?" she asked.

I shrugged. "I don't really know. Just something other than hearts and chubby babies with bows and arrows. Something a little different."

"Define 'different,'" Charlotte said with a smile.

"I can't quite do that yet," I said.

Her eyes twinkled. "Can I ask Avery to help me?"

"I don't know. Can you?" I said.

Charlotte laughed.

"If I say 'yes, go ahead,' am I going to regret it?" I asked.

"Possibly."

"Go ahead," I said, smiling back at her. "I trust you."

I went out to the workroom and showed Avery the box of cups and saucers I wanted her to clean and fill with potting soil. Our tiny teacup gardens were a perennial hit with the tourists, and I wanted to have more ready for the next bunch of Canadian skiers.

"Want me to do the planting, too?" she asked.

"That would be a big help," I said. "Thank you."

She slipped off the stack of bracelets she was wearing on her left arm—some of them her own creations and some from her collection of vintage jewelry—and stacked them on the workbench. "Is it okay if I help Charlotte with the front window when I'm done?" she asked, picking up the box of teacups.

I nodded. "As a matter of fact, she'd like your help," I said. "She's looking for ideas."

Avery grinned. "I'm full of ideas," she said.

She was definitely full of something.

Mac was just coming out of the tiny staff room with two cups of coffee when I got to the top of the stairs.

"Umm, is one of those for me?" I asked.

"Yes, it is," he said, holding out one of the mugs.

We spent the next hour going over our scribbled list of items we'd seen at the Thomas house that might work in the store. I was surprised by how many of the items I had scrawled on my handwritten list had ended up on Mac's as well.

"Great minds think alike, I guess," I said when we got to the sixth thing in a row.

"It's better than fools seldom differ," he said, raising an eyebrow at me.

I shifted sideways in my chair and tucked one foot up underneath me. "Speaking of fools," I said. "I told Rose I wasn't going to give them a hard time anymore about their investigations."

"Why?" he asked, narrowing his dark eyes.

I stretched my shoulders, hunching them up around my ears. "It took me a while, but I realized that I'm wasting my time. They're either going to nod and smile and do what they want anyway. Or argue until they wear me out and do what they want anyway. I decided to eliminate that whole part in the middle." I pulled my hand back through my hair. "It's the part that makes my hair fall out, so it seemed like a good part to get rid of."

Mac tented his fingers over the mouth of his cup. "What about Nick?"

"He can fight with them if he wants to," I said, stretching my arms out in front of me. "Let Nick's hair fall out for a little while and see how he likes it."

Mac stood up. "For what it's worth, I think it's a good decision," he said. He looked toward the hallway. "I'd better go see how Avery is doing." He gestured at the notepad on my lap. "Let me know if you want me to check the numbers before you put the final offer together."

I nodded. "Thanks. I will."

He hesitated in the doorway. "Sarah, what about the chandelier from Doran's department store? What do you want to do with it? It doesn't look like the North Landing project is going to happen, so are they still going to want to buy it for some other project?"

I sighed and rubbed the back of my neck. "Is it ready?"

"I've cleaned it up and replaced the missing screws. I don't want to do much more without some money on the table. What do you think?"

I looked up at the ceiling, but there weren't any answers there. "I agree with you." I got to my feet. "I think I'll call Jon West's office. If he's not interested anymore, I'll call the guy I told you about who's renovating that restaurant."

He nodded. "Let me know what happens."

"I will," I said.

Mac left, and I moved over to my desk. The door opened a little more and Elvis wandered in, giving a start of surprise when he saw me. "Merow?" he said inquiringly.

"Hey, it's my office, too," I said.

He looked around as if he were going to dispute my words. Then he walked around the desk, jumped onto my chair and gave me a look that was decidedly smug.

"That doesn't prove anything," I said. I scooped him up and sat down in the chair, and he settled himself happily on my lap. I had the feeling I'd just been conned.

I called the North by West office and left a message with Jon West's assistant. She promised she'd have him call me back as soon as possible. That was the kind of promise I tended to view with a lot of skepticism, so I was surprised when my phone rang only twenty minutes later and it was the North by West developer on the other end.

"Thank you for getting back to me so quickly, Jon," I said. "I wanted to check with you before we put the chandelier from the Doran's department store up on our website or sold it to someone else."

"Oh, I'm still interested in it," he said.

"You are?" I couldn't quite keep the surprise out of my voice.

"I could be there in about half an hour to take another look at it," he said. I heard what sounded like the slam of a vehicle door.

"That would work," I said. "Do you remember how to find us?"

"I do," he said. "I'll see you in thirty minutes."

I hung up the phone and leaned back in the chair, stroking Elvis's fur with one hand. "Jon West is going to be here in about half an hour," I said.

He turned his head and looked at me with one green eye.

"Yes, I know Rose will be all over him like you on a can of Tasty Tenders."

He lifted his head and licked his lips.

"I don't actually have any right now," I said.

That got me a glare before he dropped his head again. Elvis may have been a cat, but he seemed to have a better command of the English language than some people did.

I looked at the papers I'd just laid on my desk. "I'll work on these later," I said to Elvis. "Let's go see what's happening downstairs."

He jumped to the floor before I could set him down. I got up, brushed the cat hair off my lap and put on a little rosy lip gloss. Elvis, meanwhile, was washing his face.

"Ready?" I asked.

He made one last pass behind his left ear.

"You look good," I said.

He tipped his head to one side and eyed me. Then he meowed again and started for the door.

Apparently we both looked presentable.

"You know, I read somewhere that the longer people live together, the more they start doing the same things," I said as we started down the stairs. "Do you think that happens with cats and people?"

Elvis stopped on the second step and gave me a look that could only be interpreted as "Don't be ridiculous."

Chapter 12

Charlotte and Avery had their heads together at the cash desk, but Avery bounced over to me before I could cross the floor to them.

"Sarah, can we do KISS in the front window?" she asked. She was like a puppy in her enthusiasm, and Elvis made a wide berth around her and headed for the back room.

"Do you mean candy kisses or people kissing?" I asked.

"Number one, no. And number two, ewww!" she said, making a face. "I mean the retro band. You know, the guys in makeup."

I looked over at Charlotte. "You said you wanted something that wasn't the typical hearts and flowers," she said with a completely straight face.

"What exactly do you want to do?" I asked warily.

"We want to do the band in the window," Avery said, making a gesture in that direction with one hand. "We could use those mannequins we got from Doran's."

I'd known that trip would come back to haunt me. When we bought the huge chandelier from the lobby of the Portland department store, we'd also purchased several old-style glass-front wooden display cases and six mannequins.

"You can't let these go to the dump," Avery had insisted when she'd come across a row of the plastic people. "These are art."

The vintage figures looked like giant Barbie dolls. Mac had come to stand beside me. "It's not the worst idea," he'd said quietly.

"Okay," I said. "Have you lost your mind?"

Mac had given me an enigmatic smile and held up his phone. "People collect just about everything, including store mannequins from the 1960s, which I'm almost certain these are."

We'd ended up buying six of the dozen figures, disassembled in three large cardboard cartons, for five dollars apiece, and then we'd turned around and sold two of them for two hundred and fifty dollars to a collector in Florida who had stowed them in the back of his Winnebago RV. As he'd driven off, it had looked like one of them was waving out the back window.

"What are you going to do for costumes and wigs?" I asked.

"That's why this idea is so totally brilliant," Avery said, throwing her hands into the air. "It's not going to cost anything, if that's what you're worried about, and I know it is."

"Nothing?" I said.

"I swear," she said, pressing one hand to her chest with a melodramatic flourish. "Mr. P. said that Sam and the guys in his band dressed up as KISS for some kind of charity thing and we could probably use their stuff if we asked. So could we ask?"

Before I could say yes or no, she waved her other hand. "And I can borrow whatever makeup stuff I need from Phantasy. I already called Elspeth and asked her. Could you just please say yes so we can get on with it?"

A life-size KISS re-creation in my front window for Valentine's Day? It was just plain weird.

I looked over at Charlotte, who smiled back at me. I looked at Avery, who looked like she was going to bounce out of her skin.

"Yes," I said.

Avery turned to Charlotte and did a fist pump in the air. Then she turned back to me.

"Thanks, Sarah," she said. "I promise you're going to love it."

"You're responsible for asking Sam about borrowing those costumes."

"Deal," she said at once.

"And you have to do all the heavy lifting, not Charlotte."

"I promise," she said, crossing her heart with one finger like a five-year-old making a playground swear.

She pulled out her cell phone. "I'll call Sam right now."

I walked over to Charlotte. "KISS?"

"Would you like to see the list of ideas I vetoed?" she asked.

I shook my head. "I don't think so."

"You have to admit, our more . . . exotic windows are the ones that seem to bring in customers," Charlotte pointed out. "Remember the Christmas goat?"

I laughed. The Christmas goat came from the Scandinavian holiday tradition. Our Christmas goat in robes like an old-fashioned Santa Claus had brought a lot of people into the store, if only to ask why a goat was playing Saint Nick. It had been worth the thirty dollars I'd paid for the toy goat at a Bangor toy store.

"Just don't let it get too exotic," I said.

In the back room Mac had the chandelier laid out on a clean tarp. He was at the workbench. I walked over to him. "Jon West is on his way over," I said.

"Now?" he said.

His gaze went to the end wall where Mr. P. and Rose were doing something on Mr. P.'s laptop.

I sighed. "This is the universe testing my resolve because I said I wasn't going to try to stop them from being detectives if that's what they wanted."

Mac nodded and smiled, his gaze coming back to me. "The universe has a perverse sense of humor sometimes," he said.

I smiled back at him and then looked over at the old light. "You still feel comfortable about the price we agreed on for the chandelier?"

He turned the screwdriver he was holding over in

his fingers. "I do. I added a cushion for any expenses we didn't think of. We can make a nice profit off this piece and Jon West will do all right as well. The light's almost an antique, and it is a piece of Maine history. Not to mention he'll be spending a lot less than a new chandelier would cost him."

"I think I'll just stand back and let you handle things, then," I said.

"Based on the last time he was here, I think he prefers your charm just a little more than mine."

I laughed. "Jon is a bit of a flirt, isn't he?"

Mac's expression got serious. "He also goes hard after what he wants. Don't forget that."

"Thanks," I said. "I won't."

Jon West arrived exactly twenty-nine minutes after I'd spoken to him.

"Hi, Sarah," he said, holding out his hand as he stepped into the store. "I'm glad you called. I'm looking forward to seeing the light fixture all cleaned up."

He was wearing jeans and a rust-colored denim work jacket with a heavy pile lining and the corduroy collar turned up. His shaggy dark hair was pulled back, like it often was, in a ponytail.

"C'mon back to the workroom," I said, leading the way.

Mac met us at the door. "Jon, it's good to see you again," he said, offering his hand.

"You too," the developer said. The two men shook hands, and then we walked over to the tarp.

Mac and I waited without speaking while Jon West walked around the chandelier.

"Is that the original ceiling chain?" he asked. "I forgot to ask you before."

I nodded. "And the original ceiling rosette."

He crouched down to get a closer look at the cutwork and the glass shade. "What about the shade?"

"I don't think so," Mac said. "It's the shade that was with the light, but we think it was a replacement for the original, probably circa 1930."

"Are you firm on the price?" West asked, training his blue eyes on me. "Or is there some room to move?" He smiled.

"There's some room to move," I said with a smile of my own. "I wouldn't argue if you wanted to give me more than we're asking."

He laughed, straightened up and named a figure that was less than half the amount I'd originally quoted him.

"I'm sorry," I said. "I can't do that when I have other buyers interested."

West circled the light. Based on the architect's drawings for the hotel that he'd shown us several weeks before, it would look spectacular in the lobby.

"Can I ask who your other buyers are?" he said.

I patted the pocket where I'd put my cell phone as though I'd just felt it vibrate even though it hadn't. "Of course you can," I said. "I can't tell you, but I don't mind you asking." Then I smiled.

He named a number that was ten percent more

than his previous figure. I just shook my head. He walked over and stood beside me, his hands in his pockets. "C'mon, Sarah. You know how this works. You name a number. I name a number. We volley back and forth a little and settle on a price."

"We already did that," I said. "When you originally called me about the light. I've given you my best price."

West turned to look at the chandelier again. "That light's a piece of history. It was cast at a foundry just outside of North Harbor. I really want it to be the focal point of the hotel in the harbor development."

"Do you even have a development?" Rose asked.

I'd seen her start over toward us out of the corner of my eye, but short of tackling her and wrestling her to the floor, I didn't see any way to stop her. My resolution to let the Angels do their thing was about to be tested.

Jon West turned to face Rose. "Excuse me?" he said.

Rose gestured to the chandelier. "You're right. That light is a piece of our history and I would like to see it stay in town, but you don't have all the property you need to start building. You don't have Lily's Bakery." She studied him for a long moment, then gave her head a slight shake and offered a smile along with her hand. "Where are my manners?" she said. "I'm Rose Jackson, Mr. West."

Jon West shook her hand and returned her smile with a smooth, professional smile of his own. "I'm guessing you shopped at Doran's," he said.

"Yes, I did," Rose said. "I remember being in the

lobby of the Portland store just before Christmas when I was about five. They had a huge evergreen tree set up under that light. It must have been eight feet tall, maybe higher. My father picked me up so I could have a candy cane from the tree, and to me it looked like that chandelier was the star on the top."

"That's a wonderful memory," he said, tapping one hand against his leg.

Knowing Rose, it was possible it was actually a wonderful fabrication.

"Yes, it is," she said. "But it doesn't have anything to do with my original question, which you haven't answered. How are you going to build North Landing without the bakery?"

Elvis had come in from somewhere and jumped up on the workbench behind us. He bumped Jon West's arm with his head, and West reached over and absently began to pet the cat. "I hope to buy the bakery from Lily Carter's estate," he said.

"Did you kill her so you could do that?" Rose asked in the same tone of voice she might have used to ask if he wanted a cup of tea. "Lily wouldn't sell to you when she was alive."

New resolve or not, I couldn't just stand there while she accused the man of murder. I stepped between them. "Rose, this isn't the place for this conversation," I said.

Jon West held up the hand that wasn't stroking Elvis's fur. "It's all right, Sarah. I don't mind answering Mrs. Jackson's question. No, I did not kill Lily Carter. I wasn't anywhere near that bakery."

Rose had had one hand in her pocket the entire time she'd been talking. Now she pulled it out. She was holding Mr. P.'s cell phone. "When I was a child we had an expression—'liar, liar pants on fire,'" she said. She glanced down. "I think yours are about to start smoking."

She held up the phone so we could see it. It was playing what looked like some kind of security video. It was black-and-white, and the quality could have been better. Even so, I recognized the back of Lily's Bakery.

"What is this, Rose?" I asked.

"Just watch, please," she said.

I saw a figure then, just at the edge of the picture. He or she slipped out the back door of the bakery and disappeared out of the frame. Whoever it was had on a heavy denim work jacket and a knitted cap. What looked like a long, dark ponytail poked out from underneath the hat. The person was careful to keep his or her face turned away from the camera.

"Where did you get this?" Mac asked.

"I have my sources," Rose said primly.

I had a feeling her source was over at the other end of the room.

"That's you," she said to Jon West.

West shook his head. "No, it's not." He looked at me. "You all can't seriously think I killed Lily Carter over the North Landing development." He jabbed a finger at the cell phone. "This is fake."

He'd stopped petting Elvis, who bumped him

again with his head. He reached out and stroked the cat's fur again.

Rose shook her head. "No, it's not. It's from a security camera on the building next to the bakery." There was a slight edge of accusation to her voice. "You were the one playing all those childish tricks on Lily, and when they didn't work, you killed her."

"Stop," I said sharply, holding up both hands. "Just stop." I took the phone out of her hand. "Jon, this does look like you," I said. "I'm not saying you killed Lily, but did you go there to talk to her?"

The muscles along his jawline were tight, and I could tell he was gritting his teeth together. "I didn't go talk to Lily the night she died. I wasn't the person harassing her, and I didn't kill her. I wasn't even in town the night she died." Anger made his voice rougher.

He pulled his free hand back over his neck and turned to look at Rose for a moment. "You're incorrect. The entire project is *not* in danger of falling apart. It never was. The town was going to expropriate that piece of land. All that's happened now is that the timeline has been pushed back. The estate will be settled. We'll buy the property instead of going to expropriation, and North Landing *will* go ahead. So yes, Lily made me angry enough that I had a moment or two when I wanted to strangle her, but I didn't actually do it. I had no reason to."

Elvis shook himself and walked along the workbench to sit by Mac.

West wrestled his emotions back in check. "Sarah, the project is still a go. It's just on hold while everything is settled with the bakery property. Please, would you hold the chandelier for me? I'll cut you a check for a quarter of the price as a deposit."

I nodded. "Yes."

"Thanks," he said. "I'll be in touch." He headed for the front door.

Rose gave Mac and me a self-satisfied grin. "I think we solved Lily's murder," she said.

I looked at Elvis, who was poking his nose in a box Mac had set on the workbench.

"I don't think so," I said.

"What do you mean, you don't think so?" Rose frowned at me.

"The hair," I said, gesturing to the cell phone she still held in her hand. "It looks fake. But before we get to that, where did you get that video? How did you get it?"

"I have my sources," she said. Her eyes met mine, and there was a stubborn set to her shoulders.

I tipped my head in Mr. P.'s direction. "I'm guessing your source is sitting over there."

"If you think you know, then why did you ask?"

I counted to five, took a breath and let it out slowly. "I told you I wasn't going to fight with you about your investigation, but you can't keep hacking into people's computers when you want information."

"We didn't," Rose said placidly. "After Carl Levenger was here yesterday, I remembered what Charlotte had said about the bookstore having an old security camera that recorded Caleb Swift the night he disappeared. So I went to see him."

"So Carl gave you that video?"

She shook her head. "No. The police already have it. I don't think there was anything on it that was any use." She held up her phone. "This came from the gift shop on the other side of Carl." The look she gave me was more than a little smug.

"I'm sorry," I said.

She leaned over and patted my arm. "You're forgiven, dear. Now tell me why you think that hair isn't real."

Rose played the video again, and Mac leaned over to watch it with her.

"You think it's a wig?" she said.

I nodded. "I do. I know it sounds crazy, but watch." I pointed at the small screen. "See? There. Whoever that is just adjusted their hair." The person in the video put his or her hand up and moved their entire head of hair slightly forward. "That hair is probably not real at all."

Rose studied the video as she weighed my words. "I can't tell," she said finally, "but I trust your judgment."

"So if that's not Jon West, someone put in some effort to make it look like he was at Lily's," Mac said.

Rose took off her glasses and cleaned them on the hem of her sweater. "I think Alf and I need to do a little more digging." She bustled back toward Mr. P., who had been diligently typing on his laptop for the previous ten minutes while sneaking little peeks in our direction.

Mac leaned over and scratched the top of Elvis's head. "Stay out of that," he said quietly. The cat immediately dropped his paw and stopped rooting in the box.

"Why does he listen to you when you tell him to stay out of something but ignore me when I tell him?" I asked.

"It's a guy thing," Mac said.

Elvis meowed his agreement.

"So are you going to tell Rose the other reason you think Jon West is innocent?" Mac asked.

"What would that be?" I said, feeling my cheeks get warm.

Elvis, with his uncanny sense of timing, meowed loudly.

Mac didn't say a word. He just looked, pointedly, from the cat to me.

"Fine. I was watching while Jon was petting him." I glanced at Elvis, who seemed to smile at me. "I don't think Jon West had anything to do with Lily's death because my cat, the feline lie detector, told me so. Nothing crazy about that."

"It's not so far-fetched," he said. "Elvis has better night vision than we have. He has a better sense of smell. Why is it so crazy that he can sense the physiological signs that someone is lying?" He nudged me with his shoulder. "You think it was a coincidence that Elvis seemed to know who killed Arthur Fenety before the rest of us did?"

"I was kind of hoping it was," I said.

Mac laughed. "Elvis being able to tell when someone is lying is *not* the strangest thing that's happened around here," he said. We headed out into the shop.

Avery and Charlotte were standing by the front window. Actually, Avery was standing in the window, gesticulating wildly while Charlotte nodded from time to time. Mac raised his eyebrows.

"Point taken," I said.

I went back up to my office and spent the next hour putting together an offer for the items we wanted to buy from Malcolm Thomas's family. When I came back downstairs, Charlotte was waiting on a customer who was holding two quilts and Avery was dusting a set of bookshelves that Mac and I had made from an old pantry cabinet.

I was glad I'd said yes to her window display idea. I didn't know a lot of the details behind Avery's problems at home, but I could see it had been good for her to be with Liz and spend time with Rose and Charlotte as well, just the way it had been good for me when I'd been her age.

Avery came over to me. "I talked to Sam," she said. I could see from the grin on her face that he'd said yes, she could borrow the KISS costumes. I made a mental note to thank him the next time I saw him.

"And he said yes?" I said.

She nodded.

"I can't wait to see what you and Charlotte come up with."

Her expression grew serious, and she slid the stack of bracelets up and down her arm. "If you like it, could I maybe do a window all by myself sometime?"

I nodded slowly. "Yes."

She threw her arms around me. "Thank you, Sarah," she said.

I hugged her back. "You've been doing a good job," I said. "I'm glad I hired you."

She pulled back out of the embrace and rolled her eyes at me. "You mean because Nonna forced you into it."

"Your grandmother didn't make me hire you, Avery," I said.

She looked surprised. "Really? I thought maybe she knew some embarrassing story about you or something."

That idea made me laugh. "Avery, there are dozens of embarrassing stories about me floating around. So many there's no blackmail potential left. Nobody made me hire you."

The woman at the cash register had picked up one of the teacup gardens. "Look," I said. "Your teacup gardens sell out as fast as we get them made. They were your idea."

"I'll bring the rest of them out as soon as I finish this shelf," she said.

I nodded and headed for the storeroom.

Mac was still at the workbench talking on his

phone. The top of a mantel clock was lying in three pieces, and I could see he'd gotten a couple of clamps out. The clock had been another yard-sale find, the wooden case in several pieces, but for two dollars it seemed worth the investment of a little time. Mac set his cell on the workbench, pulled one hand over his neck and uttered a couple of swearwords almost under his breath.

"What's wrong?" I asked.

He made a face and shook his head. "The place where I've been renting my apartment has been sold. I have six weeks to find a new place." He gave a humorless laugh. "Maybe I should see if Rose is interested in being roommates."

"I'm sorry," I said. "If I had another apartment, I'd let you have it. If I had any space other than the little storage closet you saw under the stairs, it would be yours."

Mac managed a smiled. "Thanks. I appreciate the thought."

"Why don't you let Mac move in here?" Avery was standing behind us, probably on her way to get the tiny planters.

I looked around the space. "Avery, this is a storage room," I said. "Mac can't live here."

She gave me the look teenagers have been giving adults for millennia. That "how dumb can you be" expression.

"Not down here, duh," she said. "There's that big space upstairs that we don't even use half of for storage. Why can't Mac live there?"

Chapter 13

Mac said, "No," at exactly the same time as I said, "What do you mean?" He spoke first the second time. "No," he said again.

I pictured the second-floor storage area Avery was talking about. The big room that faced the side parking lot was actually two rooms with doors that slid back into the wall. In one of the building's previous incarnations, it had been a private smokers' club. There had been a wet bar at the end of the bigger of the two rooms, and the plumbing was still in place.

"Hang on a minute," I said. "Avery might be onto something."

"I am," she said. She didn't lack confidence in her ideas. "There's not that much stuff up there. I know because I was just upstairs to get a couple of the quilts for Charlotte—nothing really big because it's too hard to get big stuff up the stairs in the first place. And we still have under the stairs and even the sunporch until spring because the Angels have their office in here now anyway. And Mac could even use the back staircase because it's only sort of blocked off, and then he wouldn't have to go through the store all the time."

I held up both hands. "Avery, take a breath."

"No," Mac said for the third time.

It could work, I realized. "Mac, we should at least take a look."

"We should," Avery echoed. She tucked her dark hair behind one ear. "I already have some ideas for how you could do the layout."

"And I'm sure they're good ones," I said. "But we're just going to take a quick look. I need you down here with Charlotte for now."

She nodded. "Okay."

"Come take a look," I said to Mac, inclining my head in the direction of the stairs.

He shook his head in resignation. "All right."

He didn't say a word until we were at the top of the stairs. Then he turned to me. "Okay, we're here. Just count to ten and then we'll go back downstairs and say it won't work."

I pulled my keys out of my pocket and took a moment to study Mac. He looked uncomfortable, shifting his weight from one foot to the other. "You want to keep your work life and your private life separate. I understand that," I said. "As you pointed out a little while ago, this isn't a typical workplace. But if you're interested at all, I think Avery might be onto something."

After a long moment, he nodded slowly. "I guess it doesn't hurt to take a look."

I unlocked the door and we stepped inside. Overall, the space was bigger than the studio apartment Jess had lived in downtown before she found her current place. It was definitely bigger than the first apartment she and I had shared in university. And Avery was right. We really didn't have much stored up here at the moment because it was just too much of a hassle lugging things upstairs and then having to cart them back down again a week or so later.

"I know those sliding doors work," I said. I walked across the room and looked at the space on the other side of the two panel doors. "There's room for a bed and a dresser in here. Maybe even a chair."

Each of the rooms had a good-sized window that let in lots of light. And the old house had been well insulated during the original conversion years ago from a home to a business, so it was warm.

"The floors are in decent shape," Mac said, reaching down and swiping a hand across the wide wooden boards.

I pointed at the end wall. "There's plumbing in that wall. It wouldn't be that hard to make a galley kitchen there and then go through that closet and connect to the bathroom in the hall."

"What would we do for a staff washroom?"

"Do a little work on the one downstairs. We could put in a new sink and a new toilet, maybe find an end of vinyl or some tile for the floor and let Avery paint the walls." I pulled a pen and a scrap of paper that had a short grocery list scribbled on it and sketched out a rough floor plan with a tiny galley kitchen on the back. I handed him the piece of paper. "Could you build that?"

Mac studied my drawing for a moment, pulling a hand over his mouth.

"We worked pretty well together on Rose's apartment," I said.

He smiled. "Yeah, we did, didn't we?"

"So can you build it?" I repeated.

He nodded. "Uh-huh. Except for the basic rough-in of the plumbing, I can do this."

"So now the big question—do you want to do it?" I said.

Mac looked around the room. I knew he was intrigued by the way he was eyeing the end wall as though he were picturing a run of cupboards. "We could think about it," he said. "On the condition that I pay the going rent. No special deals, Sarah."

I nodded. "Agreed. And I have a condition."

"What is it?"

"If this arrangement doesn't work out for either of us for any reason, we say so—no hard feelings." I held out my hand. "What do you say? Do we have a deal?"

Mac hesitated, but only for a second or two. He took my hand, smiled and said, "We have a deal."

Mac and I spent about an hour after the shop closed measuring the storage space and roughing out a floor plan with measurements scribbled on the side. Avery had wanted to stay and help, but I'd promised she could help us work on the downstairs washroom.

That evening, after a scrambled-egg sandwich and a clementine for me, and some Tasty Tenders for Elvis, I got a pad of grid paper and a pencil and started turning my rough drawing into a rudimentary floor plan. Elvis sat beside me, craning his neck and poking his head in my field of vision every few minutes. He put his paw on the page at one point and looked at me. "There for the sink?" I asked.

"Merow," he answered.

I took a look at the spot on the drawing where he'd rested his paw. He was right. I set my pencil down, stretched my right arm over my head and reached for the phone. Elvis stretched as well and then sprawled over the floor plan as I punched in my parents' number.

"That's not helping," I said. He gave me a look that seemed to suggest he wasn't trying to help.

My dad answered the phone. "Hi, sweetheart," he said. I knew he was smiling, and it seemed to me that I could feel the warmth of that smile coming through the receiver.

"Hi, Dad," I said. "Is it cold there?" My parents lived in New Hampshire, where my dad taught journalism at Keating State College.

"It's two-flap weather," he said.

"That's some serious cold," I said with a laugh. Dad had a mangy pile-lined leather aviator hat with earflaps, which he wore only when it was really, really cold. My mother hated that hat. She said it made him look like he'd been out in the bush about a week too long. She and I had both bought him other hats over the years, but he liked his aviator hat more than any of them.

It had disappeared once under mysterious circumstances, and the entire neighborhood had been treated to the sight of my dad in a holey sweatshirt, pajama bottoms and unlaced Red Wings racing down the street after the garbage truck and then striding back, triumphantly holding the hat over his head like he was some kind of marauding Viking with a head on a pike. The hat had never been safer after that.

"Is Mom around?" I asked.

"She is," he said. "Hang on and I'll get her."

"Love you," I said.

He'd already set the handset down, but I heard him call, "Love you, too!"

After a few moments of silence Mom picked up the phone. "Hi, baby," she said.

"Hi, Mom," I said. "Dad said it's cold there."

"You've heard the expression 'a three-dog night.' Well, we had an ugly-hat day."

"I heard that," my dad called out in the background.

Mom and I both laughed.

"So what's new with you?" she asked.

I explained about Mac losing his apartment and Avery's idea to create an apartment up above the shop. "That could work," she said, and I pictured her reaching across the kitchen counter for a pencil and a pad of paper. "What were you thinking of for a layout?"

I shifted Elvis with one hand and pulled my drawing from underneath him while he muttered and murped with annoyance. I described my plan, and Mom made a couple of suggestions for the galley kitchen. I managed to scribble them on my sketch without having to make Elvis move altogether. He'd rolled onto his back and was watching me with a bemused look that seemed to say, "I'm not going anywhere."

"I talked to your grandmother this morning," Mom said. "She's going to call you later. She's worried about Liz."

"She doesn't need to be," I said, stroking the fur under Elvis's chin, which immediately put me back in his good graces. I explained what Michelle had told me.

Mom gave a soft sigh of relief. "Isabel will be happy to hear that."

We talked for a few more minutes and then we said good night.

I was about to set the phone up on the counter when it rang. "Gram," I said to Elvis. He reached over and put a paw on the phone, cat for "well, hurry up and answer it."

I picked up the receiver. "Hi, Gram," I said.

"Hello, dear," she replied. I found myself smiling all over again.

"Before you say anything else, Liz isn't a suspect anymore in Lily's death," I said. "I had supper with Michelle, and they know Liz wasn't anywhere near the bakery that night."

"Thank heavens!" Gram exclaimed. "Liz would never hurt anyone. She's all bark and no bite."

"That's because her bark is usually enough," I said.

She laughed. "So are the Angels dropping the case?"

Elvis butted my hand with his head, and I began to scratch behind his left ear. "Not likely. Rose is determined to figure out who killed Lily."

"She was a lovely girl," Gram said quietly.

"Yes, she was," I agreed. I swallowed a couple of times because all of a sudden there was a lump in my throat. This was the first time I'd let myself acknowledge that I missed Lily. We'd started to make a connection, as far as I was concerned, and I was sorry it was never going to become more than that now.

I cleared my throat. "Gram, what do you know about the Swift family?"

"What do you want to know?" she asked. I pictured her leaning forward, propping her elbows on her knees. "You're thinking about Caleb Swift, I'm guessing."

Elvis had started to purr. "Charlotte gave me the bare bones. And I seem to remember you mentioning it when Caleb went missing."

"He seemed to just vanish off the face of the earth," Gram said. "They found his sailboat drifting just past the mouth of the harbor the next day."

"Liz said that Daniel Swift believed Lily knew more than she was telling."

She sighed softly. "The Swifts founded this town. They're old money, and sometimes with old money there's a certain sense of entitlement. Or maybe 'arrogance' would be a better word."

"Elspeth called Caleb a jerk," I said. I started scratching behind Elvis's other ear. There wasn't even a momentary break in the purring soundtrack.

"I can't really say about Caleb," she said. "But his grandfather, Daniel, he's an arrogant, entitled man."

I'd seen Daniel Swift over the years. He was a tall, imposing man with a lined face from years of being out on the water and a deep voice. I knew his son and daughter-in-law had been killed in a plane crash years ago. Caleb was his only grandchild.

"Daniel couldn't accept the fact that the police weren't able to figure out what had happened to Caleb. He hired his own investigators, but they didn't turn up anything either. He refused to even entertain the idea that Caleb had staged the whole thing and just walked away from his life, which was the speculation around town. Daniel was certain there was some kind of foul play."

"Do you think he was right?"

She hesitated. "I don't know," she finally said. "I don't buy the idea that Caleb got bored with the money and the influence being a Swift gave him. I think it's possible he was drinking and fell off the boat, but Daniel wouldn't even think about that possibility. He'd always had blinders when it came to that boy. Understandable, I guess. Caleb was all he had left.

"Lily was one of the last people to see Caleb, and Daniel became obsessed with the idea that she knew something she wasn't telling. He kept pushing the police to search her bakery. Finally, one day Lily just got fed up. She stopped Daniel on the street, probably much the way I hear she did with Liz, and told him he could search the building anytime he wanted to because she had nothing to hide."

I remembered the anger in Lily's voice when she'd accosted Liz. I wonder what it had been like when she'd confronted Daniel Swift.

"Did he?" I asked.

"He had the good sense not to," Gram said. I could picture her ruefully shaking her head. "But that didn't mean he let it go, either."

I talked to Gram for a few more minutes and then we said good-bye. "Stay safe, my darling," she said.

"I will," I said. Just because the Angels were still in the private detective business didn't mean I still was.

I took my floor-plan drawings to the shop with me in the morning. Mac had only a couple of tweaks. "Want me to start pricing materials?" he asked.

I nodded. "I'll go down after lunch and do the paperwork for the building permit. Do you have any plans for Friday night?"

"Are you asking me out?" he said, the beginning of a smile playing across his face.

"No," I said. "I'm asking you in. Do you want to start moving things out of the space upstairs?"

"You mean you don't have a date?" he teased.

"Only with a furry guy whose idea of a good time is getting scratched under his chin while watching *Jeopardy!*." Elvis was sitting in the middle of the love seat, working on a knot in the fur on his tail. He paused long enough to meow his acknowledgment that it was him I was talking about and went back to it.

Jess and I had agreed to meet at her shop after work and walk over to Thursday-night jam together. She was just finishing a display in the tiny front window when I walked in. I waved at Elin, one of her two partners, who was behind the cash register. Jess hugged me, and I began peeling off my outdoor things. "How was your day?" I asked.

"Very good," she said. "I started a quilt with those vintage rocker tees from that last box I got from you guys. Come take a look."

I followed her into her sewing space, which was a small room off the main store. The quilt she had started piecing was spread over her worktable. "Oh, that's nice," I said.

She grinned. "I think so. Will you tell Mac thanks for me? He's the one who found the shirts."

I nodded. "I have some news that involves Mac."

"What is it?" she asked, leaning back against the table.

"He's going to move in to the shop. We're going to make an apartment on the second floor."

"Seriously?"

"Seriously."

"What prompted that?" Jess asked.

I explained about the building where Mac was living being sold and how Avery had suggested we turn the storage room into a small apartment.

"I think that's a great idea, having Mr. Tall, Dark and Mysterious living above the shop," Jess said, resting her hands on either side of the table. "You won't have to worry about security, and the rent will help you get the building paid off faster." She narrowed her eyes at me. "He *is* paying rent, right?"

I nodded. "Yes, Mac is paying rent. We're being very professional about the whole thing."

She gave me a saucy grin. "Would it be a bad thing to get a little unprofessional with Mac? Since you don't want to start something with Nick."

"You're incorrigible," I said.

She flipped her long hair over her shoulder. "Yeah, that's part of my charm."

I looked at my watch. "We should probably get going if we want to get a decent table."

"Do you know if Nick is coming?" Jess asked as she pulled on her coat.

"He said he is," I said. "Oh, and he said to tell you the nachos and salsa are on him."

She clasped both hands under her chin and gave me a moony, love-struck look. "I love it when a guy buys me things to impress you. You think I could convince him that buying me a pair of diamond earrings is the way to your heart?"

"No," I said, feeling in my pocket to make sure I had my phone. "And Nick isn't buying nachos to impress me. He's buying them because you bought them last time."

Jess laced her fingers together and rested her hands on top of her head. "Yeah, you just keep telling yourself that."

I was out of witty comebacks. I stuck my tongue out at her.

Nick showed up just before Sam came out for the jam, sliding onto a chair between us that Jess had been guarding for the previous half hour.

"Tortilla chips and salsa are on the way," he said.

"Nicolas Elliot, I may love you," Jess said with mock seriousness, one hand pressed to her chest with her usual melodramatic flair.

"Are you sure it's not just my hot salsa you love?" he asked, drawing out the word "salsa" and making it sound a little risqué.

"It is spicy," Jess crooned, winking at him.

I rolled my eyes at them. "Will you two knock it off?" I said.

The waiter came to the table then and set the food between Nick and Jess.

Jess propped one elbow on the table and rested her chin on her hand. "Ignore her," she said to Nick. "She's just jealous because there's a little heat between us."

I covered my face with both hands and shook my head while the two of them laughed. I was saved from any more of their wit by Sam slipping onto a stool onstage and starting on the intro to Clapton's "Wonderful Tonight."

We didn't talk at all during the first set, although

more than once Nick's eyes met mine when we were both singing along with the music.

Finally Sam said, "Thank you very much. We're going to take a little break and we'll be back."

The noise level in the pub immediately rose. Nick pushed back his chair and looked around for our waiter.

Jess leaned forward and caught my eye. "So when are you going to start work on the new apartment?" she asked.

"As soon as I get the building permit," I said, grabbing the last tortilla chip from the basket.

"You mean the place Rose is going to move into?" Nick asked. He caught the eye of our waiter and pointed to the table. "Mom told me," he added.

"No, she's adding an apartment over the shop," Jess said. "Mac's going to live there."

"You're not serious?" Nick said. Even though Jess had been talking, he was looking at me.

"I am," I said. "Do you have a problem with Mac?"

Nick wiped a hand across his chin. "No," he said, but I noticed it had taken just a little bit longer than it should have for the response. "But make sure you get Josh Evans to draw up a rental agreement, you know, just to be on the safe side."

He got to his feet. "Excuse me a second. I see someone I need to talk to."

"Somebody's jealous," Jess said in a singsong voice.

I made a snort of annoyance. "More like some-body stays in touch with Liam and when my broth-er's not around starts acting like him."

"How is Liam?" Jess asked. She picked up the empty salsa dish, sighed softly and set it back down.

"He's good," I said. "Busy. He had dinner with Mom and Dad on Sunday, and Mom said he may be in town soon, something about a project he's going to consult on." I reached for my cup and drank the last of my coffee. "That reminds me, what's the sta-tus of North Landing?"

Jess made a face. "I'll know more tomorrow. There's a meeting scheduled for six thirty."

"Any idea what's going to happen?"

She shook her head. "Not a clue."

Over by the stage I spotted Vince Kennedy talking to Asia. Jess followed my gaze. "If it all falls through, it isn't going to be good for Vince," she said.

"Liz, either," I said.

"Not to mention Jon West himself," Jess added. "You think he killed her?"

I knew she meant Lily. "No," I said, turning my empty cup in a circle on the table.

"Why so sure?"

"He just doesn't strike me as the type."

She frowned. "Wait a minute. Don't tell me. Elvis didn't do that thing he does when people are lying, did he?"

"Maybe," I hedged.

"Well, good for our little feline Sherlock Holmes," she said with a grin. "You know, just because it wasn't Jon West who killed Lily doesn't mean it couldn't have been someone connected to the development."

Adam brought more nachos and salsa to the table. I thanked him while Jess grabbed a chip.

"What do you mean?" I asked.

"Jon West has investors," she said around a mouthful of a lot of salsa and a little chip.

"Like?" I reached for a chip before Jess got them all.

"I don't have a clue," she said. "But rumor has it whoever they are, they have enough influence that the bakery property will just be expropriated if Caroline doesn't sell to Jon West."

I remembered West saying he could get the land by expropriation. At the time I'd thought he was bluffing to get Rose off his case.

"So who could do that?" I said.

Jess shrugged. "I don't know, but whoever it is, they're walking around in big shoes."

Chapter 14

After the band's last song of the night, Sam made his way over to me, still carrying his guitar.

"I have a couple of boxes for you in my office," he said as he reached the table. "You're really going to let Liz's granddaughter re-create a seventies hair band in your front window for Valentine's Day?" he said with a smile.

"C'mon, where's your sense of romance?" I teased.

He laughed.

"Is it all right if I pick them up in the morning?" I asked. "I didn't bring the SUV."

"Sure," he said.

"Glenn McNamara told me you stepped in to help fill Lily's place in the hot-lunch program," I said. "Thank you."

"It's no big deal," he said with a shrug.

"It is to the kids," I said.

"How's the detective business?" Sam asked with a sly smile.

"You heard?"

He nodded. "Eric's art class came for supper last night. Alfred Peterson was with them." He leaned in a little closer. "Are he and Rose a couple?"

"They're seeing each other," I said, pushing my hair back from my face. "I've kind of been afraid to ask exactly how much of each other they've seen, if you know what I mean."

Sam's smile got a bit wider. "Hey, love's grand at any age."

Vince Kennedy had been working his way over to us. "Sorry to interrupt," he said. He looked at Sam. "They need you in the kitchen."

Sam made a face. "Please tell me it's not the bread slicer again."

Vince shrugged. "Sorry. I don't know."

Sam handed him the guitar. "I'll see you in the morning," he said to me, and headed toward the kitchen.

Vince turned to me. He'd trimmed his gray-streaked beard into a goatee and he was wearing his hair a little shorter. It made him look a little younger, although I could see worry lines around his brown eyes.

Vince was a tall, wiry man who never seemed to be completely still. His hands or his feet were always moving. I sometimes wondered if he was keeping time to a song only he could hear. "I just wanted to say thanks for the deal you gave Asia on that guitar she bought from you last week."

"It's a good beginner guitar," I said. "I'm glad she

likes it." We both looked over to the stage, where fifteen-year-old Asia Kennedy was talking to Eric, The Hairy Banana's bass player when he wasn't giving art lessons or creating graphic novels. Asia's spiky blond hair was sticking out all over her head. I could see her strong rower's shoulders and legs under her long-sleeved blue T-shirt and the argyle leggings Jess had made.

"I know you gave her the family rate and I appreciate that," Vince said.

I turned back to face him. "I'm glad Asia likes music," I said. "It got me through my teenage years more or less unscathed. She's a good kid."

Vince's expression turned serious. "She really is," he said. He shook his head. "I'd better get this back to Sam's office," he said, holding up the guitar. "Thanks again, Sarah."

I smiled. "You're welcome."

I stopped at the pub in the morning to pick up the boxes of KISS gear for Avery, and Elvis and I had breakfast with Sam. The conversation eventually turned to the development proposal and Lily's death.

"Do you think someone could have been that upset with her refusal to sell that they could have killed her?" I asked.

Sam raked his fingers through his beard. "On purpose? Nah. I can't see it. Take Vince, for example. That development goes ahead, his problems are pretty much solved." He reached for his coffee. "If he could just get market value for that old building of his father's, the old man would be able to stay in that nursing home until he dies." He took a sip from his mug. "But could you imagine Vince killing Lily—killing anyone—over that?"

I couldn't.

"Or what about Liz? The Emmerson Foundation holds the mortgages on two buildings that would come down for North Landing and they're both in default, but I don't see Liz shoving Lily down a set of stairs."

I didn't say that wasn't exactly what had happened. I just nodded in agreement.

Friday turned out to be a busy day at the store. The Angels spent most of the day working on a timeline for the last twenty-four hours of Lily's life, when they weren't waiting on customers. I saw Charlotte and Rose on their cell phones at different times. Mr. P. was still digging into Jon West's background.

I'd waffled all morning, but in the end I hadn't told them what Jess had told me. An unsubstantiated rumor that someone with enough influence to push through the expropriation of Lily's Bakery and had invested in North Landing didn't have anything to do with Lily's death, as far as I could see.

I knew Mr. P. and Rose were up to something I probably wasn't going to like, my new hands-off policy or not. They left so quickly at the end of the day that Rose left her big tote bag behind.

When she wasn't waiting on customers, Avery spent all of her time cleaning up the mannequin parts and putting the figures together. By the end of the day, all four of them were assembled in the workroom. They gave me a start when I came around the corner and discovered the four figures standing there, naked except for their wigs.

Liz came to pick up Avery and Charlotte at the end of the day.

"There's a meeting tonight about the status of the harbor-front project," Charlotte said to me as she came down the stairs carrying her coat. Avery had taken her grandmother out back to see the mannequins. "I'm going with Liz."

"I heard," I said, holding her heavy wool peacoat so she could slip her arms into it. Jess and Nick had talked a bit about the meeting at The Black Bear. "Jess will be there, too." Charlotte's bright yellow scarf had fallen to the floor, and I bent to pick it up. "What do you think is going to happen?"

She took the scarf from me and tied it loosely at her neck. "I truly don't know," she said.

Mac and I agreed to meet back at the store at seven thirty to start clearing out the upstairs storage room. When I got back to the shop about twenty-five after, the Ellisons, father and son—whom I'd hired to do snow removal—were in the parking lot with a front-end loader and a dump truck, taking away some of the massive snow pile at the end of the small lot, so I had to park on the side street. A shooting star arced across the harbor, and I closed my eyes and made a wish. Aaron Ellison waved from the cab of the loader as I hurried across the empty lot.

Mac was waiting for me by the back door. "Where did you park?" he asked.

"Around the corner," I said, pointing up the hill.

"I'll walk you back to your car when we're done," he said.

I unlocked the back door, and when we stepped into the workroom, I gave a start of surprise. Avery had moved "the band," and for a moment I thought there were two people standing at the far end of the room.

"They better be going in the window tomorrow," I said to Mac. "I thought someone had broken in."

"I know what you mean," he said as he unzipped his heavy jacket. "I caught sight of one of them out of the corner of my eye this afternoon and for a moment I wondered why you and Charlotte were doing the wave."

I laughed.

The first thing we did in the upstairs space was move the few pieces of furniture down into the workroom. "I think we should take all the quilts downstairs as well," I said, looking at the stack of boxes by the door. "They've been selling like hot-cakes." I waved a finger at him. "Oh, and I forgot to tell you. Jess is making some kind of rock-and-roll quilt with those old T-shirts we sold her."

"That sounds like something we could hang on the wall next to the guitars," Mac said.

I nodded. "I thought the same thing." One of the reasons Mac and I worked so well together was that kind of similar thinking often happened.

He picked up two boxes of glassware that were

also going downstairs. Even under his gray T-shirt I could see his muscles move. He'd pushed back his sleeves, and I could see the smooth, dark skin of his forearms and smell his clean scent of Ivory soap and peppermints as I reached for one of the boxes of quilts. I wiped the back of my hand over my forehead for a moment. What the heck was I thinking? Maybe Jess was right. Maybe it had been too long since I'd been on a date.

When Mac came back upstairs, I was still standing in the same place, staring at the same box.

"Sarah, are you trying to move that with the power of your mind?" he asked.

I smiled and shook my head. "No. It wouldn't get very far. I was just thinking."

"About what?" He rested one hand on the top box of quilts.

"If we take the chair out of my office, we can move the credenza backward and over a little bit, which means we can access the storage space in the eaves."

"That's not going to give you a lot of seating space in your office," Mac pointed out.

"I don't think I've had a single customer up there in the last seven months," I said, glancing through the open door to the hall. "Aside from Elvis, and he seems to think the desk chair belongs to him, the only other person who spends time in my office is you, when we're working on a quote."

"Okay. Let's at least take a look," he said.

We crossed the hall and went into my office. "See what I mean?" I said.

He nodded slowly. "And if we angled your desk just a little, that would give you a bit more space for the love seat."

"Let's try it."

We set the chair in the hall, and then Mac adjusted my desk a little to the left so it was on a slight angle. The credenza was moved down and the love seat forward, and suddenly we had easy access to the storage space in the eaves.

"Perfect," I said with a grin.

Then we heard the sound of something falling downstairs.

Mac and I exchanged a look and he went out in the hallway to listen. After a moment there was another sound I couldn't quite identify.

"Stay here," Mac said in a low voice. "And call 911."

He was on his way down the stairs before I could tell him not to do anything stupidly heroic. I pulled out my cell and was about to call the police when I remembered Rose's bag. She'd been in such a hurry to leave with Mr. P., she'd left it behind on the desk chair in the Angels' "office." It was probably her we'd heard. She'd borrowed my gram's spare keys from Charlotte to get into the apartment. I knew there was an extra key to this building on that ring. Rose had probably borrowed the keys again.

I remembered how I'd launched myself into the apartment bedroom and almost knocked her head off. I didn't want Mac to tackle Rose and maybe break her hip. And I certainly didn't want her to be arrested for B and E. I hurried down the stairs, moving quickly and quietly just in case it wasn't Rose moving around downstairs. Mac was just disappearing around the door to the storeroom.

"Hey!" he called out sharply. That was followed by the sound of a scuffle. I bolted across the shop, thinking this whole thing was stupid. We should have just called 911 and stayed put.

Mac had the intruder on the floor, one knee in the small of the person's back. He looked up at me. "Sarah, what are you doing down here? Did you call 911?"

"I thought it might be Rose," I said. I could see that it wasn't and I felt my knees begin to shake. The intruder was taller and male, based on his build. I reached over and flipped on the overhead light.

And discovered it was Vince Kennedy lying on the storeroom floor.

Chapter 15

My mouth hung open for a moment before I could speak. "Let him up," I finally managed to say to Mac. "I know him."

Mac got to his feet and pulled Vince up with him by one arm.

Vince was wearing jeans and a black hoodie. He was disheveled, his hair standing on end and the sweatshirt twisted to one side.

"What the hell are you doing, Vince?" I said, the fury rising in my chest leaving a sour taste in the back of my throat.

I was right in front of him, but he wouldn't look at me. "Last night you were thanking me for Asia's guitar, and tonight you're breaking in to my store."

"I'm sorry," Vince said, and finally he did look at me. "Things have been a little tight."

"So you decided it would be a good idea to rob a friend?" Mac asked, his voice tight with anger.

"I knew you had at least a couple of guitars here that were worth some money," Vince said. He couldn't meet my eyes for very long. His gaze kept sliding away.

"Why didn't you ask someone for help?" I pulled a hand down over the back of my head. I was angry and troubled all at the same time, the emotions churning in my stomach. "I would have helped you. Sam would have helped you. Why would you do something like this?"

Vince swallowed hard and didn't say anything.

"What do you want to do?" Mac asked. He was still holding Vince by the neck of his hoodie. "I know what gets my vote."

Part of me wanted to let Vince walk out the door. Another part wanted to call the police and let Vince spend the night in jail. I was furious. I was sad. I felt . . . betrayed. Then something sticking out of the kangaroo pocket of his hoodie caught my eye. It looked like . . . hair?

I reached over and snatched the dark wig—because that's what it was—from his pocket. It was one of the wigs that went with the KISS costumes I'd gotten from Sam. My hand was shaking as I held it up. I took a step closer to Vince. "I hear these things bring big money on the street."

The color drained from his face.

"Cut the crap, Vince," I said, my voice suddenly raw-edged with angry intensity. "Why did you really break in here?"

I could think of only one reason, and it made my stomach sick.

He didn't answer.

I looked away. "You can tell me or you can tell the police," I said softly.

"I came to get that . . . wig."

I focused on him again. "Why?"

"Because when the old guy Peterson was having lunch at the pub the other day, I heard him say he'd found security footage of the person who'd been hassling Lily Carter before she died." His eyes met mine and stayed there this time. "I was afraid if you saw the video and then took a close look at the wig, you'd realize it was me."

Mac muttered an oath and let go of Vince's arm.

"The mouse?" I said, staring at him. It couldn't be true. "The mixed-up salt and sugar? The eggs thrown at the front window? Everything? That was you?"

Vince nodded.

"Why?"

"Because Lily wouldn't sell." His voice rose. His emotions were right at the surface. "She just kept using the same lame excuse that the development would be bad for the downtown. Do you know what it costs to keep my old man in that nursing home?" He didn't wait for me to answer. I knew he wasn't expecting me to. "Thousands every month. His savings are just about gone, and his pension just isn't enough. I've looked at other places, and believe me, you wouldn't put a dog in them." His right hand was flexing and then squeezing into a fist at his side. Flexing and squeezing, flexing and squeezing. "The money Jon West was offering would have meant my father could spend the rest of his life living with a little dignity. And he damn well deserves that."

"I can't believe you would do something like that to Lily," I said hoarsely, shaking my head.

"Yeah, well, I'm desperate, Sarah," he said, and his mouth twisted to one side. "I hope you never know what that feels like."

I got right in his face. "You don't have a monopoly on bad things happening to you, Vince," I said. "Don't move. Not an inch. You try to leave and you won't have to worry about Mac handing you your head because I'll personally lay you out like a welcome mat at the front door."

I gestured to Mac. We took a few steps away from Vince.

"What do you want to do?" he said.

I couldn't read his feelings in his face.

"We can call the police."

"I don't know," I said. Sam had been like a father to me ever since my biological father died, which in a weird way made Vince feel like family. I looked away for a moment and then met Mac's gaze again. I still had the wig in one hand, and I fingered the dark hair. "I'm having a really hard time believing that Vince was the one pulling those stupid tricks on Lily."

Mac rubbed his left shoulder with his other hand. "I don't know the guy, so I'm not making excuses for him, but when people are desperate, they do things they would never do in other circumstances."

"I'm going to call Sam," I said. Maybe it wasn't

exactly logical, but I thought possibly Sam could talk some sense into Vince.

Mac's expression didn't change. "All right."

"Do you think I'm wrong?" I asked as I pulled out my phone.

"Not my place to judge, Sarah," he said.

"You never do," I said. "Thank you for that."

I turned and punched in Sam's number. When he answered, I explained what had happened. "If you can come and get him, I won't call the police."

Sam muttered a couple of choice swearwords. "I'm on my way."

I hung up and walked back over to Vince.

"Sam's coming to pick you up," I said. "My options were him or the police. And the only reason I didn't call the police is because Sam's been like a dad to me and I know he considers you a friend."

"Thank you," Vince said so softly I could barely make out the words.

"I'm not done, Vince," I said. My arms were folded across my chest, hands clenched. "You have twenty-four hours to tell Detective Andrews that it was you who was harassing Lily. I don't want her to waste her time in that direction when she doesn't need to."

He nodded wordlessly. We waited the rest of the time for Sam in silence.

Sam didn't say a word to Vince, at least not in front of Mac and me.

"Thank you," he said to Mac, offering his hand.

"Thanks for coming up here," Mac replied. They shook hands.

"I'm not going to make any excuses," Sam said, but he looked over his shoulder to where Vince was standing, shoulders slumped in his sweatshirt, by the back door.

"Good plan," I said. I could hear the anger in my voice. I hadn't made any effort to hide it from Sam.

He leaned in and hugged me. "Thank you," he said softly against my ear. "I know you did this for me."

After they were gone, Mac and I walked back inside.

Mac studied me, narrowing his eyes. "I can see the wheels turning," he said. "What's up?"

"I'm not certain yet," I said slowly.

"You think Vince really did break in here to steal a couple of guitars?"

I shook my head. "No, I don't."

"So he came to get that wig. So you wouldn't figure out he was the one harassing Lily Carter."

I set the wig back in the box on the workbench. "Maybe. I'm not certain. I need to check on a couple of things."

Sam had clearly been expecting I'd show up for breakfast the next morning. He had everything ready for blueberry pancakes, along with a chopped-up sardine for Elvis.

"Sam, what was that fund-raiser you loaned Vince the Rickenbacker for?" I asked.

He came over and poured me another cup of coffee. "Fairy Godmothers. They grant wishes to kids who are seriously ill. Vince and Eric subbed for a couple of guys out of Boston who couldn't make it for the show."

He topped up his own cup. "Vince donated his time. All he took was gas money, and not all of that. It's really hard to believe he was the one pulling those stupid stunts on Lily."

"When was the concert?" I asked.

I could feel Elvis's green eyes on me, watching me as though he knew I was gathering information.

"The twenty-first, in Portland," he said, returning the coffeepot to its burner. "Vince and Eric drove down, crashed with someone Eric knows and drove back the next morning. Why the third degree?"

"The twenty-first? You're positive? And they stayed all night?"

He slid into the booth on the seat opposite me. "Sarah, what's going on?"

"It wasn't Vince."

"What wasn't Vince?" he said.

I speared the last bit of my pancake and ate it. "He wasn't the one who pulled those tricks on Lily. The twenty-first was the night someone egged the front window of the bakery. I know because I was there early the next morning. Vince couldn't have done it if he was playing in Portland."

"So why would he say he did, then?"

I nodded as I set down my fork and reached for my cup. "Exactly. Why would he do that?"

"You think you know."

"Maybe," I admitted. I finished my coffee and

stood up. "I need to check something out. I'll call you."

It was bitingly cold, so I'd arranged to pick up Rose. She was waiting outside Legacy Place with Mr. P.

"Hello, sweet girl," she said. "Alfred is coming with us."

"Good morning, Mr. P.," I said as he got in the backseat with Elvis.

He was wearing a striped stocking cap and scarf that Rose had made for him, along with a heavy brown parka and the same kind of heavy, insulated gloves that Aaron Ellison wore when he plowed the parking lot. He reminded me of a ceramic garden gnome.

"Good morning, Sarah," he said as he fastened his seat belt. "Thank you for picking us up."

"You're very welcome," I said.

"Good morning, Elvis," Mr. P. said as I pulled away from the curb. I glanced in the rearview mirror in time to see him sneak the cat a tiny fish cracker. I shifted my eyes back to the road.

Avery and Liz were waiting for us in the lot. When I got out of the SUV, Avery climbed out of her grand-mother's car and skidded across the parking lot to-ward me. She was wearing high-top sneakers instead of boots. "Sarah, can I work on the window today? Please, please, please. You don't have to pay me. I just want to get it done."

It made me feel good to see her enthusiasm. "Yes, you can work on the window," I said.

Mr. P. was carrying Elvis. I saw him exchange a smile with Rose.

"Yay!" Avery said, jumping up and down and almost falling. "I'll tell Nonna that she can get me at lunchtime." She made her way back over to the car, arms windmilling, and somehow managed not to fall.

I put my things upstairs in my office, went into the staff room and filled the kettle before I went back down.

"The water's on," I said to Rose.

"Would you like coffee, dear?" she asked.

I'd already had two cups at Sam's. "I think I'll have tea, please," I said.

"I'll bring you a cup," she said, patting my arm as she passed me.

I went into the storeroom. Avery was at the workbench. "Could you watch the front for a few minutes for me, please?" I asked.

"Sure thing," she said. She'd left her usual stack of bracelets at home, but she had a new henna tattoo, a flowering vine that wound around her wrist and disappeared up the sleeve of her black T-shirt.

Alfred was already settled at the desk in the Angels' "office" along the back wall.

"Mr. P., could I take another look at that security video, please?" I asked. "The one from the camera at the bookstore."

"Of course," he said.

I waited while he clicked keys, and then he turned the laptop so I could see the screen. I studied the figure carefully, trying to guess how tall the "fake" Jon West was based on the height of the door to the bakery. It wasn't Vince. It couldn't be. By my rough calculations the figure was shorter than Vince, who topped out at about six feet.

"Would you like to see it again?" Mr. P. asked.

I nodded, rubbing the bridge of my nose with two fingers. "Please."

The second time through I was certain. "Thank you," I said.

"Is there anything I should tell Rosie?" he asked.

I gave him a tight smile. "Not yet."

He nodded. "All right," he said. I could see the gleam of curiosity in his eyes.

I headed back to the store. It wasn't Vince in the security footage, but my suspicion about the person he was covering for was right. The figure in the denim jacket and long wig was Asia Kennedy. I was sure of it. It was Asia who had pulled all those stupid, childish tricks on Lily. What the heck had Vince been thinking, trying to cover for her by stealing that wig?

And then I had an awful thought. Was there more to it? Asia had been harassing Lily. I tried to swallow down the lump at the back of my throat. No. It wasn't possible. It wasn't. Asia was just a kid, a teenager. She couldn't have killed Lily, could she?

Chapter 16

When Liz came to pick up Avery at noon, she brought Charlotte with her. She also brought food—roast-beef sandwiches from McNamara's. Since I had spent a big chunk of the morning priming the hutch, I was happy to see I didn't have to figure out lunch. Avery was still working on the front window. "I'll watch the store," she said, "and the rest of you can go sit down and eat."

Mac and I found a couple of small tables to push together, and then we carried over several chairs. Chairs were never a problem at the shop. It sometimes seemed as though they multiplied in the dark corners of the room.

Once we were all seated with sandwiches and tea—or coffee for Mac and me—Rose turned to Liz. "Tell us about the meeting last night."

"It was just a lot of empty promises," Liz said, making a dismissive gesture with one hand.

Charlotte nodded in agreement. "They seemed to have only two answers for any questions they were asked—we're working on that and that's something we're still negotiating."

"Do you think the project is dead?" Mr. P. asked.

"Yes," Liz said, pulling the pickle out of her sandwich. "The only thing that's left to do is order flowers and plan the wake. Jon West was talking about expropriation again. I don't see how that's going to happen."

I didn't say that maybe she was wrong. "What about you, Charlotte?" I asked instead.

"I'm not as certain as Liz is," Charlotte said, playing with the teaspoon that was resting on her saucer. "Caroline was there. I talked to her for a minute."

"I'm guessing Lily left the bakery to her," I said, fishing an olive round from my sandwich and popping it in my mouth. "Did she say anything that made you think she might be willing to sell? Not that she'd be able to do that for a while."

Charlotte shook her head. "No. But she didn't say she's not willing to sell, either. She is getting a lot of pressure from Jon West. At least that's what she told me. You know that there are rumors someone with money has invested in the project?"

"I heard," I said.

"Do you know who this mystery investor is?" Rose asked.

Charlotte picked up her tea. "All I can tell you is that I've heard the Wellington Group mentioned, but that could be just a rumor."

"That's somewhere to start," Mr. P. said, glancing at Rose.

Rose leaned over and patted his arm. "Alfred will find something. Don't worry."

Mr. P. smiled back at her. He had the look of a love-struck teenager, and I had no doubt he would do whatever it took to justify Rose's faith in him—which was not necessarily a good thing.

The conversation turned to other possibilities that had been floated over the years for development of the harbor front.

"You know what I don't understand," Liz said, shifting sideways in her seat. "What changed for Lily?"

"What do you mean, what changed?" I asked.

"Well, it must be close to five years ago now," she said. "There was another plan for revitalizing the waterfront. It didn't get as far as this one has, but I don't remember Lily having any problem with that idea."

I remembered Jess mentioning the other waterfront proposal. "Maybe that project was smaller," I said.

Charlotte looked at Liz. "Are you talking about that development company out of Vermont?" she said.

Liz nodded over her teacup. "That's the one."

Charlotte shook her head. "Then no," she said to me. "That plan for the harbor front was actually bigger than the North Landing project is. There was a problem with the development company. Their financing was a little too creative for some people. There was a lot of behind-the-scenes maneuvering, and suddenly the whole project was quashed."

Liz brushed a few crumbs from the sleeve of her cashmere cardigan. "Lily definitely had no problem with that idea," she said. She shrugged. "And there's no reason to keep it a secret. The person doing what Charlotte so diplomatically called 'behind-the-scenes maneuvering' four years ago was me."

"You, Elizabeth?" Charlotte said, her eyes widening with surprise.

"Why on earth would you do that?" Rose asked, her cup paused in midair.

"The Trinity Group were the main investors in that deal. I did a little digging into their finances," she said. "Their portfolio was very shaky, not to mention they were being investigated by the IRS. They went bankrupt not long after."

"Pyramid scheme," Mac said quietly. "I remember the SEC investigation."

"The whole thing was a house of cards," Liz commented, looking around for the teapot.

"Maybe Lily just changed her mind about any kind of development," Mr. P. said. "That kind of thing happens."

Rose had gotten up to get the teapot, and she paused with it hovering over Liz's cup. "Alfred, are you saying that women just change their minds on a whim?"

Mac caught my eye across the table, and the corners of his mouth twitched.

"Of course not," Mr. P. said smoothly. "I'm saying that as some people mature, what's important to them changes. Maybe that's what happened to Lily."

Rose smiled. "You could be right." She turned to Charlotte. "Do you think you could sound out Caroline and see if she knows what changed Lily's mind?"

"I can try," Charlotte said. She folded her napkin and set it on her plate. "I just don't want Caroline to feel like she's getting the third degree. She's Lily's mother, remember."

"You're the most diplomatic person I know," Rose said as she poured another cup of tea for Liz. "I know you can figure something out."

"Are you going to give her a trowel along with that line, Rose?" Liz asked.

Charlotte turned her head to look at her friend. "Liz, what on earth are you talking about?"

"Rose is laying it on a little thick," Liz said.

"Are you trying to tell me I'm not diplomatic?" Charlotte said. Her hackles were up.

Liz waved the question away with one hand. "Heavens, no. You're far more diplomatic than I am."

"Everyone's more diplomatic than you are," Rose retorted.

Avery burst into the room then. Her hair looked like something Elvis might have dragged around the parking lot. There was a smudge of dirt, or maybe it was makeup, on one cheek and a huge smile on her face.

"The window's done, and you have to see it!" she exclaimed.

I got to my feet. "Okay, then. Let's go."

I took a step toward the shop doors, and Avery put up both hands to stop me.

"No," she said. "You have to go around and see it from the front to get the full effect."

"Then that's what we'll do," Rose said. "I can't wait to see what you've done." She patted Avery on the cheek and started for the back door.

"Kiddo, do you know how cold it is outside?" Liz asked.

Avery's face fell.

Mr. P. got to his feet. "A little cold can be very invigorating," he said.

Mac smiled as he stood up as well. "Yes, it can, Alfred," he said.

Liz pushed back her chair. "I like to be invigorated as much as the next guy." She smiled at her granddaughter. "Let's go."

We all cut through the parking lot and went to stand on the sidewalk in front of the store.

"Oh. My" was the only thing I could think of to say.

"I like it," Rose proclaimed. "Do you think Avery could do an Aerosmith window?"

Liz had her arms folded across her chest. "You're not going to remind us about the time Steven Tyler's mouth had two tongues and yours didn't have any—are you?"

"You're just jealous," Rose said with a saucy grin.

Alfred looked puzzled. "You dated Steven Tyler, Rosie?" he asked.

"It was just a fling, dear," she said, patting his arm.

Avery had faithfully re-created all four of the members of KISS down to Paul Stanley's Starchild makeup and—heaven help us—his chest hair. She'd stenciled A KISS IS STILL A KISS on the window in red letters.

Mac turned to look at me. He didn't even try to stifle a grin.

"Don't you dare say the word 'interesting,'" I hissed.

"I like it," he said.

"She managed to connect a metal band, *Casablanca* and Valentine's Day," I said. "I like it, too." There wouldn't be another Valentine's-themed window like it anywhere in town.

"Can we go back inside?" Liz said. "My girls are freezing."

"I'm all right," Rose said as we made our way up to the front door.

"I wasn't talking about you," Liz said, pointedly crossing her arms over her chest.

Rose rolled her eyes as she figured out Liz's meaning. "Oh, for heaven's sake," she said.

Avery was waiting for us in the shop, too twitchy to stand still.

"Sweetie pie, you did a wonderful job," Rose exclaimed, wrapping her in a hug. "You make me want to run off and become a groupie." She turned and smiled at Mr. P. "Not that I'm going to."

"Charlotte helped a lot," Avery said. "She did the Paul guy's chest hair, and she styled all the wigs."

Rose turned her smile on Charlotte. "Good job," she said, eyes twinkling.

"Absolutely," Liz said. One eyebrow went up and she gave Charlotte a sly smile. "Nice work with the chest hair."

"What about me, Nonna?" Avery asked. "Do you really like it?"

"It's fantastic," Liz said.

Avery threw her arms around her grandmother. "Do you mean it?"

"Of course I mean it," Liz said. "Would I lie to you?"

"Uh, yeah," Avery said. "You said you liked the smoothie I made for you yesterday and then I caught you pouring it down the sink."

Liz kissed the top of Avery's head. "Smoothies have fruit and yogurt, ice cream even. They do not have kale. Kale is not something we're supposed to drink."

"It's going to get people's attention," Mac said. He gave her a fist bump.

Avery looked at me. "Do you like it, Sarah?" she asked.

"Yes, I do," I said. "You did a great job."

I glanced at Charlotte. "You too."

Rose was standing beside me, and I put my arm around her shoulders. "You know what this calls for?" I said.

"Cake!" Avery, Mr. P. and Liz said at the same time.

I raised my eyebrows and looked down at Rose. "Tomorrow's moving day, but maybe after that you could christen the oven in your new apartment."

Rose clasped her hands together. "What a wonderful idea." She linked her arm through Avery's and started for the storeroom. "What do you think we should make?" I heard her say. "Lemon chiffon or maybe angel food with fruit and whipped cream?"

"I'll go clean up," Charlotte said.

I smiled at her. "Thanks."

"I'm going to see what I can find out about this Wellington Group," Mr. P. said.

The phone started to ring. "And I'm going to get that," Mac said.

Only Liz and I were left, standing just inside the door. "Thank you, Sarah," she said.

"For what?" I asked.

"For letting Avery fill your front window with four aging rock and rollers, or at least a reasonable facsimile of them."

I looked over at the window. "I like it. I'm not just saying that. She did a good job. It'll get people talking. It'll bring in business."

"I'm so glad you came home," Liz said.

I smiled. "Me too."

I was right about the window. Another ski tour on the way out of town after lunch stopped when someone on the bus spotted the "band" in the window. Forty-two people piled out and stood on the sidewalk to check out the band. The tour guide, a man in his twenties wearing a navy ski jacket and a knit Red Sox hat, came inside.

"Your window display's fantastic," he said.

"Thank you," I said. Out of the corner of my eye I

could see Avery by the cash register, grinning and looking like she was about to come out of her skin with excitement.

A middle-aged woman opened the door and poked her head inside. "Can we take a look around?"

"Of course," I said.

"Did you do the band?" she asked, walking over so she could see the display from the back.

I shook my head. "Two of my staff did." More people were coming in behind her.

The woman took a couple of steps closer to me. "I did them, you know," she confided. "Well, two of them." She turned down the waistband of the gray spandex pants she was wearing. KISS was tattooed on her left hip.

"Good for you" probably wasn't the most appropriate answer, but it was the only thing I could think of to say.

We ended up doing more business than we'd done in the store in the entire month of January.

Avery stayed to help, eating up the compliments on her work and answering questions with enthusiasm and maturity.

It was a few minutes after closing time when the bus pulled out of our parking lot.

"I can't believe they all liked the window," Avery said with a satisfied smile, leaning against the cash counter.

"I told you that you'd done a good job," I said.

"I'll get the vacuum and start cleaning up," she said, pushing herself upright.

I walked over to Charlotte, who was straightening up a display of wineglasses and charms.

"Thank you for helping Avery," I said. "She's so excited."

"I didn't really do much." Charlotte smiled. "Avery did most of the work."

I leaned over and kissed her cheek. "You always say that," I said. "And you're always wrong."

Mac came in from the storeroom. "What time are we starting in the morning?" he asked.

Sunday was moving day for Rose, the only day we were all free to help her.

"Eight thirty," I said. "Do you want me to pick you up?"

He shook his head. "Thanks. I don't mind walking."

I looked at Charlotte. "I could pick you up," I said.

She nodded. "If it's not too much trouble. I'm bringing a thermos of hot chocolate and some muffins so we can take a break after a couple of hours."

"I'm borrowing Glenn McNamara's cube truck," I said. "That way we should be able to move the big stuff in just one load."

I'd tried to rent the truck from Glenn, but he wouldn't hear of it. "Just put some gas in it, Sarah," he'd told me. "And we'll be square."

"What are you going to do with the SUV?" Mac asked, reaching for the bottle of hand sanitizer we kept by the cash register.

"Leave it in Glenn's parking lot. That way we can back the truck close to the steps at the house," I said.

"Do you want me to drive it?" he said. "We could put a lot of the small things in the back."

I nodded. "That's a good idea. Could you drop me at Glenn's? It's faster than if I walk over there."

"Sure," he said. "In that case, is eight o'clock too early?"

I shook my head. "Not for me."

Charlotte came downstairs in her coat and boots.

"I'll see you in the morning," I said.

She nodded. "I'll be ready."

Avery pulled on her hat, a purple monkey with ears and tufts of black hair. "Yeah, don't worry, Sarah. I'll make sure to drag Nonna out of bed in time."

Liz made a face at her. "I'm not drinking anything with kale in it," she said as the three of them went out the door.

Rose was winding Mr. P.'s scarf around his neck. "Rose, would you two like a ride?" I asked.

"No, thank you, dear," she said. "It's not that cold. We're going to walk."

I turned to Mac, who was pulling on his parka. "What about you? Could I drop you somewhere?"

He smiled. "Thanks, but I think I'll walk. Rose is right. It's really not that cold." He fished his gloves out of his pocket. "I'll see you in the morning."

I nodded.

Rose and Mr. P. were ready to go, so the three of them set off down the sidewalk together. I locked the door behind them and walked around shutting off the lights. I found Elvis upstairs, sitting on my desk chair. "That's not your chair," I said.

He blinked at me and then lay down on the seat.

"Still not yours," I said, reaching for my coat.

He looked down at the fabric seat and then up at me as if to say, *I'm sitting here and you're not.*

In the back of my mind all day I'd been trying to figure out what to do about Vince. I understood his impulse to protect Asia. But it wouldn't do her any good if he went to jail for something he didn't do. And if she'd had anything to do with Lily's death, it needed to be dealt with, not hidden, as painful as that would be.

"I'm going down to Sam's," I said.

Chapter 17

I hadn't been certain of what I was going to do until I said the words out loud. Elvis jumped down from my chair and went and stood by the office door. "You can come," I said. I looked around even though the cat and I were the only ones left in the building. I felt odd about what I was about to admit. "I need you to help me figure out if it was really Vince's daughter who was harassing Lily."

"Merow," the cat said. I decided to take that as agreement.

"You have to go in my gym bag," I said. "I can't walk into The Black Bear carrying a cat."

Elvis put a paw over his nose and ducked his head.

"It does not smell," I said. He did this every time I wanted him to get in the bag. "You spend more time in that bag than my running clothes do. If anything, the bag smells like cat."

He looked at the bag. He looked at me. What he didn't do was move.

I crossed my arms. Elvis started washing the fur on his chest.

"Okay, don't come, then," I said with an elaborate shrug.

I pulled on my hat and picked up my gloves. Elvis made a squinty face at me. Did he think I was bluffing? I was asking that question about a cat, I realized. Luckily for me, Elvis caved at just that moment. He got up, went over to the empty gym bag sitting on the floor and pawed at the zipper. I bent down, opened the top, and he climbed in.

"Thank you," I said, giving the top of his head a little scratch.

This wasn't me getting involved in the Angels' investigation, I told myself all the way down to The Black Bear. This was just me looking out for a friend.

The pub was busy. No surprise. It was Saturday night, and I knew Sam had a local band playing later. He came across the room to me when I walked in. "Hi," he said. "Are you meeting Jess?"

"No," I said. "I was hoping Vince might be here."

Sam's expression changed. "He is here. He talked to Michelle Andrews this morning, by the way."

I sighed softly. "I was hoping he hadn't."

He looked confused. "I don't understand. I thought you wanted Vince to tell her what he did."

I sighed. "It's complicated."

"Most things are," he said. "What's going on?"

I shifted the gym bag from one shoulder to another, hoping Elvis wouldn't choose now to meow and give me away. "I just want to talk to him for a minute, Sam. Can you just trust me?"

He nodded slowly. "He's in my office, but Asia's with him, Sarah. Think carefully about what you say."

I nodded. "I promise."

He inclined his head in the direction of the kitchen. "You want a bowl of sausage and penne soup?" he asked.

"Ummm, thanks. That sounds good," I said. I kept one hand on the bag as a warning to Elvis that he needed to stay still and quiet if he wanted any of the tiny sausage meatballs that would be in my soup.

Vince and Asia were on the couch in Sam's office. Vince was playing Sam's twelve-string. Asia was eating something—the Italian penne and sausage soup, my nose told me.

"Hi," I said.

"I'm feeding Sarah in here because she has her cat with her," Sam said.

So much for fooling him.

Vince looked up and nodded in my direction but didn't say anything.

Asia smiled. "Hi, Sarah," she said. "Can I see your cat?" She was wearing a Queen T-shirt and skinny jeans, her short blond hair brushed back off her face.

"Sure," I said. I took off my coat and tossed it over the back of an armless chair Sam had bought from my shop. Then I set the bag on the floor, opened the top, and Elvis poked his head out and looked around.

"Hello," Asia said, holding out one hand. Elvis

walked toward her, nose twitching. After sardines and Tasty Tenders, meatballs were one of his favorite foods. He sniffed Asia's fingers and then licked her thumb. She laughed. "Is it all right if I give him a meatball?" she asked.

"Go ahead," I said. I knew I'd have a better chance of wrestling a bobcat away from one of those meatballs than I would Elvis.

She fished one out of her bowl and held it out. Elvis sniffed it delicately, and then the whole thing went in his mouth. He ate it, licked her fingers and then meowed softly.

"You don't need any more," I said. He didn't even look at me. I was on ignore.

Asia patted her lap, and to her delight Elvis jumped up, settled himself and sniffed the air.

I laughed. "He's not exactly subtle."

"He so friendly," she said, stroking his fur.

"That's because he's a ham bone for attention," I said.

Vince continued to play Sam's guitar, but I'd seen him dart little looks in my direction from time to time.

Sam came back in then with a bowl of soup for me. I could smell the oregano and tomatoes and see slivers of mozzarella and croutons in the bowl.

I thanked him and settled in the chair. Asia snuck Elvis another meatball when she thought I wasn't looking. I was trying to figure how to start the conversation, let alone steer it to the development, when Asia solved the problem for me.

"Sarah, is it true that you bought the old chandelier from Doran's that used to be right inside the front doors and the people from North by West want to buy it for their project here?"

"It's true," I said, chasing a crouton around the bowl with my spoon.

"So that means they really are going to build it, right?" She was still stroking Elvis's fur. He was curled up on her lap, front paws tucked up under his body.

"Nothing's decided yet," Vince said. "I told you that." I could hear the tension in his voice.

"Your dad's right," I said. "Things are still up in the air."

"Lily's . . . dead," Asia said. "She can't stop everything anymore."

I nodded. "I know, but Lily felt pretty strongly about not selling the bakery. Whoever she left it to may decide they want to honor her wishes." I didn't want to get into the concept of eminent domain with a teenager.

The color rose in Asia's cheeks. "But that's not fair," she said hotly. "Lily's reasons were her own, and she's gone now so . . . so everything's different now."

"Don't," Vince warned. He stopped playing and put a hand on his daughter's shoulder.

"Why?" she said, looking from me to her father. "Lily was the reason we couldn't sell Gramp's building. I'm sorry she's dead, but she is, and now there isn't any reason to not fix up the harbor front."

"Enough," Vince said. "You're being disrespectful." He didn't raise his voice, but something in his tone made Asia drop her head. He wiped the side of his mouth with the edge of his hand and leaned Sam's twelve-string against the couch.

"I get that you're angry," I said.

Asia glanced at Vince before she spoke. "If Lily didn't like all the plans, why didn't she just move the bakery somewhere else?" she said. "That's what a lot of people were saying. A lot of them were mad."

Here was my opening. "You think someone was angry enough to kill her?"

"You mean somebody who lives in North Harbor?" Her eyes widened in surprise. "No way. I know people were pissed but not that pissed."

I watched Elvis. Asia was stroking his fur as she talked. His eyes were half-closed and he was purring. If he thought Asia was lying, I couldn't see any sign of it.

Vince nudged his daughter. "Hey, kiddo, would you go get me a refill?" He held out his cup.

"Sure, Dad," she said. She set Elvis on the floor and took Vince's mug. "Would you like more coffee, Sarah?" she asked.

"Please." I handed her my own cup.

"I'll be right back," she said.

"I know what you're doing," Vince said as soon as the office door closed behind Asia. Annoyed that he'd been moved from the warmth of Asia's lap, Elvis stalked over to me and head butted my leg. I reached down and lifted him onto my lap, where he kneaded my legs with his paws before stretching out.

"I know what you're doing, too," I said. "It wasn't you wearing that wig, was it?"

He looked away and then his gaze came back to me. "I already told you that I was the one who pulled those stunts on Lily. I told Detective Andrews the same thing." The muscles along his jawline were tight, as though he was grinding his teeth together.

"You made yourself a suspect, Vince," I said.

"I didn't have anything to do with Lily's death."

"I know. And neither did Asia."

"So we're done?" Vince finally said after what seemed like a long silence.

I nodded. It wouldn't have made sense to anyone else—it didn't really make sense to me—but somehow Elvis knew when people were lying, and Asia wasn't. The worst she'd done was play some childish pranks on Lily, which made sense. She wasn't that far from a child herself.

The office door opened and Asia came back with our coffee. She handed me my mug. "Thanks," I said.

She smiled. "You're welcome." Then she hesitated and took a deep breath. "How did you know it was me?"

"Asia!" Vince said, his voice edged with warning.

She turned around and held out his coffee. "Give it up, Dad," she said. "I just heard you and Sarah talking."

"What? You were listening at the door?" He took the mug and got to his feet.

"So *that* you get pissed about?" she said, rolling her

eyes in that way that only an exasperated teenager could do. She turned back to me. "How'd you know?"

"Body shape," I said. "And I figured out the hair was a wig."

She nodded and sat on the corner of Sam's desk. "It was kind of lame of me to try to look like Mr. West. I didn't want to get him in trouble . . ." Her voice trailed off.

"You just didn't want to get yourself in trouble, either," I finished.

Her cheeks got red and she nodded. "Pretty much. I didn't figure anyone would think anything about him being around."

Vince put a hand on her shoulder. "Asia, stop talking, please," he said.

She turned and looked up at him. "What's the point, Dad? Sarah knows what I did. There's no point in lying about it."

"There's no point in going on about it, either," he said.

"Just for the record, I didn't kill her," Asia said.

Vince swore softly and raked his hand back through his hair.

"Well, I didn't," she said, giving him that aggrieved-teenager look again.

"I didn't think you did," I said. "But thank you for telling me."

Asia shrugged. "She caught me." She hung her head, shame-faced.

"She caught you?" Vince said. "Why didn't you tell me?"

Asia gave him an incredulous look. "Right, Dad. There's a good idea. I should have said, 'By the way, Daddy, I've been breaking into Lily's Bakery to harass her, and the night she got killed she caught me.'"

Vince blew out a breath.

"What did she do?" I asked.

Asia looked away for a moment.

I waited.

"She yelled at me," Asia said. "She said she should call the police on me."

"But she didn't."

She shook her head. "She asked me why I'd done all those things to her, and I told her about Gramps. She said she was sorry, but her reasons for not selling were just as important. I asked her what they were, but she said she couldn't tell me. She said she had family to look after, too." She shrugged. "I asked her why she couldn't just move the bakery someplace else, but she said it was complicated. I said that's what adults always say when they want things their way and they don't want to explain why. Then I left."

"What time was that?" I asked.

"I dunno," she said. "Sometime after midnight."

"Did you see anyone else?"

She twisted her mouth to one side. "No. Lily was in the kitchen at the back, feeding her starter."

"Feeding her what?" I asked.

"Her starter. For sourdough bread. You have to feed it regularly or it won't work right." She smiled. "My gram used to make that kind of bread, and she'd let me help her feed the starter. It's basically fermented flour and water. You can keep it going forever if you do it right." She shrugged sadly. "I guess it's like Lily now. Dead."

"I guess it is," I said.

I picked up Elvis and set him in my gym bag. Then I stood up. "As far as I'm concerned, this conversation stays between us," I said. I was looking at Asia, but I was really talking to Vince. "You know what you did was really stupid."

She nodded.

"I'll walk you out," Vince said.

I nodded.

He looked at Asia. "Don't bother listening at the door," he said.

Her face flooded with color again.

"You satisfied?" he asked once we were back in the hallway.

"I meant what I said in there," I said.

"So you're not going to tell Detective Andrews I lied?"

I shook my head. "I'm not even going to tell Sam you lied, but I'm betting he'll figure it out. As far as I'm concerned, this is done."

I turned and started for the front door.

"Sarah," Vince called after me.

I turned.

"Thank you," he said. I nodded and started for the door again.

Sam was behind the bar. He walked over to me. "Did you get what you needed?" he asked.

I nodded. "I did." I stretched up and kissed his cheek. "Thanks for supper."

He smiled. "Anytime." Then his expression changed. "I don't know if I need to say this or not, but I'm going to. Whatever else Vince did or didn't do, he didn't kill Lily. The night she died, we were all at Eric's after I closed up. He had a new guitar. We played half the night."

"I know Vince wouldn't hurt anyone," I said. "But thanks for telling me. He's lucky to have you for a friend."

Mac tapped on my door at exactly eight o'clock the next morning. "Hi," he said when I opened the door. "Are you ready?"

"Do you mean ready to go get the truck or ready to be living in the same building as Rose?"

. "Both, I guess," he said with a smile.

I laughed. "I'm ready to get the truck as soon as I grab my jacket, and I don't think I'm ever going to be completely ready to live with Rose."

"She's a great cook," he said. His mouth twitched. "Maybe on Sunday morning Alfred will come out in his bathrobe and bring you a plate of Rose's waffles."

"Not listening," I said. I put my fingers in my ears and started humming.

Mac just laughed, and when I looked at Elvis, perched on one of the stools at the counter, it seemed to me that he was laughing, too. I made a face at Mac and took my fingers out of my ears. "Now how am I going to look Mr. P. in the eye when I see him?"

Mac folded one arm over his chest and pressed the other hand over his mouth.

"What?" I said. "You want to say something, so you may as well go ahead and do it."

"You want to know how you're going to look Alfred in the eye?" he asked. "How about just lean down the way you usually do?"

"You're so not funny," I said, but I was laughing, which pretty much negated what I'd just said.

We picked up the truck at McNamara's and then I drove over and picked up Charlotte. She was carrying two thermoses and a quilted tote bag. She climbed in the cab of the truck and set the bag carefully on the floor mat before she fastened her seat belt.

"I smell cinnamon," I said.

"That's because I made cinnamon rolls."

"You're my favorite person in the entire world," I said as I pulled away from the curb.

"Funny how you always remember to tell me that when I have cinnamon rolls," she said with a smile.

"Just a happy coincidence," I said, working hard to keep a straight face.

Liz and Avery were just arriving as we pulled up in front of Legacy Place.

"I'm here," Liz said as I joined them on the sidewalk. "And I ate scrambled tofu, which I do *not* intend to ever eat again."

"It's good for you, Nonna," Avery said.

"At my age I don't want good for me," Liz groused. "I just want good."

"Eating a healthy diet can add years to your life," Avery retorted, a tad self-righteously.

"It doesn't really add years to your life," Liz retorted. "It just feels like that because it takes years to chew the darn stuff."

I laid my head on her shoulder. "Charlotte has cinnamon rolls," I whispered in her ear.

Liz smiled and rubbed her hands together. "Let's go, people," she said. "Rose is waiting. Charlotte, let me help you carry something."

Rose and Mr. P. were waiting in Rose's third-floor apartment. There were boxes in every room labeled in Alfred's angular printing.

"Good morning, everyone," Rose said when she answered the door. "Alfred was just going to take my bed apart, and that's the last thing to do."

Mac shot me a look. "I'll go see if he needs any help," he said.

Glenn had loaned me a small wheeled platform, about four feet by three feet. I rolled it into the kitchen.

"Do you want to start in here?" I asked Rose.

She nodded. "Wherever you think, dear," she said.

"Okay. Furniture goes in the truck and boxes in the SUV." I handed Liz the loop of rope that acted as a handle for the makeshift dolly. "Let Avery do the heavy lifting."

"Rose and I could carry down the towels and the bedding," Charlotte said. "Shall we use the backseat of the SUV?"

I nodded. "I'm going to see how Mac and Alfred are doing."

Mac was just taking off the second side rail on Rose's iron bed frame. "I'll help you carry this down," Mr. P. said.

"I was kind of hoping you'd supervise Avery putting boxes in my SUV," I said. "I mean, if you don't mind. I don't want her to break anything."

He smiled. "Of course. I don't mind at all." He headed for the kitchen.

"Does this mean you're my muscle?" Mac asked, raising an eyebrow.

"Let's do it," I said. I grabbed one end of the metal headboard and he picked up the other.

"Thanks for giving up your Sunday to do this," I said as we started for the kitchen. "There have to be a lot of other things you could be doing."

Avery and Mr. P. were just heading out the door on their way to the elevator with a precarious-looking pile of boxes on the dolly and Alfred draped over them like he was trying to hug the whole stack.

"We're good," I heard him say as we cleared the doorway.

Mac smiled at me. "What else could I be doing that would be more . . . interesting than being here?" he said.

I stuck my tongue out at him.

We had the truck and the SUV loaded before ten o'clock. We made an odd little parade on the way over to the house with Liz's car driven by Avery in the lead, a pile of curtains in the backseat, followed by Charlotte and me in the cube truck and Mac with Rose and Mr. P. in the SUV full of boxes bringing up the rear. Everyone had to have a tour of the apartment, and then we stopped for hot chocolate and cinnamon rolls. Even so, we had everything upstairs by lunchtime.

"How about grilled cheese and tomato soup for lunch?" I said when the last box came in.

"Were you going to cook?" Charlotte asked, exchanging a look with Liz. "Because you don't have to do that. Really."

"I know I don't have to," I said. "But you've all worked so hard. You must be hungry."

"I think it's a little early for lunch," Rose said.

"Sarah's teasing you," Mr. P. said. "She's not cooking. I am."

"Thank you, Lord," Liz said. "That scrambled tofu stuff was starting to look good."

"You can buy tofu cheese," Avery chimed in.

"Fascinating," Mr. P. said. "How are you at buttering bread?"

Elvis was waiting for us, perched on the top of the cat tower. Everyone exclaimed over the quality of Alfred's work.

Mr. P. and Avery washed their hands and then I showed them where everything was.

"Everything's under control," the old man said to me. "I'll call you if I need anything."

"Can I help?" Rose said behind me.

"We're fine, my dear," Alfred said. "Why don't you take a break for a minute?"

I steered Rose over to my rocking chair. "Wasn't this your grandmother's?" she asked.

I nodded. "It was in my dad's nursery when he was a baby."

She sat down in the wooden chair and leaned back against the pillow Jess had made for me. "I remember sitting in this chair with your father when he was about a year old," she said. "He was such a beautiful baby. So good-natured." She reached up and gave my hand a squeeze.

Mr. P. and Avery served grilled-cheese sandwiches toasted golden brown and cut into long fingers for dipping in our tomato-rice soup. Everything was delicious, far better than if I'd tried to cook, which is what I told them.

"We really need to speed up your cooking lessons," Rose said.

"It's a losing battle," I said. "But I'm willing to keep going if you are."

Charlotte left after lunch. She was making supper for all of us back at her house. I took the truck back to McNamara's lot and Mac followed to drive me back.

"Thank you for your help," I said to Mac. "It would have taken a lot longer without you."

"I don't mind," he said. "Like I said before, I like Rose."

"Are you coming to Charlotte's for supper?"

He shook his head. "I already told Charlotte thank you, but I have plans."

"I'll miss you . . . I mean, we'll miss you," I said.

Mac smiled. "Another time." He tucked his scarf a little tighter at the neck of his coat. "I'll see you tomorrow morning," he said.

By four o'clock Rose's apartment look pretty good. Mr. P. left with Liz and Avery to get cleaned up. We were all meeting at Charlotte's at five. I stood in the middle of the kitchen with Rose.

She turned to me, her eyes bright. "I don't know how to say thank you, sweet girl," she said.

"Just be happy here," I said.

She hugged me.

Back in my own apartment I showered while Elvis did a circuit of the backyard. I had no idea what he did on his little tours of the yard—he had a litter box inside—but he insisted on prowling around back there once a day no matter how cold it was.

About a quarter to five I got my canvas tote. "Hop in," I said to him. "I've been instructed to bring you."

"Bring Elvis with you," Charlotte had said at lunch. "I have a little something special for him."

The cat had been sitting on Avery's lap, but he'd smiled across the table at Charlotte as though he'd understood every word she'd said—and for all I knew maybe he had.

Nick was setting the table when we got to the house.

"Hi," I said. "What are you doing here?"

He was wearing a black turtleneck sweater and jeans, and for a moment I could see the teenage boy I'd had a major crush on.

"I stopped in to see Mom and I was invited for supper, provided I earn my keep."

I reached for a pile of napkins on Charlotte's sideboard and handed them to him as he worked his way around the table.

"How's Lily's case coming?" I asked.

"Our part is almost finished. You know about Vince?" he asked, lowering his voice a little.

"I do."

Nick shook his head. "Hard to believe."

"When people get desperate they do things they wouldn't otherwise even think about." I handed him the last napkin. "Nick, Vince didn't kill Lily," I said.

"I really hope you're right," he said.

"He was with Sam and Eric and some other people making music half the night at Eric's place after the pub closed."

I saw a flash of relief cross Nick's face. Vince was in the clear, and as far as I was concerned, so was Asia. Which meant we still didn't know who had killed Lily.

Chapter 18

Elvis and I didn't stay late at Charlotte's. It had been a long day and I was tired. I stretched out on the couch and Elvis watched me from the top of the cat tower. We'd talked about the North Landing development at supper. Actually, everyone else had talked about it and I'd listened and tried to find a connection between it and Lily's death. Because I was convinced there was one.

For all his computer skills, Mr. P. hadn't been able to find out who Jon West's investors were who had enough influence to push the project forward. "There has to be a way to find out," I said to Elvis.

Mr. P. had explained that if Jon West's company were a public company, it would have been easy to find out who was backing North Landing, but it was a private company and he hadn't found any way to access the records that would tell me what I wanted to know.

"I'm sorry, my dear. I'm afraid I'm not Woodward or Bernstein," he'd said, referring to the *Washington*

Post reporters who had broken the Watergate scandal.

I looked over at Elvis, the realization dawning on me that I still had one more option. One that might just work. "I know what to do," I said, getting to my feet.

I walked over to him and reached up to scratch the top of his head. "I know what to do," I stage-whispered.

I sat on a stool at the counter and reached for the phone. My dad answered. "Hi, sweetie," he said. "I thought you were moving Rose today."

"All done," I said. "She has a bunch of unpacking to do, so she's staying on Charlotte's couch for a few nights."

"I'm glad she's going to be there," Dad said. "Now you won't be alone so much."

I smiled. "I'm not alone, Dad. I have Elvis." The cat lifted his head at the sound of his name, looked around and went back to washing his face.

"I just mean if there's any . . . trouble."

I couldn't help laughing. "I love Rose, but she's barely five feet tall. What exactly is she going to do if trouble shows up here?"

He laughed, too. "Okay, so she isn't exactly Amazonian. I'd still rather take on a grizzly bear than I would an angry Rose. I feel better knowing she'll be there. Humor your father."

"All right," I said. I propped an elbow on the counter. "I need a favor."

"Sure. What is it?"

"Remember me telling you about the problems with the North Landing project?"

"I do," he said.

"Well, now it seems that if Caroline doesn't sell the bakery to the developer, the town will be able to expropriate the land."

"I don't think so," Dad said slowly. "I don't think it fits the criteria, from what I know."

I leaned forward and snagged the edge of the container of cookies Charlotte had sent home with me and pulled it closer. "Word on the street is that Jon West has a silent partner or partners with enough influence to make it happen."

"And you want to know who that is," he said.

I fished an oatmeal-butterscotch cookie out of the can and took a bite. "Uh-huh. Both Jess and Liz stand to benefit if North Landing goes forward. I just want to know everything is legit."

"And you think this secret-investor thing might somehow be tied to Lily Carter's death." He paused for a moment. "I didn't just fall off the turnip truck, you know."

I let out a breath. "Okay. Yes. It might—might—have something to do with what happened to Lily."

"So why aren't the police doing this?" he said.

I stuffed the rest of the cookie in my mouth and ate it before I answered. "Maybe they are," I said. "I can't exactly ask Michelle."

"Point taken," Dad said. I could picture him making a face as he mulled over my request. "All right. I have a couple of contacts I can ask. Just based on what you've told me, there might be a story in all of this."

Dad taught journalism now and still regularly wrote longer feature pieces for several magazines, but he'd been a newspaper reporter for many years and that drive to chase a story was in his blood.

"Thank you," I said.

"Hang on. I haven't told you my conditions."

I stuck out my tongue even though he couldn't see me and reached for another cookie I was pretty sure I was going to need. "Fine. What are your conditions?"

"You know if you keep making that face it's going to freeze like that," he said.

"How do you know I'm making a face?" I said.

"I know you, sweetie," he said with a laugh. "Condition number one: You don't do anything stupid with anything I manage to find out for you."

"Agreed." Rose and the others were more likely to do that, and I wasn't planning on sharing anything I found out.

"Number two: If you come across anything, anything that might be connected to Lily's death, you take it to Nicolas or the police."

After what had happened with the Arthur Fenety case, that was easy to agree to.

"Let me see what I can do," Dad said. "I'll call you tomorrow."

"I love you," I said.

"Love you, too, baby."

I hung up the phone and turned around to find a

pair of green eyes staring up at me. I hopped off the stool and scooped Elvis into my arms. "The game is afoot," I told him.

Exactly five minutes after nine on Monday morning the phone rang at the shop. Mac answered it and then came out to the workroom where Charlotte and I were going through the linens I'd washed.

"Sarah, it's your dad," he said.

"Why don't I just start ironing?" Charlotte said.

I smiled at her. "That would be great. Thank you."

"I think I'll take this in my office," I said to Mac.

Elvis followed me up the stairs, jumping up onto my desk as I reached for the phone.

"Hi, Dad," I said.

"Hi," he said. "Did I catch you at a bad time?"

I sat on the edge of the desk and Elvis made himself comfortable next to the phone. "No. I was just sorting tablecloths with Charlotte. Did you find out something already?"

"I did," Dad said. "Remember when I said it sounded like there might be a story in this whole North Landing business?"

Elvis rubbed his head against my free hand and I began to stroke his fur. "I remember," I said. "Are you saying someone is writing an article about the development?"

"Yeah," he said. "A pretty in-depth one, too."

"You found out who that investor is, didn't you?"

"Uh-huh." He hesitated for a moment. "You're not going to do anything stupid, remember?"

"I promise," I said.

"The major investor in North by West is Swift Holdings."

"You're certain."

"Absolutely. On paper the company is being funded by the Wellington Group, but that's owned one hundred percent by Swift Holdings."

Swift Holdings. Daniel Swift. Caleb Swift's grand-father. Everything kept coming back to them.

"I've e-mailed you everything I could find about the Wellington Group," Dad said.

"Thanks," I said. "I have go."

"Okay, sweetie. Stay safe. I'll talk to you soon."

I hung up and looked at Elvis. "Daniel Swift," I said.

"Mrr," he said. It was hard to tell if he was sur-prised or not.

I walked around the desk, sat down and pulled my laptop closer. Dad had e-mailed me a lot of back-ground information on the Wellington Group, includ-ing the history of the company and its organization. I scanned the pages, not really sure what I was look-ing for. About halfway down the third page on the company's corporate structure, a name caught my eye.

"No," I said.

Elvis leaned around the computer as though he were trying to see the screen.

"Sloane Redding," I said, touching the screen with a finger.

Elvis looked at me. Suddenly his whiskers twitched,

and he jumped down from the desk and headed out into the hallway. I was guessing that Charlotte had opened the can of cookies she'd brought with her. Elvis not only had lying radar, he also had cookie radar.

I looked at the computer again. I'd been friends with a Sloane Redding in college. We'd lost touch after she spent a semester in Mexico as part of an exchange program. What were the odds that this Sloane was the same person? I crossed my fingers and pulled up a search engine.

For once, things were going my way. I found a photo from a benefit underwritten by the Wellington Group. Sloane Redding was in a group photo. Her hair was different and her clothing looked to be a lot more expensive, but it was the same person.

Was it really going to be that easy? Mr. P. hadn't had any luck so far. Could I call Sloane and find out once and for all if the North Landing development had had anything to do with Lily's death? There was only one way to find out. I scrolled up the screen and found the number for the Wellington Group in Boston.

"I'm sorry. Ms. Redding is in our North Harbor, Maine, office," the young man who answered the phone told me.

The Wellington Group had an office here in town?

"Could you give me that number, please?" I asked.

"I'd be happy to," he said. He read off a string of digits to me, and I wrote them down.

I leaned back in the chair and studied the numbers. Was this a wild-goose chase? Was I sticking my nose in where I shouldn't be? Gram would have said, *In for a penny, in for a pound.*

I reached for the phone.

"Ms. Redding's office. Charmaine Kellogg speaking," the voice on the other end of the phone said when I reached Sloane's office.

"Good morning," I said. "Is Ms. Redding in? It's Sarah Grayson calling about the North Landing project."

"I'm sorry. Ms. Redding is in a meeting all morning," Charmaine Kellogg said, her voice all smooth professionalism. "May I help you?"

"Thank you," I said. "I have a business here in North Harbor. I was hoping to talk to Sloane about what's going to be available as far as space in the project. We went to college together." Strictly speaking, that was all true.

"I could give you an appointment to see Ms. Redding next week."

I couldn't wait until next week. "I'm sorry," I said, "the only time I have available is eleven thirty this morning."

I sounded a little pretentious even though I was telling the truth for the most part. On Tuesday Mac and I were going to look at a house with a garage and a couple of outbuildings just outside of town. The owner was in the hospital with a broken hip and would be coming out to an apartment. His son wanted an estimate for us to take care of emptying the house and readying it for sale.

"Eleven thirty will be fine," Charmaine Kellogg said. I was already forming an image of the woman as someone sleek and elegant in a beautifully tailored business suit and dark-framed glasses. She'd probably turn out to look nothing like that.

"Do you know how to find our office?" she asked.

"No. I don't," I said.

She gave me directions, and I realized that the Wellington Group was in the same building as North by West's North Harbor office.

Interesting.

I went back downstairs. Charlotte was showing a customer the chair that had been in my office a few days ago. Mac was out back at the workbench.

"Mac, did you remember the other day when Charlotte mentioned the Wellington Group as a possible investor in North Landing?" I asked as I walked up to him.

He put down the sanding block he'd been using. "I remember," he said. "They invest primarily in real estate on the East Coast." His dark eyes narrowed. "You think they are involved in the development here?"

"Maybe," I said. "I have an appointment with Sloane Redding at eleven thirty."

"I don't recognize the name," he said.

I didn't bother telling him that I did. "You can manage things here?"

He smiled. "Take as much time as you need."

Since the North by West office was just a few minutes' walk from Jess's shop, I called her to see if she'd like to have lunch.

"I'd love to," she said. "I'm rolling a hem on an overskirt, and by lunchtime I'll be cross-eyed."

"I'll stop for sandwiches," I said. "See you later."

Charlotte stuck her head around the storeroom door. "Mac, could you carry out a chair for a customer?" she asked.

"Of course," he said.

Since Charlotte was busy, I decided I might as well start the ironing. I'd just plugged the iron in when Rose and Mr. P. came in the back door.

"Hi, Rose," I said. "I thought you were taking the day off."

"I was," she said, "but Alfred and I have learned a little more about Caleb Swift." She looked at her watch. "Liz should be here in a minute."

Mr. P. was already getting settled at his desk.

"I'll just go put the kettle on," Rose said.

I wondered if they were the only detective agency in the world that seemed to run on tea.

I had time to iron two lace-edged tablecloths before Liz arrived. We all gathered around Alfred, with the exception of Mac, who was waiting on a customer.

"So what did you find out?" Charlotte asked.

Rose and Mr. P. exchanged a look and he spoke first. "Well, it seems that young Mr. Swift wasn't quite the young man of character he seemed to be on the surface."

I thought about Elspeth calling Caleb the proverbial, entitled rich kid. "What do you mean?" I asked.

"I talked to three young women he dated. At first

they were rather noncommittal, but eventually they opened up."

Rose smiled at him. "Alf has a very nurturing way about him," she said.

"They all told me the same thing," Mr. P. said. "Caleb Swift had a very dark, possessive streak. One of the girls told me that Caleb smashed the screen of her laptop because he thought her history professor was flirting with her. Another told me that she was up late studying and discovered Caleb was sitting outside her dorm room in his car."

Charlotte shook her head wordlessly.

Liz held up a hand. "So how exactly does this help us figure out who killed Lily? Do you think Caleb Swift's been alive all this time and suddenly decided to come back and kill Lily?"

"It's not impossible," Rose said.

"It's not damn likely, either," Liz countered.

I couldn't help noticing the tight lines around her mouth.

"It's one more piece of the puzzle," I said. I looked at Mr. P. "Any luck so far with the Wellington Group?"

He shook his head. "I'll keep digging," he said, turning back to his laptop.

I put my arm around Liz's shoulder. "Let's have some tea," I said, starting toward the door into the shop.

"What makes you think I want a cup?" she said.

"I wasn't asking," I said. "What's with you today?"

She brushed a curl of hair away from her face. "This is just ridiculous. Caleb Swift most likely fell off that sailboat of his and drowned years ago, and now Rose thinks he came back from the dead to kill Lily?"

I sighed. "Okay. I know that part isn't very credible, but now we know something about Caleb Swift that we didn't know before. Maybe it'll be useful."

"I don't see how and I don't care how nurturing Alf is. I don't think we should be prying into those girls' lives."

"You're right." I gave her shoulders a squeeze. Charlotte had started dusting a set of bookshelves. "Charlotte, would you make the tea?" I asked. "Liz could use a cup."

"That's a good idea," she said.

Liz reached over and laid her hand against my cheek. "I'm sorry I'm such a crabby old hag."

I put my hand over hers. "Love you," I said.

I walked over to Mac. "Everything okay?" he asked.

"I need to make a phone call," I said. "Can you hold down the fort for a few more minutes?"

"Sure. I've got this," he said.

I went upstairs to my office and closed the door behind me. Liz wasn't being completely straight with me and I was pretty sure I knew why. I stared at the phone for what seemed like a very long time. And then I picked up the receiver.

Chapter 19

Elspeth Emmerson showed up about twenty minutes later. As always, she looked perfectly put together in knee-high caramel-colored boots and a pumpkin-colored coat, with her blond hair pulled back from her face on one side. Only the fact that she kept sliding a narrow gold and silver twist ring up and down her right index finger let on that she was nervous.

I walked over to her. "Are you sure about this?" I said.

She nodded. "Yes. It's time for me to stop acting like I have something to be ashamed of."

"You don't," I said.

There were no customers in the store. Charlotte was standing next to the rack Mac had mounted on the wall, hanging the tablecloths that were already ironed and talking to Liz. They both turned around at the sound of Elspeth's spike heels on the wide plank floor.

"Hi," Charlotte said with a warm smile.

Liz fixed her gaze on Elspeth, but her eyes flicked to me for a moment. "What are you doing here?" she said.

"I came to talk to Charlotte and Rose and everyone else about Caleb."

"But you already told Sarah that you and Caleb went out for a short time."

"I didn't tell her everything," Elspeth said.

Concern was etched into the lines on the older woman's face. "I know this is painful for you," she said quietly. "Why don't you let me do this?"

Elspeth crossed the space between them and put a hand on her aunt's arm. "I know you want to protect me," she said. "But I'm okay. And why should I act like I have something to hide when I didn't do anything wrong?" She turned to Charlotte. "Would you ask Rose and . . . and everyone to come out here, please? There's something I want to tell everyone about Caleb Swift."

Charlotte looked at Liz and then at me. "All right," she said slowly. She headed for the back room. Liz didn't say a word.

Elspeth waited until Charlotte had left the room. Then she focused her attention on Liz again. "This is all me, Aunt Liz. I can see it on your face. You're angry at Sarah, and the person you should be angry with is me."

Liz shook her head. "Why would I be angry at Sarah? The only person I'm angry at is young Mr. Swift."

Elspeth put her free hand, clenched in a fist,

against her chest. "I should have spoken up a long time ago about what Caleb did to me. What if . . . ?" She stopped, swallowed hard and looked away for a moment. "What if what happened to Lily is somehow connected to him? If I'd gone to the police, maybe Lily would—"

"No." Liz and I both said the word at the same time.

I shook my head. "What happened to Lily has nothing, *nothing* to do with you," I said.

Liz grasped Elspeth's forearms with both her hands. "It is *not* your fault that Lily is dead," she said. "Do you understand me?"

After a moment Elspeth nodded. Rose came out of the workroom then, followed by Mr. P. and Mac. She came right over to Elspeth and gave her a hug.

"Charlotte said there's something you wanted to tell us about Caleb Swift," she said. She studied the younger woman, concern etched in the lines on her face.

"There is," Elspeth said. She cleared her throat, and when she spoke again, her voice was stronger. "Caleb and I went out a few months before he started seeing Lily. At first things were wonderful. He was charming and very attentive. He wanted to spend every minute with me." She paused for a moment. "But soon he didn't understand why I had to keep going to my study group and why I was applying for an internship that would take time away from him." She continued to twist the ring on her right hand.

"Take your time," Liz said gently.

"One night I canceled a date with him because my economics prof had dumped a surprise test on the class and a bunch of us had decided to get together and study. Caleb was waiting outside the library when I came out. I told him it was creepy and he should go home. He grabbed my wrist . . . and . . . and he broke it."

"Oh my word," Rose whispered.

"The reprobate," Mr. P. said, the furrows between his eyes deepening.

"I snuck out of my dorm room in the middle of the night like I was the criminal," Elspeth continued. "I came to Liz because I knew she wouldn't push me to tell her what happened. Then I called Caleb and told him if he ever came near me again, I would tell her what he'd done. A few weeks later he started seeing Lily. I, uh . . ." She cleared her throat again. "I went to see her. I told her what Caleb had done to me. She told me he wasn't that kind of person with her and asked me to leave. When he disappeared, well . . . I've always wondered if she knew more than she was saying about what happened to him."

Rose immediately wrapped Elspeth in another hug. "Oh, my dear, I'm so sorry you had to go through that."

Charlotte reached over and squeezed her shoulder. "It's brave of you to tell us," she said. "Thank you."

"I should have been braver sooner," Elspeth said. "I didn't tell Aunt Liz what happened for a long time, and when I did, I made her promise not to tell anyone else."

A look I couldn't decipher passed over Charlotte's face. "You're braver than I am," she said.

We all looked at her. She looked at each one of us, a grave expression in her brown eyes. "My first year of teacher training, I had a boyfriend a lot like Caleb Swift," she said. "He didn't break my wrist. But he did hit me." She stopped and pressed a hand to her mouth. Elspeth reached out and caught her hand, and something passed, unspoken, between the two women.

"I've never told this to another living soul," Charlotte said.

"You could have told us," Rose said gently. "We know it's not your fault."

"It was hard to say this happened to me," Elspeth said. "I'm supposed to be smart."

Charlotte nodded. "I know."

"It has nothing to do with smart," Mr. P. said. "I'm sorry this happened to both of you."

"Thank you, Alfred," Charlotte said.

Elspeth took a deep breath and let it out. She seemed a bit lighter somehow. "There's one more thing," she said.

"What is it?" Rose asked.

"The night Lily was killed? Maybe it doesn't mean anything, but that was Caleb Swift's birthday."

Before Elspeth left, Liz came over to me. I remembered what she'd said the day we'd had tea at her house: "I protect the people I care about."

"You should have told me she was coming here," she said, crossing her arms over her chest.

"She asked me not to."

"You really think I would have tried to talk her out of telling everyone what happened?" One eyebrow went up.

"No, but it wasn't my call," I said. "I asked Elspeth if Caleb had been abusive, because I noticed how protective you got when his name came up, but it was her idea to come and tell everyone what happened to her. She asked me not to tell you, and I didn't. She thinks you feel guilty for not going after Caleb at the time." I pulled hand over my neck. "You do, don't you?"

Liz looked at me for a long moment. "I didn't know for sure," she finally said. "I suspected, but I wasn't positive. Like she said, it was a long time before she told me everything." She looked past me out the big front window and then her gaze came back to me. "I should have pushed. I definitely shouldn't have agreed to keep it all a secret. I should have strung that young man up by his . . ." She didn't finish the sentence.

"You took care of Elspeth," I said. "That's what needed to be done."

Liz looked over to where her niece was standing with Rose and Charlotte. "It was good for her to talk about what happened," she said. "She doesn't have anything to be ashamed of."

I nodded. "No, she doesn't."

"I need to talk to her before she goes."

I gave Liz's arm a squeeze as she passed me.

"The date has to mean something," Rose said once Liz and Elspeth were outside.

"It is an awfully big coincidence," I admitted, crossing my arms over my chest and rubbing one shoulder with the other hand.

"I keep wondering, could Caleb Swift be alive?" Rose asked. "And I know how far-fetched that sounds."

"You don't seriously think he came back here and killed Lily, do you?" Charlotte said.

Alfred frowned. "That is a bit of a stretch."

"Someone should talk to Daniel Swift," Rose said.

"I'll go." Liz had come back inside after walking Elspeth to her car. "I know Daniel. He was on the board of the Sunshine Camp at one time."

Rose opened her mouth to say something, and Liz reached over and caught her hand. "I need to do this," she said. "Four years ago, when Elspeth showed up on my doorstep in the middle of the night with her arm in a cast, I should have made her tell me what really happened. I knew she wasn't telling me everything."

"She came to you precisely because she knew you wouldn't push," Charlotte said. "She wouldn't have told you."

Liz gave her a sidelong glance. "Excuse me, have you met me, Charlotte?" she said. "I don't usually take no for an answer."

"If you're going, I'm coming with you," I said. "I

met Daniel Swift once, years ago. Gram worked with him on the refurbishment of the Opera House."

"Fine," Liz said. "What time works for you?"

"How about late this afternoon?" I said. "I have a meeting with someone from the Wellington Group later this morning. It looks like that rumor Charlotte heard was right. They've invested in North Landing."

Rose looked at me. "When did all this happen?"

"A little while ago," I said. "It'll be a sales pitch, but I thought maybe we could learn a little more about Jon West and the company if I went."

"Good thinking, Sarah," Mr. P. said, smiling at me and giving me a thumbs-up. "Since we haven't been able to find out anything from the outside, we'll just have to infiltrate them."

"We should talk to Caroline," Rose said.

Liz shook her head. "It won't work. She isn't going to tell you anything."

"Maybe not," Rose said. "But it won't hurt to try." She looked at Charlotte. "Will you come with me after work?"

"Yes," Charlotte said. "I have a pot roast in the slow cooker. We can have supper afterward."

"I'm going to see what else I can find on young Mr. Swift's disappearance," Mr. P. said.

"All right," Rose said. "Everyone has a job. I'll go put the tea on." She headed for the front.

Charlotte smiled at me. "I'll go give Mac a hand." She must have seen something in my face because she leaned closer to me. "And I'll keep an eye on Rose when we go see Caroline."

"Thanks," I said.

She headed for the shop.

I leaned over and bumped Liz with my shoulder.

"I meant what I said," I told her. "It's not your fault. And Elspeth is fine. Don't lose sight of that."

She took a deep breath and slowly exhaled. "I would have pounded that young man into sand," she said in a voice edged with venom.

"I don't doubt that for a second," I said as we started for the door.

"We're onto something," she said. "I can feel it in my bones."

"Well, I'm not going to argue with your bones."

She smiled. "Don't get saucy with me, missy. I changed your diapers."

I laughed. They'd all changed my diapers.

Liz's expression grew serious again. "Elspeth said the day Lily died was Caleb Swift's birthday. I think it means something."

I didn't say anything, but so did I.

Chapter 20

The Wellington Group office was in a brick building just up the street from the library. I recognized the young man at the reception desk. He'd worked as a waiter at The Black Bear for several summers. "Hello, Ronan," I said.

He smiled up at me. He was wearing dark-rimmed glasses and a gray suit. "Hi, Ms. Grayson," he said. "Ms. Kellogg will be out to get you in just a moment. May I get you a cup of coffee?"

"No, thank you," I said. I looked around. "How long have you been working here?"

"It's actually an internship," he said, "and I've been here since January fifth."

"Well, good luck," I said.

He smiled again. "Thank you."

Charmaine Kellogg looked exactly the way I'd envisioned her. She was wearing a black suit with a vibrant pink blouse. Her hair was slicked back in a high ponytail and, like Ronan, she was wearing glasses; hers had dark tortoiseshell frames.

We shook hands. "Ms. Redding is in her office," she said. She pointed over her head. "I'll take you up."

The wooden staircase to the second floor couldn't have been original, but the mellow wood fit the tone of the restored space.

"This is a beautiful building," I said.

She gave me a professional smile. "Mr. West worked on this project."

I ran my hand over the polished wood of the banister. "I didn't know that."

She nodded. "Just over two years ago. Everything from the studs out is new. That's when he got the idea for the North Landing project."

I stopped at the top of the stairs and looked around. Ahead there was an open area with chairs and two large multipaned windows that overlooked the harbor. Several of what I assumed were offices opened off the space.

"Jon does beautiful work," I said.

She gave me that polished smile again. "Thank you. I'll tell him you said that."

"How long have you been in North Harbor?" I asked.

"Not long," she said, leading me over to the chairs by the window. "Mr. West and I drove up from Boston together on the twenty-third."

"This is very different from Boston."

The professional smile got a little warmer. "I grew up in a small town. I like it here." She tipped her head to one side. "Were you at The Black Bear last Thursday night, by any chance?"

I grinned at her. "Weren't they terrific?"

"Incredible," she said. "Do they do that every Thursday night?"

I nodded. "In the off-season, yes." I gave her an appraising look. "So maybe we'll see you this week?"

"Absolutely." She gestured at the chair. "Have a seat and I'll let Ms. Redding know you're here."

"That's all right, Charmaine," a familiar voice said behind me. "I'm here."

I turned around to find my freshman-year college roommate standing there smiling at me.

"Hi, Sarah." Sloane Redding crossed the few feet between us.

"I can't believe it's you," I said. I hesitated and then hugged her. We broke out of the hug and grinned at each other.

Charmaine Kellogg was still standing beside me, a polite smile on her face.

Sloane turned to her. "Thanks, Charmaine," she said. "I'll take it from here."

The younger woman nodded and headed for the stairs.

"You look wonderful." Sloane gave me a quick appraising look.

"So do you," I said. Her auburn hair was short, casually tousled in a cut that had probably cost more than a hundred dollars. Her wire-framed glasses had been replaced with nerd-chic black frames. She was wearing a slim brown pencil skirt with a jewel-toned turquoise blouse and heels that brought her up to my height.

"Come back to my office," she said. She led me down a short jag of the hallway to an office with one exposed-brick wall and another beautiful view of the harbor. "Have a seat," she said, indicating a pair of armless upholstered chairs in front of a long distressed table that she was using as a desk. I took one chair and she sat down in the other.

"What are you doing here?" I asked. "The last time I saw you, you were going to be a teacher. How did you go from that to all this?" I gestured at the room.

She smoothed her skirt over her knees. "Do you remember that semester I did in Mexico?"

I nodded.

"I worked at a school three days a week." Her mouth twisted to one side for a moment. "I was lousy at it. I knew by the end of the first week that teaching was not going to be my life's work."

"It was really that bad?" I asked.

She leaned forward and nodded. "My adviser suggested I consider another major."

"Ouch!"

"Tell me about it," she said with a roll of her eyes.

"So what happened?" I asked. "The last thing I heard, you were taking a semester off and staying in Mexico."

She leaned back, crossing one leg over the other. "That's what I did, for a couple of months, until my dad said he wasn't sending me any more money." She laughed. "He told me I had to get a job. So I came home and found one working the reception desk at an investment firm. When it was time to come back to school, I knew I wanted to study business." Her expression changed. "Sarah, I'm sorry."

"For what?" I said.

"For pretty much disappearing without an explanation. I thought about you a lot. I should have written or called or something. I spent a lot of time sulking." She shrugged. "I was a brat."

"I did wonder what happened to you," I said. "I'm glad that now I know." I smiled at her.

"And I'm sorry I didn't try to find out whether you were in town. It's not an excuse, but I didn't get here until the twenty-third."

"It's okay," I said.

Sloane smiled and leaned back in her chair. "So tell me why you wanted to see me."

I folded my hands in my lap and started in on the spiel I'd planned as I was driving down. "I have a business here in town—Second Chance—it's a repurpose shop. A couple of my friends are planning on moving into North Landing, assuming it goes ahead, and I wanted to know more. I knew the Wellington Group was one of the investors in the project, and when I saw that you worked for them, I thought maybe I could get the inside track on the project." So far nothing I'd said wasn't true.

"You know the project has had some problems?" she said.

I was surprised by her bluntness, which must have shown on my face.

"I didn't think there was any point in beating

around the bush with you," she said. "Unless you've changed a lot."

"I appreciate that."

"I remembered you talking about spending your summers here," Sloane said. "I didn't know you were living here or that you have a business."

The woman sitting next to me was far more polished and professional than my college friend had been, but I could see the girl I used to know underneath the beautiful clothes and expensive haircut.

"Sarah, the Wellington Group has a lot of money already invested in this development idea and the potential to make a lot more if it's as successful as we believe it can be. We have a responsibility to our investors to make this work, and I can promise you North Landing is back on track."

"Because Lily Carter is dead?" I asked.

Sloane was clearly prepared for my question. She didn't so much as blink. "What happened to her is very sad, but it has nothing to do with the development. Yes, it would have been easier if she'd been willing to sell the bakery to us. We were willing to compensate her very well."

She tipped her head to one side and studied me. "You run your own business, so you know that there's nothing personal in a business decision. Yes, the Wellington Group stands to make money if North Landing is successful, but so does North Harbor, and since the project clearly benefits the town, sometimes compromise has to be made."

"You mean the town was going to expropriate

Lily's land," I said, trying to sum up her two long sentences into one.

"That was one of the options talked about," Sloane said.

"I thought that was something that couldn't be done in this case."

She gave me a professional smile that had no real warmth in it. I was reminded that the fact that we had once been friends didn't mean we still had a connection. "We have a lot of resources and staff with experience in this kind of thing."

It was as close as she was going to come to admitting somehow they were using influence behind the scenes.

Sloane turned and picked up a cardboard accordion file from the desk behind us. "Take this with you, Sarah," she said. "It has all the details about the North Landing project—specs, financials, projected ROI. If you think it's a good deal, then I hope you'll think about moving your business downtown, but if you don't, I'm still happy I got to see you."

She stood up, and I realized the meeting was over. I got to my feet as well.

"Could we maybe have lunch sometime?" she asked. "Not for me to give you the hard sell, just to catch up."

I nodded. "I'd like that."

We walked out together. "If you have any questions, please call me," she said. She indicated the cardboard folder. "My card's inside with my direct line on it."

"I do have one question," I said. "Who exactly is the Wellington Group? Who are your investors?"

Again I got the cool, professional smile. "I'm sorry," Sloane said. "The Wellington Group is a private corporation. I can't give you that information, but I can promise you that you'd be in good hands with us."

I wasn't going to get any information from her, I realized. It had been a fishing expedition and I hadn't caught anything. But it wasn't like I hadn't already gotten what I needed from my dad.

"I'm glad I got to see you," I said with a smile. "We do have a lot of things to catch up on. Do you still like country music?"

Sloane put a hand over her heart. "I've seen my man Ronnie Dunn six times in concert."

I grinned. "So I don't have to ask if you're still a fan."

"I am," she said as we started down the steps. "Do you still play?"

"Not as much as I should."

She gave me a sly grin. "So if I make it to one of those Thursday-night jam sessions I've been hearing about, will I hear you?"

I shook my head, laughing. "I wouldn't count on that," I said.

Sloane walked me to the front door and we exchanged another hug. "I'll call you when I've had a chance to read all of this," I said, holding up the folder of information.

"I'll look at my calendar and we'll have lunch soon. I promise," she said.

It was a little early, but I drove over to Mc-Namara's, got a couple of roast-beef sandwiches and headed back to Jess's shop. I was halfway down the street when I saw Jess hurrying down the sidewalk. She waved at me and we met in front of the store.

"Hey, am I late?" she said, pushing back her hood. "I had to go deliver a dress to a customer."

"No, I'm early." I held up the takeout bag. "Roast beef with pickles and extra mustard."

"You are my favorite person in the entire world," Jess said.

"Right," I said as I followed her inside. "As long as the sandwich lasts, I am."

Jess said hello to Elin and then we moved into her sewing room. "What's that?" she asked, pointing at the folder Sloane had given me as she took off her jacket and hung it over the back of a chair.

"The prospectus for North Landing."

"I have one of those," Jess said. "Why do you?"

"Long story," I said. "Let's eat first."

Jess got coffee for us both and we sat on opposite sides of her desk. I set the folder on the floor by my chair.

"So dish," Jess said, after she eaten about half her sandwich. "Why do you have a North Landing prospectus?"

I took a sip of coffee before I answered. "Let me see if I can give you the short version," I said. "I had a meeting with Sloane Redding from the Wellington Group, which is an investor in the North Landing project. I was hoping—" I sighed and shook my head. "I don't know what I was hoping, actually. Maybe that I could find out something that would prove who killed Lily."

Jess frowned. "Wait a sec. Is this the same Sloane Redding who was your roommate before me?"

My mouth was full, so I just nodded.

"So did you pump her for information?"

I wiped a dab of mustard from the side of my mouth. "I tried," I said. "I didn't get anywhere."

Jess shrugged. "All I've got is my coffeemaker broke and I stabbed myself about ten times working on that rolled hem, so you win for most interesting morning," she said.

As we finished eating, I told Jess about the meeting.

"Sarah, I know you want to see the person who killed Lily pay for what they did, but it's not your job. That job belongs to the police and Nick." She grinned and wiggled her eyebrows at me. "You're trying to be Wonder Woman without the boots and the lasso."

I laughed, and coffee almost went up my nose. Jess had a way of cutting right to the point of things.

"I never met Sloane," Jess said. "What is she like?"

"When we were in college, she was fun. And smart. I was sorry we lost touch."

She pulled a pickle out of her sandwich and popped it in her mouth. "What's she like now?"

"Very polished and elegant. Expensive clothes and gorgeous red hair in one of those casual haircuts that probably cost a fortune to get to look that way."

Jess frowned. "Wait a sec. I think I met her. Buddy Holly black-frame glasses?" she asked.

"Yes," I said. "When did you meet her?"

"If it was her, I gave her directions about a week and a half ago. It was the night Lily died, as a matter of fact."

I stared at her. "The night Lily was killed. Are you sure? Sloane told me she got here on the twenty-third."

"Of course I'm sure," she said. "She was looking for the Owl & the Pussycat bookstore."

The bookstore, which was right next door to Lily's Bakery.

Jess must have had the same thought. "What? You think your old roommate snuck into town and killed Lily? Seriously?"

I shook my head. "Seriously. I don't know. Like you said before, I'm not Wonder Woman."

I was back at the store just after one o'clock. Mac was at the counter, waiting on a customer. Once he was finished, he walked over to me. "I sold those four ladder-back chairs," he said. "The buyer will be back with his SUV to pick them up."

"Did you get the full price?" I asked.

He nodded. "The guy didn't even try to dicker." He gestured to the portfolio I was carrying. "How did the meeting go?"

"It was interesting."

"I thought we weren't going to use that word anymore," he teased, his dark eyes sparkling.

"It applies in this case," I said, pulling off my hat. I took Sloane's business card out of the folder and then held out the papers. "I know you had a look at the simplified prospectus, but would you take a look at these financials for me? You can decipher them a lot faster than I can."

"I'd be happy to. Am I looking for anything in particular?"

I shook my head. "I just want to know if the project really is a good investment." I looked around. Avery was dusting the musical instruments on the back wall. "Where's Rose?" I said.

Mac pointed in the direction of the storeroom. "Finishing those tablecloths."

I found Rose at the ironing board in the workroom.

"Hello, dear," she said. "How was your meeting?"

I almost said "interesting" again. "Informative."

"In what way?"

"I think you can officially eliminate Jon West from your suspect list," I said. "I talked to one of the administrative assistants, and she mentioned that she and Jon drove up from meetings in Boston the morning after Lily's death."

"You and Elvis were right about him," she said. "He's a very smart cat."

"What about me?" I said with mock indignation.

She reached up and patted my cheek. "You're smart, too, dear."

I went up to my office. Elvis was sitting in my

chair. "I'm a person. I sit in the chair," I said. "You're a cat. You sit on the floor. What part of that do you not understand?"

He tipped his head to one side as though he were pondering the question.

I picked him up, sat down and set him on my lap. He studied my face.

"Sloane lied to me," I said.

His green eyes narrowed.

"Yes, I know you don't know who she is. The thing is, she lied. Do I call her on it?" He swung his head around to look at the phone on my desk. That was definitely a yes.

I reached for the phone. Sloane must have been at her desk. She answered on the third ring.

"Hi, Sloane. It's Sarah," I said.

"Hi," she said. I could hear the smile in her voice. I felt a pang of guilt, and then I remembered she'd looked me right in the eye and lied to me. "You're a fast reader."

"I have a question."

"Shoot."

"Why did you lie to me about when you got into town? And don't say you didn't. I know you went to talk to Lily Carter."

There was silence on the other end of the phone. "Please don't tell me another lie," I said.

"My job was on the line," she said after a moment's silence.

"I know Daniel Swift owns controlling interest in the Wellington Group. Did he send you to see Lily?"

"Don't ask me that," she said, her voice low and guarded.

It was as good as a yes.

"Did you hurt her?" I asked.

"Sarah! I can't believe you'd ask me that." Her voice rose in indignation.

"Did you?" I repeated.

"No," she said. "When she realized who I was, she told me to get out. And she told me to tell Mr. Swift that he was wasting his time sending other people to do his dirty work." Sloane cleared her throat. "I left. I swear she was alive, Sarah."

Elvis was watching me. "I really hope you're telling the truth," I said. I didn't have anything else to say. I hung up.

Chapter 21

The shop was fairly busy after lunch. That meant I didn't have a lot of time to think about what I was going to do with what I'd learned from Sloane, not to mention whether I should tell the others what I knew about the Wellington Group and Daniel Swift. Midafternoon I got a call that the building permit was ready for Mac's apartment.

Liz walked in about twenty minutes to four.

"Why don't we take the SUV and I'll bring you back for your car?" I said to her. "I have to come back to get Elvis."

"That's fine," she said.

"I don't think we'll be that long," I said to Mac.

He smiled. "Take your time. Rose and Avery are taking the wallpaper off that screen you bought from the pickers, and I'm waiting for the man who bought those chairs to come back and look at a table."

Elvis was sitting on the cash desk. "Merow," he said.

"And Elvis will be working the cash desk," Mac said with a completely straight face.

"Good to know you have everything under control," I said.

"Did you make an appointment?" I asked Liz as we pulled out of the lot, headed for Daniel Swift's office.

"No, I did not," she said.

"And that would be because?"

"I didn't want to give him time to come up with a story or say the only time he could see us was three weeks from next Thursday."

"What if he's not there?" I asked.

She flipped down the passenger-side visor, opened the lighted mirror and checked her lipstick. "He's there," she said. "Monday through Friday, if he's in town, he's at the office from eight a.m. to four thirty. He takes a half hour for lunch between twelve thirty and one o'clock."

I glanced over at her, and she met my gaze with the tiniest of shrugs. "I'm old. I ask questions. People tell me things."

I laughed. "So do we have a game plan?"

"Yes," Liz said. "We go in and ask him what the Sam Hill is he up to."

"Just like that?"

"Just like that," she said, closing the mirror and flipping the visor back up. "Daniel Swift is a no-nonsense, cut-to-the-chase and all those other clichés, direct sort of person. So am I."

My grandmother had essentially said the same thing when I'd called to ask her about the Swift patriarch. "Okay," I said.

"You'll be Gabrielle to my Xena, Warrior Princess," Liz said.

"The sidekick?"

She shrugged.

"I'm not even going to ask what you and Avery have been watching," I said.

She fluttered a hand at me. "Avery has been studying Greek history at school. Xena is Greek history."

I shot her a look, raising one eyebrow.

"More or less," she added.

"There's something I need to tell you."

"I'm listening," Liz said.

"Daniel Swift *is* the Wellington Group."

Out of the corner of my eye, I saw Liz shake her head. "I guess that shouldn't surprise me," she said. "Daniel Swift always was a secretive old coot."

I waited for two cars to go by before I turned left.

"I take it you found this information and not Alfred."

"I did," I said. "So far you're the only one I've told."

"So far I'm the only one you need to tell," she said.

Swift Holdings was on the top floor of a three-story building, almost at the end of Bayview Street at the far end of the harbor. There was no boardwalk, no businesses catering to tourists, no slips for harbor cruises or kayak rentals.

We took the elevator to the third floor. The business occupied the entire space. The elevator opened to their reception area. The floors looked to be the original hardwood, and there was an accent wall of what I was guessing was reclaimed barn board. It was impressive in an understated way that whispered old money.

Liz walked over to the reception desk, a curved expanse of wood without a single bit of paper to disturb the shiny surface. She smiled at the young woman on the other side. "Mrs. Emmerson and Ms. Grayson to see Mr. Swift."

The receptionist gave her a bright smile. "Do you have an appointment with Mr. Swift?"

Liz smiled back at her, and I thought her expression looked a lot like a snake about to unhinge its jaw and swallow a small farm animal, whole.

"Mr. Swift and I have known each other longer than you've been alive, my dear," Liz said. "He'll see us."

"I'm sorry," the young receptionist said. "Mr. Swift is extremely busy. I can give you his assistant's phone number, and I'm sure she'll be able to help you with whatever you're collecting for." She made the mistake of stressing the last two words.

She had spunk. I had to give her that. Unfortunately for her, Liz ate spunk for lunch.

"Oh, dear child," Liz said. "You clearly don't know who I am." She leaned over and actually patted the young woman's shoulder. It was a condescending gesture, but I couldn't help thinking about all the times I'd been stymied by a gatekeeper like this at a reception desk. Then she flipped one end of her cashmere scarf over her shoulder and strode down the hallway just to the right of the reception desk. I hurried behind her.

"Hey! Hey! You can't go back there," the young woman called after us. She may as well have been calling out the previous night's hockey scores behind us. Liz didn't give the slightest indication she'd heard. She went to the last office door on the left, opened it and sailed inside.

A woman in her mid-fifties was standing beside a long black table that was clearly being used as a desk. I wondered where people who used tables for their desks stashed all their junk. Maybe they didn't have any.

"Hello, Liz," the woman said. "I didn't realize you had an appointment today." She was about my height, plus-sized, with short blond curls, simply but elegantly dressed in a blue-and-black block Mondrian-print dress.

Liz smiled. "Hello, Jane," she said. "I don't have an appointment, but I just need five minutes of his time. It's foundation business."

The receptionist, who couldn't have been more than five feet tall, literally slid to a stop at the office door. "Mrs. Evans, I'm sorry," she began.

Jane Evans held up a hand. "It's all right," she said. "I'll take care of Mrs. Emmerson."

The younger woman shot Liz a daggers look, nodded and went back down the hallway.

Jane Evans smiled at me. As soon as I'd heard her last name, I'd recognized her. She was Josh Evans's mother.

"Hello, Sarah. How are you? Josh told me he'd seen you." She took both of my hands in hers.

"It's good to see you, Mrs. Evans," I said.

"Please call me Jane," she said. She glanced at Liz. "So Liz has gotten you involved in the foundation?"

"Isabel is out of town," Liz said. She lied so smoothly. I hoped it was just because there was a grain of truth in everything she was saying.

Jane Evans turned back to me. "How is your grandmother?"

"Wonderful," I said. "She and John are in New Orleans for the next month and a half, working on a Home for Good project, and she says she's learning a little Cajun cooking."

"That sounds like your grandmother," Jane said with a smile. She let go of my hands and turned to Liz. "Give me a minute. I think Daniel can probably see you."

Liz smiled back. "Thank you, Jane," she said. "I appreciate it."

There was a door behind and to the right of Jane Evans's desk. She tapped on it and slipped inside.

"You didn't tell me Jane Evans is Daniel Swift's assistant," I hissed at Liz.

"What difference does that make?" Liz retorted.

I didn't have the chance to tell her I didn't like lying and I especially didn't like lying to Josh's mother before Jane came back out and beckoned to us.

Daniel Swift's office was an imposing space—designed to be, I was betting. The wall to the left was floor-to-ceiling bookshelves. I saw legal references and several first editions. The centerpiece of the right wall was a beautiful framed photograph of the North Harbor waterfront taken early in the morning, with the sun sparkling off the water. It was surrounded by several photographs, several of them clearly of Caleb Swift.

Daniel Swift was at his desk, but he stood up and came around to take Liz's hand in his own. He had a very slight limp, I noticed, but he was still an imposing man. The desk was massive, walnut or black chestnut, I guessed. Behind it a wall of windows looked out over the water. Swift was wearing a gray suit, a crisp white shirt and a muted blue tie. He looked every inch the successful businessman.

"Elizabeth, how are you?" he asked.

"I'm well, Daniel," she said. "You've met Isabel's granddaughter, Sarah Grayson?"

Swift turned his blue-gray eyes on me. "I have," he said, offering me his hand. "Nice to see you again, Sarah."

"You as well," I replied, shaking his hand. He had large hands and a correspondingly strong handshake.

I saw him exchange a look with Jane Evans. "If you need anything, let me know," she said, and then she quietly left.

Daniel Swift indicated the two black leather club chairs in front of the desk. "Please sit down," he said. He walked back around the massive desk and sat in his leather executive chair. "Jane said you wanted to talk to me about the Emmerson Foundation."

Liz undid her coat and sat down. She crossed her legs at the ankles and folded her hands in her lap. Swift hadn't offered to take our coats, and I knew we wouldn't be in the office very long.

"I do," Liz said. "You know that there's a conditional offer on the table from the North Landing developer for both of the harbor-front buildings the foundation holds the mortgages on."

"I'm aware of that," he said. "Would you like me to look at the paperwork?"

Liz tipped her head to one side and studied him. "No, Daniel," she said. "I'd like to know why you've been keeping the fact that you're the major investor in the development a secret?"

He didn't blink; he didn't flinch; he didn't twitch. I wouldn't have wanted to play poker with the man, not that I could imagine a circumstance where that would come up. He seemed to have no tells.

"Swift Holdings invests in a lot of development projects, Elizabeth," he said. "North Landing is really just a tiny part of our portfolio."

"Horse pucky," Liz said. "You invested in that development for a reason, and you kept it secret for a reason."

"Are you here to play detective, Elizabeth?" Swift asked. He seemed amused by the whole conversation.

"You're a condescending ass, Daniel," Liz said.

"You think I don't know that you bankrolled this project as a way to harass Lily Carter?"

There was an almost imperceptible twitch at the corner of Swift's right eyelid. Liz had struck a nerve.

"You're making a fool of yourself, Elizabeth," he said.

She laughed. "It's not the first time, and it won't be the last."

The lines in his face tightened.

He stood up. "This meeting is over," he said.

Liz got to her feet as well. Her eyes locked on Daniel Swift's face. "Technology is a wonderful thing, Daniel," she said. "When you and I were young, it was easy to sneak out a window or in one for that matter. Now there are security cameras everywhere. Which means a secret visit to the bakery the night Lily died won't stay a secret forever."

Swift came out from behind his desk. A smile played around his mouth, but there was no warmth in it, only cold humor. "Do you really think I care about some small-town baker making her little loaves of sourdough bread and hoping we'd all hold hands and sing 'Kumbaya'?"

"I don't think you care about anyone but yourself," Liz said. She pulled on her gloves very slowly and deliberately. "I'm making it my mission to find out what happened to Lily. And if I find out that you had anything to do with her death, no matter how indirectly, I will break you like a baseball bat making contact with a mailbox."

"Are you threatening me, Elizabeth?" he asked.

Liz smoothed one glove over her hand. She looked up at Swift. "I'm sorry," she said. She paused for effect. "I thought I'd made that clear."

He looked at me for the first time since I'd entered the room. "Elizabeth is clearly suffering from some kind of dementia," he said. "I think you should take her home and contact her family."

I wanted to slug the old coot with my purse. But all I said was "Good afternoon, Mr. Swift." And Liz and I left.

Jane Evans wasn't at her desk in the outer office, but the pretty blond receptionist was at her place in the foyer.

Liz walked over to her. "You have spunk," she said. "Which I generally don't care for. You're also loyal, which I do like very much." She gestured over her shoulder. "He doesn't deserve your loyalty." She held out a business card. "I'm Elizabeth Emmerson French. I'm chair of the board of the Emmerson Foundation. And by the way, you should know who the movers and shakers are in town if you're going to do this kind of job. If you'd like to make a career change, call my office."

The startled young woman took the card. "Uh . . . uh . . . thank you," she said.

Liz nodded and made her way over to the elevator. I followed.

When the elevator door closed, Liz turned to me. "Dementia, my ass . . . ets," she said.

I clapped.

Liz narrowed her eyes. "What's the applause for?"

"Remind me never to get on your bad side," I said. "Baseball bat making contact with a mailbox? You were fierce. Way to go, Xena."

She laughed as the elevator doors opened onto the building's lobby. "Now all we have to do is figure out how the Swifts are tied in to Lily's death," she said, "because I'm certain they are."

I nodded. So was I.

Chapter 22

Liz and I drove back to the shop. Rose was waiting by the back door.

"Well?" she said to Liz as I stopped to stomp the snow off my boots on the mat.

"We rattled his cage," Liz said, heading into the storeroom.

Rose trailed her. "But did you find out anything?"

"Daniel Swift is mixed up in this somehow," Liz said.

"But do you know how?" Rose persisted.

Liz stopped, turned and looked at her friend. "Not yet."

Rose looked at me.

"Liz is right. Daniel Swift has a connection to Lily's murder. But I don't know what it is, either." I hated to think that Sloane might have done something to Lily. Could she have changed that much?

"There's something else I need to tell you," I said. "Daniel Swift is the investor behind the Wellington Group. I got my dad to do a little digging."

Rose turned her attention to Mr. P., who was in his usual seat in the Angels' "office." "The answer has to be in the footage from the security camera at the bank on the end of the street. Alfred just got it this afternoon."

"Do I want to know how?" I said.

Liz rolled her eyes.

"Probably not, dear," Rose said, patting my arm.

I looked at Mr. P. "Keep going," I said.

"Don't worry. Alf can do this," Rose said.

He sat up a little taller in his chair.

"I'm going to go find Mac," I said. "Let me know if you find something."

Mac and Avery were in the shop, both waiting on customers. Avery raised a hand when she caught sight of me and walked over to meet me. "She's interested in the twelve-string," she said, indicating the woman she'd been talking to who was holding a Gibson guitar very similar to Sam's and trying a few chords. She was mid-fifties, wearing jeans tucked into leather boots and a dark red duffle coat. "She's looking for a deal, but don't be fooled by the clothes. She can afford to pay more than she's offering."

"Why do you say that?" I asked.

Avery glanced back at the woman and saw she wasn't paying any attention to us. "She's wearing a vintage watch that's worth about three times the cost of that guitar. She also has a rose gold bracelet and earrings that aren't exactly cheap."

"Very observant," I said. "Do you want to close the deal?"

She nodded.

"Go ahead, then," I said.

I nodded to Mac, who was showing a customer my favorite slipper chair, and headed upstairs. Elvis was sitting in the middle of my desk. "Merow?" he said.

"I think Daniel Swift's fingerprints are all over this," I said, peeling off my jacket and dropping onto my office chair. The cat lifted a paw, studied it for a moment, then licked it.

I laughed at the symbolism. "And, yes, he does seem to think that he doesn't have any dirt on his hands." I sighed. Maybe we'd get lucky and Mr. P. would find something.

When I went back downstairs, both Avery and Mac had made their sales. "I'll get the vacuum," Avery said.

Mac came over to me. "How was your meeting with Daniel Swift?"

"You should have seen Liz," I said, pulling a hand through my hair. "She was fierce."

"Did you find out anything useful?"

"Aside from the fact that I wouldn't want to play poker with Daniel Swift? No." I sighed. "He's mixed up in this, though," I said. "Do I sound like Rose if I say I just know it? In here." I put one hand on my chest.

"No," Mac said. "I think in the end you have to go with your gut." He gestured in the direction of the storeroom. "I forgot to tell you. I have someone interested in that hutch you've been working on."

I'd ended up painting the big piece of furniture. The shelves were a pale gray called Foggy Morning and the rest was a deep marine blue. The salvaged ring pulls had worked perfectly on the louvered doors.

Mac named a figure that made me blink. "That's twice what I expected to get," I said. I grinned at him. "Didn't you say something about me making a mistake buying that hutch from Cleveland?"

"No comment," he said with a smile.

I locked the front door, and Mac and I straightened up while Avery vacuumed. When I went out into the workroom, I found Rose and Liz looking over Alfred's shoulder. I walked over to them.

"Did you find anything?" I asked.

Rose shook her head. She gestured at Mr. P.'s laptop. "Just a woman."

"Let me see," I said.

Alfred hit several keys, and black-and-white footage began to play. It took me a moment to orient myself; then I saw I was looking down at an angle at a section of the street that included the front door of the bakery. How on earth had the old man gotten the bank security video? Once again I decided that ignorance was bliss.

After a moment I saw a woman at the door. Was it Sloane? She turned her head, and I saw that it was. My heart began to race

"Keep watching," Mr. P. said softly.

I kept my focus on the screen, and then I saw Lily as well. From her body language, it was clear she was ordering Sloane out. Just the way she had said. I felt the knot of anxiety in my stomach loosen.

"Is there any sign of Daniel Swift?" I asked.

"Not so far," Mr. P. said. "But I have a lot of this to fast-forward through."

"Could I give you two a ride home?" I asked. Rose shook her head. "Thank you, dear," she said, patting my arm absently. "Charlotte is going to pick me up. We have plans."

"I'd better go hurry Avery along if I want to get home and dig into a big plate of kale and chickpeas," Liz said. She reached over and patted my cheek. "Thanks for coming with me, toots."

"I will be your sidekick anytime," I said solemnly, leaning in to kiss her cheek. She headed for the shop.

"Love you, Liz," I called after her.

"Yeah, yeah, yeah, everybody does," she said, not even turning around.

Avery left with her grandmother. Charlotte picked up Rose and Alfred, and Mac, as usual, decided to walk. I corralled Elvis and headed home.

The cat immediately headed for the kitchen. "I'm going to change first," I said. My running clothes were folded on what I thought of as Elvis's chair. I knew I should get dressed and go for a run, but I really didn't to. The conversation with Daniel Swift kept running like a loop in my head.

I was staring at the contents of my refrigerator, wondering if there was any new way to make an egg and tomato sandwich, when I heard a knock at the door. It was Nick.

He was holding something wrapped in one of Charlotte's quilted bags.

"Care package from my mother," he said. "Ham and potato scallop." He handed over the bag. "She said it might need a minute or two in the microwave."

"Thank you," I said. "Your mother must be telepathic. I was just standing in front of the fridge, wishing there was something in it to eat . . . that I could cook and have it still be edible."

Nick laughed. "Saved by a casserole dish of potatoes."

"C'mon in," I said. He followed me inside, and I set the bag of food on the counter.

Elvis jumped down from his perch on the top of the tower.

"Where did you get that?" Nick asked, walking over for a closer look. "That's nice work."

"Alfred Peterson made it for me," I said.

Elvis meowed indignantly. "Excuse me, he made it for Elvis."

Nick ran a hand over the smooth dark wood. "Alfred did this? Wow."

"He appears to be a man of many talents."

Nick smiled. "I don't doubt that. At least this one's legal. Which reminds me: Do you know anything about a brief glitch in the firewall at First National Bank yesterday?"

I shook my head. "No." I didn't *know* anything. That was my story and I was sticking to it.

Nick crossed the room and came to stand in front of me. "So how's the detecting going?"

"They haven't given up, if that's what you're asking," I said.

He shrugged. "I've kind of given up on that happening."

I pushed back the sleeves of my T-shirt. "Were you around when Caleb Swift disappeared?" I asked.

He nodded. "I remember that. They found his sailboat adrift and no sign of him or of any foul play."

I looked up at him. "I know this is going to sound crazy, but do you think there's any chance that Caleb Swift is alive?"

"Have you been drinking?" Nick asked, narrowing his brown eyes at me.

"No," I said. "I know it sounds a little out there."

"And I think I know where the idea came from."

"You think it's impossible."

"I do," he said. "If Caleb were alive, his grandfather would have found him. Sarah, the old man broke his ankle just after Thanksgiving and had to have it pinned. He ran Swift Holdings from his hospital room. He doesn't give up. He couldn't find Caleb because Caleb is dead." He frowned at me. "Why the interest anyway?"

"Lily," I said. "I'm grasping at straws."

Nick smiled. "Yeah, you are."

Elvis jumped up on a stool, put a paw on the counter and sniffed at Charlotte's bag.

"Get away from that," I said. I turned back to Nick. "Would you like to join me . . . us? I know

Charlotte. There's more than enough food for two people."

"Thanks," he said, "but I'm meeting a couple of the guys down at The Black Bear to watch the game. Rain check?"

"Absolutely." I walked him to the door. "Thanks for bringing the food," I said.

He smiled. "You're welcome." He hesitated. "I know you want to see whoever killed Lily brought to justice. So do I. But she wasn't killed by a dead man, Sarah."

I nodded.

"How about dinner sometime next week?" he said, pulling on his gloves.

"Sounds good," I said.

"Good. I'll call you."

We said good night and he left.

Elvis was still sitting on the stool, eyeing the food from Charlotte.

"Merow!" he said.

"Give me a minute," I said.

The cat made a sound a lot like a sigh.

I warmed up half the scallop and ham and put the rest in the fridge for another night. Then I took my plate and sat on the couch with Elvis beside me mooching tiny bites of ham.

"Nick's right, you know," I said. "If Caleb Swift were alive, the old man would have found him." I remembered the elder Swift in his office, so arrogant as he talked to Liz. I tried to imagine him running his company from a hospital bed.

The potato scallop was delicious, tender potatoes in a creamy sauce with mushroom and onions. I wondered if Rose could actually succeed in teaching me how to cook. No one else had been able to. Not my mom. Not Gram. Liam could cook. The last time he'd been in town, he'd made coleslaw and pulled-pork sandwiches on Mom's sourdough bread.

Sourdough bread.

What had Daniel Swift said about Lily? I closed my eyes and tried to hear the conversation in my head. *Do you really think I care about some small-town baker making her little loaves of sourdough bread and hoping we'd all hold hands and sing "Kumbaya"?*

Elvis leaned sideways so his furry face was in my field of vision. "Murp?" he said inquiringly.

"How did he know?" I asked.

The cat looked around a bit uncertainly. I pointed a finger at him. "Asia told me that Lily was making sourdough bread. How did Daniel Swift know that if he wasn't there? She didn't make that regularly." I shifted Elvis on my lap. "He was there."

"Murp," he said.

My logic was a bit ropy, but I decided that was a yes.

"So how did he get in the building? He wouldn't have been stupid enough to walk in the front door."

As far as Elvis was concerned, if there was no more ham to mooch, the conversation was over. He jumped from my lap onto the old steamer trunk I was using as a coffee table. His back foot hit my cell phone and sent it to the floor. It skidded under the front of the club chair opposite the sofa and out the back, coming to a stop against the baseboard.

Elvis dropped his head and gave me his remember-how-cute-I-am face.

"You're not in trouble," I said, waving a hand at him in a placating gesture. My focus was on the phone. It had slid all the way under the chair and out the other side.

And suddenly I knew. "That's how he did it," I said.

Was it Liz or Charlotte who had told me about the buildings along the street by the bakery? They had all had connected basements at one time. That's how Daniel Swift had gotten into the bakery. That's how he'd killed Lily.

"He broke his ankle," I said slowly. "I don't see a man like that using crutches, but maybe a cane." I remembered the conversation I'd had with Nick, all hypotheticals. Could a cane have caused Lily's head wound? It seemed possible to me.

"I have to call Michelle," I said. I got up to retrieve my phone, and there was a knock at the door.

"I bet that's Rose," I said. She'd been planning on spending the week with Charlotte so she could get the apartment organized, but I knew she was eager to be all moved in. I scooped up the phone with one hand and turned to open the door with the other.

Daniel Swift was standing there. "Hello, Sarah," he said. Then he pointed a gun at me.

I took several steps backward. I didn't really have a choice. Elvis hissed at the man, his ears flattened against his head.

"What a stupid animal," Swift said. "I should have guessed you'd be a cat person. Cats are devious. I don't like them."

I bent down and picked up Elvis. "Maybe you don't like being reminded of your own duplicity," I said.

My heart was thumping in my chest, but if Liz could stand up to this man, then so could I.

"You know," he said flatly. At least there was no beating around the bush.

"Yes, I do," I said. "And so do the police."

His hand shot out and grabbed my wrist. My cell phone hit the floor. I saw a flash of black fur, and Swift pulled his hand back, but he had my phone now. He also had a nasty scratch, courtesy of Elvis.

"Very good," I whispered to the cat.

"I sincerely hope I didn't catch anything from that . . . animal," Swift said, pulling a linen handkerchief from his pocket and wrapping it around his left hand, all the while keeping the gun on me.

"I'm more worried about my cat getting something from you," I said.

He gave me the same smile I'd seen earlier, all ice and arrogance. "You've been spending too much time with Elizabeth."

I swallowed down the large lump in my throat. "She had you pegged," I said. "You killed Lily."

"I slipped when I mentioned what kind of bread she was making, didn't I?" he said.

I swallowed down the lump in my throat. "Why did you kill her?"

"I didn't kill her. She died. It was an accident."

"Then tell the police that." I made a move toward the phone on the counter.

He blocked my way, the gun only a few inches from my head. "Don't do that," he said. "I will shoot you."

"You can't get away with killing me, too," I said, faking a confidence I didn't feel. "And you won't get away with killing Lily, either."

"That's where you're wrong," he said. His face hardened. He tapped my shoulder with the gun. "Move."

"Where?" I said.

"Upstairs."

My keys were on the counter, and he grabbed them as we passed. Why were we going upstairs?

Swift nudged me into the entryway and up the staircase to Gram's second-floor apartment. "Which key is it?" he said.

"Figure it out yourself," I said.

He pointed the gun at Elvis. "Which key?" he repeated.

The cat glared and hissed as I found the proper key and Daniel Swift unlocked Gram's apartment.

It smelled like her, like lavender-scented talc, and I took a deep breath, finding a bit of comfort in the scent.

Swift forced Elvis and me out onto the second-floor verandah overlooking the backyard.

"Scream and I'll put a bullet directly through that mangy animal's head," he said.

It was cold on the balcony even with the shelter of the house behind me. I shivered in my sweater and leggings.

"If you're planning on pushing me over the railing, the fall won't kill me," I said. "I might break something, but I'd still be able to tell the world what you did. Why did you kill Lily, by the way?"

What did they always do in the movies? Keep the bad guy talking until the good guys arrived. "It was because of your grandson, wasn't it? Caleb." It was work keeping the fear out of my voice, and I couldn't stop shivering. Swift was wearing a gray wool coat with a scarf at the neck, a snap-brim fedora and lined leather driving gloves. He wasn't cold at all.

His mouth twisted. "You know nothing about my grandson."

"That's not true," I said. "I know you must love him very much to do everything you've done. You bought a controlling interest in that investment company and then invested in the North Landing project, all to get to Lily."

"She was beneath him," Swift said, an ugly expression on his face. "And she was the last person to see him alive. She had to know something." His voice got rougher. "I'm going to take that building apart board by board. There has to be something, some clue. Why else would she refuse to sell?"

He thought Lily had killed Caleb, I realized.

He took a step toward me. I stood my ground.

"Move," he said.

I shook my head.

"You think I won't shoot you?"

"I'm not going to help you throw me over that railing," I said.

"You're not going over the railing." He was so close I could smell the damp wool of his coat. Elvis growled low in his throat, a sound I'd never heard him make before.

"You're going to have an unfortunate fall down some icy stairs."

"I fell down more stairs than that when I was eight," I said. "It won't kill me, and I promise I'll scream so loudly they'll hear me at the police station." *Keep him taking,* I told myself, *and the good guys will get here.*

"Do you really think I didn't plan this out? Alas, you're going to hit your head on the top stair post."

He aimed the gun at Elvis again. "Move."

The deck and the steps were slippery. Usually I kept them clear and sanded, but it had been such a busy week I'd let it slide. I gave a tiny hysterical giggle at the play on words. And then one foot went out from under me. I scrambled to get my balance, one hand flailing as I clutched Elvis with the other. Swift grabbed my free arm, forcing it up behind my back. I struggled, but he was bigger and stronger and I couldn't get my footing.

He began to drag me toward the wooden newel post at the top of the stairs that led down to the backyard. He dropped his other arm. The gun was at his side. There was no reason not to scream. But he'd anticipated that. As I took a breath, he slipped the gun into his pocket and clamped his other gloved hand down hard over my mouth.

The only chance I could see was to go limp, let Elvis get free and then throw myself down the stairs. I was banking on getting to the bottom before he could pull out the gun again and shoot me. Then my left foot found a place where there was a little sand left from the last time I'd put some down. Instead of going limp, I kicked up and out, as hard as I could, aiming for his knee and making a very satisfying connection. At the same time a black paw slashed up and raked the back of Swift's hand.

He let go of me, swearing. Then, to my surprise, his eyes rolled back in his head and he dropped to the deck like a bag of water. Because the blade of my big yellow snow shovel had just made contact with the back of his head.

The other end of the shovel was in Rose's hands.

She was breathing hard, but there was a smirk of satisfaction on her face. "Are you all right, dear?" she said.

Chapter 23

The police arrived what seemed like moments later.
Daniel Swift was conscious by then. I think if he'd
tried to move, Rose would have brained him again.
One paramedic tended to the bump on the back of
his head while another checked my shoulder.

Rose sat at my grandmother's dining room table
and gave her statement to Michelle. When she'd said
that she and Charlotte had had plans, what she
hadn't said was that their plans were to follow Daniel Swift. They'd trailed him to a brick building
down the street. Formerly factory housing for the
chocolate factory workers, it now held several professional offices. Charlotte had stayed with the car in
the lot, and Rose had gone inside to see where Swift
had been going.

"That was dangerous," Michelle said sternly.

Rose shook her head. "Nobody notices an old
woman. We're about as close to invisible as it gets."

In a cosmic stroke of good luck or good timing,
Rose had seen Swift pull on a gray fedora, turn up

the collar of his coat and start down the street. When she realized he was heading to my house, she'd tried to call me and discovered she'd left her phone in Charlotte's car.

Her expression grew serious. "I'm sorry, my dear," she said. "I should have paid more attention." She reached across the table for my hand and gave it a squeeze. "If anything had happened to you . . ."

"Nothing happened to me," I said. "Because of you. Where did you learn to swing a shovel like that?"

"I played baseball when I was a girl. *Baseball*, not softball," she stressed. She smiled and patted her hair. Not a single one was out of place after all her exertion. "If Daniel Swift's head had been a baseball, that would have been a home run."

Behind her I saw Charlotte shake her head.

We ended up downstairs in my apartment. When I came back from changing into dry clothes, Mr. P. had shown up and was in the kitchen making coffee and tea. Rose and Charlotte were at the table along with Jess. Charlotte had called her. Elvis was on Jess's lap.

"Where do you keep your cookies?" Mr. P. asked.

"I don't exactly have any cookies," I said a little sheepishly.

"Crackers?" he asked hopefully. "Or muffins?"

I felt my cheeks getting red.

"Give it up, Mr. P.," Jess said from her seat at the table. "The only edible things you're going to find in that kitchen are sardines and cat kibble, and I don't fancy having either one of them with my coffee."

"Merow!" Elvis exclaimed.

"No one's going to eat your sardines," I said.

He looked pointedly around the room just to make sure we all knew they were paws off.

"Liz is on the way," Charlotte said. "She's stopping at McNamara's."

Rose got up, came around the table and put her arms around me. "As soon as that bandage is off your hand"—she gestured to the gauze the paramedic had put on the scrape on the side of my left hand—"we'll start your cooking lessons again."

"Have I told you I love you?" I asked.

She stood on tiptoes and kissed my cheek. "Only about half a dozen times in the last hour."

"Is that all?" I said.

She laughed. "I'm so glad you're all right."

I peeked into the kitchen to see how Mr. P. was doing. He seemed to be figuring things out. Charlotte came up behind me and put an arm around my shoulders.

"Is it crazy that I feel a little sorry for Daniel Swift?" I said.

"No," she said. "It just shows that you have a good heart."

"All he had was his grandson," I said. "I have all of you." I suddenly had a lump in my throat again. I looked over at the table, where Rose was telling Jess how she'd gotten the shovel and crept up the stairs.

"We're very glad we have you," Charlotte said.

There was a knock at the door.

"I'll get it, my dear," Mr. P. said.

It was Nick. He was carrying a brown paper shopping bag.

"Come join the party," Jess said, waving at him from the table.

"I just wanted to see for myself that Sarah is okay," Nick said.

"I'm fine," I said, hobbling over to the door.

He frowned when he noticed how gingerly I was moving my shoulder.

"It's just a little road rash," I said.

"I thought you were out of the detective business," he said, lowering his voice.

I shrugged. "So did I."

Nick handed me the shopping bag. "This is for you. Open it later."

"What is it?" I asked.

"It's no big deal. Just . . . just look at it later." He shook his head. "I can't believe Daniel Swift killed Lily. And tried to kill you."

"He thought she knew what happened to his grandson."

"Do you think she did?"

I rubbed my shoulder. It still ached where Swift had wrenched it up behind my back. "I don't know," I said. "I guess we'll never know now."

Nick smiled. "Did Rose really clobber Swift with a snow shovel?"

"She has a swing like Ted Williams."

Charlotte came over to us. "Come sit down, Sarah," she said. "You were supposed to stay off that ankle."

"Would you get Nick a cup of coffee?" I said. I looked at him. "Do you have time for one?"

"I'd love one."

Mr. P. had heard the conversation. "I'll get it," he said. "Nicolas, how do you take it?"

Jess got to her feet. "Sit," she said, putting both hands on my shoulder and steering me to her chair.

I sat, gratefully, because my ankle did hurt. I set the shopping bag at my feet. Jess pulled over the footstool. "Put your foot on that," she said. "I'll get you a cup of coffee. And I'm spending the night, by the way. And Rose is cooking breakfast in the morning, because I'm not eating sardines."

There was a meow at her feet. She bent down and lifted Elvis into her arms. "You are my hero, Mr. King of Rock and Roll," she said. She scratched under his chin and he started to purr. She kissed the top of his head and set him on the footstool next to my foot. "Watch her," she said, pointing at me.

Elvis immediately turned and stared at me.

Jess laughed and went into the kitchen to get my coffee. There was another knock at the door.

"I'll get that," Charlotte said before I could move.

It was Liz with Avery and Mac in tow and probably half the food Glenn McNamara had had.

"Are you all right, child?" Liz said. I could see the concern in her eyes.

"I'm fine, thanks to Rose," I said. Rose had gotten to her feet and was looking in the two large paper shopping bags Mac was carrying.

"You really clocked the old dude with a shovel?" Avery asked.

"I wouldn't quite put it that way, dear," Rose said, "but essentially, yes."

"Hot damn!" Avery said, high-fiving Rose.

Liz shot her a look. "Sorry, Nonna," she said, ducking her head.

"Take those bags from Mac and put them in the kitchen, please," Liz said, making a shooing motion with one hand.

Mac handed her the bags and then put an arm around Rose's shoulders. "I'm so proud of you," he said.

Her cheeks flushed pink. "Thank you," she said.

Liz looked at Mac. "Have a seat," she said. "Talk to Sarah. I'll get you a cup of coffee as soon as I find out if there is any."

"There is," I said. "Mr. P. made it."

Mac pulled off his gloves and dropped into the chair opposite me. Everyone else was crammed into my tiny kitchen.

"Are you really all right?" he asked.

"I am," I said. I held up my hand. "The bandage is twice the size of the scrape, and I only twisted my ankle."

"I'm glad," he said. He hesitated. "If you need anything, later on or tonight, call me? Please?"

I nodded, suddenly feeling . . . awkward.

We all managed to squeeze around the table with our coffee and tea. Liz had brought rolls and Glenn's chicken corn chowder and probably every cookie in the place. Charlotte and Mr. P. served us all while Rose told her story again, with Elvis adding commentary from his perch on the footstool. Nick managed to eat a bowl of chowder and two peanut-butter cookies before his phone rang.

"I've gotta go," he said. He came around the table, leaned down and kissed Rose on the cheek. "Promise me from now on you'll let someone else do the shoveling," he said.

She laughed, reached up and patted his cheek.

"If you or Jess need anything, I'm as close as the phone," Nick said to me. He reached out with one hand and tucked a stray strand of hair behind my ear.

The gesture felt oddly intimate. I had to swallow before I could speak. "Thanks," I said.

Charlotte walked Nick to the door. When she opened it, Caroline Carter was standing there.

"Is this a bad time?" she asked uncertainly.

"Of course not," Charlotte said.

"I'm on my way out," Nick said. "I'll call you later," he said to his mother.

I struggled to my feet. "Caroline, come in, please," I said.

"Detective Andrews called me," she said, her fingers playing with the fringe of the long, rust-colored scarf she was wearing. "I just wanted to see if you and Rose were all right."

"We're fine," I said. "Please sit down."

She took Nick's empty chair. Mr. P. quietly got up and headed for the kitchen. In a moment he was back with a cup of tea for Caroline. I mouthed a "Thank you" at him.

"You're hurt," Caroline said to me.

"A twisted ankle and some skin off the back of my hand," I said. "It's nothing."

"Did you really go after Daniel with a shovel?" she said to Rose.

Rose nodded.

Caroline smiled. "Good for you." She shook her head. "I can't believe he killed Lily."

"I'm not making excuses for the man," I said carefully. "But I think his grandson's disappearance broke something in him. He thought Lily knew what happened to Caleb, and he got fixated on that."

Caroline pressed her lips together and looked at the ceiling for a moment. I saw her swallow a couple of times, and it was clear she was fighting back tears. And in the split second before she spoke, all the pieces fell into place for me.

"She did know what happened to Caleb," Caroline said. "I killed him."

Chapter 24

I think you could have heard the proverbial pin drop.

"What happened?" I said finally.

Caroline put both hands flat on the table. "He came to the bakery to talk to Lily. He wanted to get back together, but she didn't like how possessive he'd gotten. He grabbed a knife off the counter, backed her into a corner in the basement and cut her, right here." She put hand to her collarbone. "There was a pair of scissors I'd been using to cut string to put around the recycling on top of a box. He was going to cut her again. Or worse." She dropped her head. "I stabbed him."

Liz reached over and laid a hand on Caroline's arm. "You were protecting your child. No one would have faulted you for that."

"Daniel would have," Caroline said. "Lily was terrified about what he'd do."

I thought of Swift out on the deck, determined to get rid of me. I didn't doubt Lily's conclusion. But I couldn't miss the irony that Lily was dead because Daniel Swift was convinced she knew what had happened to his grandson, and he'd been right.

Caroline swallowed hard. "We got his body into one of the tea chests we kept for storage and got it on the dolly. I put on Caleb's hoodie. I knew the Levengers had a security camera and it would record me leaving. I was banking on the fact that the quality of the image would be poor because the old man was pretty cheap."

"What did you do?" Liz asked.

"I got his body onto the *Swift Current*. I used to sail a lot when I was younger. I took the boat out to deep water at the mouth of the harbor." She stopped and swallowed again. "I weighed down the body and . . . dumped it overboard." Her voice had lowered to a whisper. "Then I swam to shore and Lily picked me up."

No one said anything. Pain was etched in every line of Caroline's face. "The knife Caleb attacked Lily with is wrapped in plastic and buried under the concrete next to the floor drain in the basement. Lily kept it in case we ever needed to prove he'd attacked her."

"That's why Lily wouldn't sell," I said softly.

"She was protecting me," Caroline said. "I didn't care about myself, but I was afraid she'd go to jail for helping me cover up what I did. She was afraid of what Daniel would do to me."

Tears began to slide down her face. "Whatever he would have done to me could never have been worse than this."

Caroline had come to tell us the truth before she went to the police. Liz convinced her to stay with us and wait for Michelle. And she called Josh Evans. By the time Josh and Caroline had left for the police station with Michelle, I was finding it hard to stay awake.

"Sarah needs to get some rest," Liz proclaimed. "Time to clear out."

Avery and Mr. P. cleaned up and loaded the dishwasher.

Mac blew up the air mattress for Jess, and Rose made her a bed with two of my grandmother's quilts.

Rose wrapped me in a hug. "I'll be in my apartment. If you need me, send Jess to get me and I'll be here with bells on . . . and a shovel in my hand."

I laughed and hugged her extra hard.

Jess ran me a bath, poured in about a third of a bottle of patchouli oil and left me to soak.

"You don't have to stay," I said, admittedly halfheartedly.

"Yeah, I kinda do," she said. "I don't think your snow shovel can take it if Rose decides to go all kung fu on someone else with it."

Once I was settled in bed, I couldn't sleep. It looked like the North Landing project would go ahead now, but there was nothing to celebrate. I kept thinking about Lily's desperation to protect her mother and Daniel Swift's to find out what had happened to his grandson. It was all so sad.

With everything going on, I'd forgotten about the package Nick had given me. I'd brought it into the bedroom and left it on the chair. I got up and brought it back to the bed. Inside the bag was something wrapped in white tissue. I undid the paper. It was a *Mighty Morphin Power Rangers* T-shirt.

I could hear Jess snoring softly in the living room. I didn't want to wake her up, but I wanted to talk to someone. The phone was on the nightstand. I reached for it and punched in a number. He'd told me to call if I needed anything. It rang three times and then he answered.

"Hi, Mac," I said. "It's me."

Read on for a special preview of
the next Second Chance Cat Mystery,

A WHISKER OF TROUBLE

Coming in February 2016 from Obsidian.

Elvis regarded breakfast with disdain.

"Oh, c'mon," I said, leaning my elbows on the countertop. "It's not that bad."

He narrowed his eyes at me, and I think he would have raised a skeptical eyebrow if he'd had real eyebrows—he didn't since he wasn't the King of Rock and Roll or even a person. He was just a small black cat who thought he was a person and as such should be treated like royalty.

"We could make a fried peanut butter and banana sandwich," I said. "That was the real Elvis's favorite."

The cat meowed sharply, his way of reminding me that as far as he was concerned, he was the real Elvis and peanut butter and banana sandwiches were not his favorite breakfast food.

I looked at the food I'd pulled out of the cupboard: two dry ends of a loaf of bread, a banana that was more brown than it was yellow, and a container of peanut butter, which I knew didn't actually have so much as a spoonful left inside because I'd eaten it all the previous evening—with a spoon—while watching *Jeopardy!* with the cat. It wasn't my idea of a great breakfast either, but there wasn't anything else to eat in the house.

"I forgot to go to the store," I said, feeling somewhat compelled to explain myself to the cat, who continued to stare unblinkingly at me from his perch on a stool at the counter.

Elvis knew that it wouldn't have mattered if I had bought groceries. I couldn't cook. My mother had tried to teach me. So had my brother and my grandmother. My grandmother's friend Rose was the most recent person to take on the challenge of teaching me how to cook. We weren't getting anywhere. Rose kept having to simplify things for me, as she discovered I had very few basic skills.

"How did you pass the Family Living unit in school?" Charlotte, another of Gram's friends had asked after my last lesson in Rose's sunny small kitchen. Charlotte had been a school principal, so she knew I'd had to take a basic cooking class in middle school. She'd been eyeing my attempt at meat loaf, which I'd just set onto an oval platter, and which I'd been pretty sure I'd be able to use as a paving stone out in the garden once the backyard dried up.

I'd wiped my hands on my apron and blown a stray piece of hair off my face. "The school decided to give me a pass, after the second fire."

"Second fire?" Charlotte had said.

"It wasn't my fault." I couldn't help the defensive

edge to my voice. "Well, the sprinklers going off wasn't my fault."

"Of course it wasn't, darling girl," Rose had said, her voice muffled because her head had been in the oven. She had been cleaning remnants of exploded potatoes off the inside.

"They weren't calibrated properly," I'd told Charlotte, feeling the color rise in my cheeks.

"I'm sure they weren't." The corners of her mouth had twitched and I could tell she had struggled not to smile.

Tired now of waiting for breakfast, Elvis jumped down from the stool, made his way purposefully across the kitchen and stopped in front of the cupboard where I kept his cat food. He put one paw on the door and turned to look at me.

I pushed away from the counter and went over to him. I grabbed a can of Tasty Tenders from the cupboard. "Okay, you can have Tasty Tenders, and I'll have the peanut butter and banana sandwich." I reached down to stroke the top of his head.

He licked his lips and pushed his head against my hand.

I got Elvis his breakfast and a bowl of fresh water. He started eating, and I eyed the two dry crusts and brown banana. The cat's food looked better than mine.

I reached for the peanut butter jar, hoping that maybe there was somehow enough stuck to the bottom to spread on at least one slice of bread, and then there was a knock on my door.

Elvis lifted his head and looked at me. "Mrrr," he said.

"I heard," I said, heading for the living room. It wasn't seven o'clock, but I was pretty sure I knew who it was at the door.

And I was right. Rose was standing there, holding a plate with a bowl upside down like a cover. "Good morning, dear," she said. She held out the plate. "I'm afraid my eyes were a little bit bigger than my stomach this morning. Would you be a dear and finish this for me? I hate to waste food." She smiled at me, her gray eyes the picture of guilelessness.

I folded my arms over my chest. "You know, if you don't tell the truth, your nose is going to grow."

Rose lifted one hand and smoothed her index finger across the bridge of her nose. "I have my mother's nose," she said. "Not to sound vain, but it is perfectly proportioned." She paused. "And petite." She offered the plate again.

"You're spoiling me."

"No, I'm not," she retorted. "Spoiling implies that your character has been somehow weakened, and that's not at all true."

I shook my head and took the plate from her. It was still warm. I could smell cinnamon and maybe cheese.

There was no point in ever arguing with Rose. It was like arguing with an alligator. There was no way it was going to end well.

"Come in," I said, heading back to the kitchen with my food. I set the plate on the counter and lifted the bowl. Underneath, I found a mound of fluffy scrambled eggs, tomatoes that had been fried with onions and some herbs I couldn't identify, and a bran muffin studded with raisins. Rose was a big believer in a daily dose of fiber.

It all looked even better than it smelled, and it smelled wonderful.

Rose was leaning forward, talking to Elvis. She was small but mighty, barely five feet tall in her sensible shoes, with her white hair in an equally sensible short cut.

I bent down and kissed the top of her head as I moved around her to get a knife and fork. "I love you," I said. "Thank you."

"I love you too, dear," she said, "and thank you for helping me out."

Okay, so we were going to continue with the fiction that Rose had cooked too much food for breakfast. "Could I get you a cup of . . ." I looked around the kitchen. I was out of coffee and tea. And milk. "Water?" I finished.

"No, thank you," Rose said. "I already had my tea."

I speared some egg and a little of the tomatoes and onions with my fork. "Ummm, that's good," I said, putting a hand to my face because I was talking around a mouthful of food. Elvis was at my feet, looking expectantly up at me. I picked up a tiny bit of the scrambled egg with my fingers and offered it to him.

He took it, ate and then cocked his head at Rose and meowed softly.

"You're very welcome," she said.

"Why don't my eggs taste like this?" I asked, reaching for the muffin. Scrambled eggs were one of the few things I could make more or less successfully.

"I don't know." Rose looked around my kitchen. Aside from the two crusts of bread, the empty peanut butter jar, and the mushy banana on the counter, it was clean and neat. Since I rarely cooked, it never got messy. "How do you cook your eggs?"

I shrugged and broke the muffin in half. "In a bowl in the microwave."

She gave her head a dismissive shake. "You need a cast-iron skillet if you want to make decent eggs." She smiled at me. "Alfred and I will take you shopping this weekend."

I nodded, glad that my mouth was full so I didn't have to commit to a shopping trip with Rose and her gentleman friend, Alfred Peterson.

It wasn't that I didn't like Mr. P. I did. When Rose had been evicted from Legacy Place, the seniors' building she derisively referred to as "Shady Pines," I'd let her move in to the small apartment at the back of my old Victorian. Mr. P. had generously made a beautiful cat tower for Elvis as a thank-you to me. He was kind and smart, and he adored Rose. I didn't even mind—that much—that Alfred had the sort of computer-hacking skills that were usually seen in a George Clooney movie and that he was usually using them over my Wi-Fi.

It was just that I knew if I went shopping with the two of them, I was apt to come home with one of every kitchen gadget that could be found in North Harbor, Maine. Rose had made it her mission in life to teach me to cook, no matter how impossible I was starting to think that was. And Mr. P. had already— gently, because he was unfailingly polite—expressed his dismay over the fact that I didn't have a French press in my kitchen.

Rose smiled at me again. "Enjoy your breakfast," she said. "I need to go clean up my kitchen."

"Do you want to drive to Second Chance with me?" I asked. "Or Mac and I can come and get you when we're ready to head out to Edison Hall's place."

Rose worked part-time for me at my store, Second Chance. Second Chance was a repurpose shop. It was part antiques store and part thrift shop. We sold furniture, dishes, quilts—many things repurposed from their original use, like the teacups we'd turned into planters and the tub chair that in its previous life had actually been a bathtub.

Our stock came from a lot of different places: flea markets, yard sales, people looking to downsize. I bought fairly regularly from a couple of trash pickers. Several times in the past year that the store had been open, we'd been hired to go through and handle the sale of the contents of someone's home— usually someone who was going from a house to an apartment. This time we were going to clean out the property of Edison Hall.

Calling the old man a pack rat was putting it nicely. Rose and Mac were going with me to get started on the house, along with Elvis because I'd heard rustling in several of the rooms in the old house, and I was certain it hadn't been the wind in the eaves.

ABOUT THE AUTHOR

Sofie Ryan is a writer and mixed-media artist who loves to repurpose things in her life and her art. She also writes the national bestselling Magical Cats mysteries under the name Sofie Kelly.

Also available from
New York Times bestselling author
Sofie Ryan

The Whole Cat and Caboodle
A Second Chance Cat Mystery

Sarah Grayson is the happy proprietor of Second
Chance, a charming shop in the oceanfront town of
North Harbor, Maine. At the shop, she sells used
items that she has lovingly refurbished and repurposed.
But her favorite pet project so far has been adopting a
stray cat she named Elvis.

But when Sarah's elderly friend Maddie is found with
the body of a dead man in her garden, the kindly old
lady becomes the prime suspect in the murder. Even
Sarah's old high school flame, medical investigator
Nick Elliot, seems convinced that Maddie was up to
no good. So it's up to Sarah and Elvis to clear her
friend's name and make sure the real murderer doesn't
get a second chance.

"A surefire winner."
—*New York Times* bestselling author
Miranda James

Available wherever books are sold or at
penguin.com

OM0149